# Any Second Now

CHRISSY HOPEWELL

# Also by Chrissy Hopewell

Hart Sisters Trilogy:

*If We Pretend*

*Unless It's You*

*Since We're Here*

*One Hundred Lights* (novella)

Fort Collins Blizzard Hockey:

*Just One Season*

*Any Second Now*

Sign up to Chrissy's newsletter for extra content, including free hockey romance novella *Zamboni Kiss* and bonus scenes for every book.

www.ChrissyHopewell.com

*to my children: I hope you get to follow your dreams*

# Finally

## ATTICUS

New Year's Eve

Before she arrived at my apartment a few days ago to visit my sister, I hadn't seen Raleigh Hayes in almost a decade.

And now, with the ink fresh on her second divorce, Raleigh's here and looking absolutely gorgeous in a maroon wrap dress with a dangerously low neckline.

"Sorry, Luce!" I call to my sister. My hockey teammate walks her out of the ballroom where the Fort Collins Blizzard NHL team is having their big New Year's Eve celebration. I just accidentally knocked into our team captain, who was holding two full glasses of champagne, both now all over Lucy.

And while I didn't do it on purpose, there's a bright side: I'm now standing alone with Raleigh.

"Are you going to vomit in a bush next?" Raleigh tilts her head and presses her lips together, her fine blonde hair shifting around her face.

"Will I never live down my first semester of college?" I groan dramatically and squeeze my eyes shut for a beat. "Even though it was twelve years ago and I was a sweet and lonely freshman?"

Raleigh laughs, her dark chocolate-brown eyes sparkling, and the sound warms me from the inside.

"First of all," she says when her chuckles die down. "You were never lonely—there were *always* girls following you around—and second, I'm pretty sure you weren't sweet."

"Hmm. You might be right." I rub my hand on my chin and pretend to look thoughtful. "But all I wanted to do was hang out with my big sister's friends. Was that so bad?"

They laughed at me back then for tagging along all the time. But at the first party I went to with the trio of my sister and her two best friends, I stumbled upon a football player who had Raleigh looking very uncomfortable cornered in a dark hallway. Or maybe I was jealous. I interrupted with the excuse that I was looking for Lucy. I had a few inches on the football player, but he probably had fifty pounds on me, so I was lucky that he only glared at me before walking away. After that, I invited myself out with them all the time.

Maybe they didn't technically need me to protect them, but I needed to know they were safe.

And okay, maybe they also made sure I got home in one piece after a long night of partying, although I often curled up on the couch in their apartment so I didn't have to drag myself back to my dorm on campus.

A server in all black approaches us with a tray of champagne, so I ditch the empty flutes and grab a pair of fresh ones.

"I promise I won't spill this on you." I hand Raleigh a glass and our fingers brush with a sharp tingle as she accepts it.

"Thanks." She takes a sip and seems to assess me, then shakes her head. "I truly don't know how you hook up with all the women that Lucy says you do. You have, like, zero charm." I mock shock as Raleigh downs half her champagne, but she's holding back a smile.

She's flirting with me. Thank god. Because right now, I *do* feel like I have zero charm, even though I've never had a problem getting women to take an interest in me. In fact, I hardly ever have to try. It just happens. I think briefly about the woman I hooked up with on the road a few weeks ago in Chicago, then the one a month before that in Dallas. It's not who I want to be, but it's who I am.

"Ouch. Zero charm?" My eyes flit down to her lips, my gaze lingering on how plump and inviting they are. I look back up and her cheeks are turning rosy.

Oops. Didn't mean to be so obvious in my ogling.

"Yeah, when we were in college—"

"Raleigh." I step toward her, shrinking the gap between us. "I am not the same person I was in college."

"You're not?" She bites her bottom lip and stares up at me, big brown eyes so wide. I force myself not to stare at her mouth.

"Well, are *you*?" I don't know. Maybe I kind of am.

I've apparently still got this thing for Raleigh. I would've thought that a decade playing professional hockey and getting the money and attention that comes with that would've cured me of this unrequited college crush.

I guess I thought wrong.

"No." She shakes her head, some of the flirtatiousness falling off her face, and her gaze lowers to the ground. "I'm much less optimistic about life."

Shit. I guess two divorces can destroy someone's optimism. How can two fucking men have let her get away? And now she's got that damn hurt look on her face... I reach over and gently touch the underside of her chin, letting my finger linger. Raleigh looks up at me.

"Well, some things are the same," I say.

I should definitely stop talking. Immediately.

"Like what?" Her voice shakes the slightest bit, and her eyes roam my face.

Like what, indeed. I don't really have a plan here. Just want to make her sad expression go away.

I lean forward and down until my lips lightly brush against her earlobe. She intakes a sharp breath.

"I still want to kiss you." I lightly touch her hip in a mostly appropriate way. In a way that if someone looked over at us, they might think I'm leaning in because the music is so loud and we can hardly hear each other.

She swallows as I lean back, and I watch her throat bob.

"Fine then." Raleigh tips her chin up.

"Fine then?" I search her face. She didn't just agree to—

"Yeah. Let's get it out of your system."

She *did* just agree.

My jaw drops. "What?"

"Come on." Raleigh grabs my hand and turns, pulling me behind her. She deposits her empty champagne glass on a small round table, and I do the same.

Is she dragging me away to kiss me?

No way.

That's not what's happening.

But she's leading me around the small stage and DJ stand to a dark nook where there's no people, just tangles of cords and empty bins. She only stops when we get to the wall, where she spins around, still holding my hand.

"I might be a little drunk. But I want to forget things tonight." Her hand trembles almost imperceptibly in mine. "And kissing you might help me do that. Maybe I can spend the next year regretting this kiss instead of my marriage, who knows."

I press my lips together to suppress a grin, then lean a hand against the wall above her head and dip my chin down toward her. Raleigh's lips are a deep pink, her red lipstick long worn off, but her natural color is just as sexy. I push a strand of her hair, curled for the dressy New Year's Eve celebration, off her forehead. My fingers graze the side of her face and my heart thumps in my chest like a bass drum. A slight flare to her nostrils shows our proximity is affecting her as much as it's affecting me.

Thank god for the drinks I had—the ones that Coach Jackson and our team captain will make me regret tomorrow. It's pathetic, but I want to project confidence, and the alcohol is helping. I'm a star NHL player, but around Raleigh? I feel anything but confident.

"You sure, Raleigh?" My voice practically cracks. I sound like a teenage boy. Fuck.

"It's just this one time." Raleigh puts her hands lightly on my waist. "Because it's New Year's Eve and the night feels, well, kinda special."

She's right. There is something in the air. It crackles around us. There's still a whole damn party going on in this ballroom, but I'd also believe it's just me and Raleigh standing here tucked behind the stage of an empty room.

"Once, and never again." I nod.

"Never again," she says, but neither of us move. A crooked smile crosses her face.

"Don't be chicken, Atticus." She tugs at my waist.

I chuckle. "I'm not chicken."

The things I want to do to this woman. My eyes flit to her bare neck and the deep V of her dress, which dips between her breasts.

But this is Lucy's best friend.

Someone I've known for so long. This is a line I've always wanted to cross, but never dared. There are a lot of reasons this has never happened. And for a guy who never gets involved with any woman, kissing Raleigh is anything but simple.

"Atticus. You're overthinking. That's my job," she huffs.

She's not wrong. I don't spend a lot of time worrying about women because I don't spend a lot of time dating. Or any time, really. Raleigh's always been methodical and clinical in her decision making.

"I'm not overthinking."

I'm definitely overthinking.

I let my gaze settle on her lips. Why am I hesitating, besides all the reasons I just went over in my head?

"Since when do *you* overthink kissing someone?" Her hands leave my waist and she crosses them on her chest. "I mean, all the girls you hooked up with in college. There was a different one every weekend. I don't know *how* you got them to hook up with you, besides the whole tall hot hockey player thing, but there were plenty of your type in college—"

I stop her mid-sentence by crashing my mouth against hers. Fuck, I meant that to be way sexier, way more romantic, because I've been thinking of kissing Raleigh since I showed up at James Madison University at eighteen years old and now it's happening and it's the only time it'll ever happen and I'm stuck in my fucking head. I nudge her back against the wall with my free hand.

A moan escapes her throat and she wraps her arms around my neck, arching forward to push her body flush against mine. My heart races with the full contact.

I step forward and press her harder against the wall, deliciously trapping her, letting my tongue slip into her mouth and tangle with hers.

This is too good. Too much.

This is Raleigh.

One of my sister's best friends.

The woman I've had a crush on for over a decade.

I reach both hands down and cup her ass, then lift her so she's up against the wall at my height. If she weren't wearing a dress, she'd wrap her legs around my waist, I know it.

I need more time, privacy, a hotel room... I'm hard as a rock and she's pressing herself against me, and we need to get out of—

She pushes me away and gasps, her eyes wide, her lips parted, cheeks flushed.

"Hey," I say and kiss her again, this time more gentle.

"Put me down before someone sees us," Raleigh says, her voice wispy and shaky, and as I stand up straight and let her slide down my body, I realize this is the end of it. She won't be sleeping in my bed tonight, she'll be sleeping in the next room with Lucy and their other friend.

She meant it.

Just this once.

I set her on the ground but press my hands on either side of her against the wall. I don't want to let her free.

"Are you going to keep me trapped here all night, or can I go find Lucy and January?" She smirks up at me and gently pushes against my chest. I love the feel of her palms on my pecs.

"They're gonna know," I growl.

"No they're not." But Raleigh rubs her mouth as if to check for smeared lipstick or swollen lips. "They're both preoccupied."

She ducks under my arm and away from me, but stops before she's five feet away.

"Did you get it out of your system, *frat boy*?" she asks, looking back over her shoulder.

I chuckle. "Sure, *chicken*."

"Good." Raleigh smooths her hair down.

"But you know I wasn't in a frat."

"Whatever." She shrugs and presses her lips together. "And Atticus? This never happened."

Then she disappears.

Of course, we should act like this never happened.

It's not like I'm a relationship guy.

## CHAPTER 1
# Would Swearing Help?

RALEIGH

Friday, June 13

I question a lot of my life decisions on a regular basis—like why I agreed to get married not once, but twice before the age of thirty—but I don't question my urge to punch my ex-husband.

"Here's the thing, Raleigh." Jacob stands on the front step of the house we once shared and mostly blocks the path to my escape vehicle as he runs his hands through his wavy blond hair. The look on his face is so serious, so earnest. "My therapist finally made me understand something about myself."

"I gotta get to work." I clench my teeth and try not to roll my eyes. I also would like to punch his therapist, for no reason other than he probably encouraged Jacob to come talk to me about whatever revelation he's about to share.

I really should've gone no-contact after the divorce.

Jacob's always texting me. Emailing me. Showing up at the house—the one I haven't gotten around to putting on the market, the one he still has a key to—to explain his latest breakthroughs or thoughts on our failed marriage.

Jacob steps aside and I trot down the two cement steps, hoping he doesn't follow me to my car.

"I'm a compulsive liar." He follows me. "Always have been."

I screech to a stop halfway down the sidewalk and spin back to him. He startles and stops right before running into me.

"Well, yeah, obviously." I throw my hands in the air. "Did you not know that? You lied about your investments, your previous gambling problem, and your entire past." I tick each one off on my fingers. "So what else have you lied about?"

Jacob stares at me, wide-eyed, so I turn back and take the last few steps to my car. He's handsome and charming, but such an idiot.

He gave me all of our joint assets in the divorce, even though he was unemployed at the time.

The house and everything in it.

Joint savings account.

Joint checking account.

What was left of them, anyway.

I took it and reminded him divorce is forever. That's the whole point. But he was—is—so convinced we're going to get back together. We're not. I'm sure of it. But he's convinced he can wear me down.

A few weeks after the divorce was final, Jacob came to me asking for money. I knew he'd be broke. He's never been a career-driven person and can't seem to manage to hold down a job for more than a year.

And I couldn't help feel guilty for taking everything from him. I feel responsible. He was my husband, and sometimes I feel like I abandoned him instead of sticking with him through his problems.

So now I send Jacob money once a month to help with his bills. My mother is horrified. And my friends. Maybe I am, too.

"That's it! I swear! It was worse when I was younger, but marrying you was the best thing I ever did—"

"Divorcing you was the best thing *I* ever did," I mutter under my breath.

"What?"

I freeze with a hand on my car door and turn to him. This can't go on. I'm exhausted and overwhelmed and I don't want to care about what anyone else wants anymore.

"You can't keep showing up here." There's a pain in my chest.

"But it's our house." He reaches for me, palms up, but I step away. "And you won't meet up."

"We've been divorced for six months." I open the car door and slide in. "I need space from you. But you keep coming here, to my work, my mom's house. You email and text and call all the time. Please, stop."

When he pops up on my phone screen, it's labeled *ex-husband—don't answer.*

"And it's *my* house."

His face falls and I feel like I kicked a puppy. My ex-husband isn't a bad person. I still love him, in my own way, but I've been working on getting over him since last summer when I found out he'd been gambling and making terrible investments over most of our five-year marriage.

Clearly, he's not in the same place as I am.

I need a serious break from this life of mine.

* * *

"Hey, hey!" My manager comes around the corner of the pharmacy counter, shoving her purse in one of the cubbies and smiling widely at me. "I have good news."

"Hey, Stacey." I desperately need some good news right now. "That sounds promising." My stomach feels all twisted and unhappy after the latest Jacob interaction. I guess I thought once the divorce was final, since we didn't have kids or anything permanent together—not even a dog—that it would be a clean break.

I was wrong.

And it seems to be getting worse.

"Corporate approved your sabbatical request." She gives a little squeal.

"What?" I spin my head to her and breathe in sharply. A shocked chuckle escapes my mouth. "No way."

"Yes way. Eight weeks. Congratulations! I really didn't think they'd approve it. They never give the pharmacists sabbaticals." Stacey plants her hands on her hips.

"I didn't think it'd go through." Like I really, really didn't. So much so that I don't have set plans to fill eight weeks with, which is not like me.

My mom and I have had a working spreadsheet outlining my life options starting back when I was fourteen years old. It was helpful then, but now? It's too much. At thirty-four years old, I feel like I should be in charge of my own spreadsheet, not a shared document with my mother.

There is one thing I've been working on secretly.

A big purchase in the works.

A spite buy.

"Just one unexpected detail." Stacey scrunches her face.

"What?" I narrow my eyes. "And what's that face for?"

"Your sabbatical starts on Monday. Yay!" She pumps a fist in the air and watches my reaction with wide eyes.

I gape at her, wondering if she's joking. But she doesn't back down.

"But... it's Friday." I swallow. "And I don't work again till Monday."

"So I guess this is goodbye." My manager winks at me. "Are you still going to Colorado?"

Colorado? Maybe. I mean, I have my own timeline sketched out, and maybe I could get my spite buy by... Monday?

Stacey and I had talked about how there was a very, very low chance of my request getting approved. I had two things in mind when I filled out the sabbatical request form.

The first is to go back out to see one of my best friends in Colorado.

I visited Lucy with our other best friend-slash-college room-mate, January, over last New Year's, and I've been itching to get back out there. I want to see Fort Collins in the summer. There was something magical about the snow-capped mountains surrounding the small college and hockey town.

Does it also have something to do with her incredibly hot younger brother who I might have kissed on New Year's Eve in a move that was so out of character for me it must've been a cham-pagne-fueled hallucination?

Maybe.

Maybe I can't get that damn kiss out of my head.

Maybe *that* was the moment I realized I was 100% not in love with my ex-husband.

Just one kiss to get it out of his system. That's what I'd said to him. Who was that woman on New Year's Eve? Not me. Not the twice-divorced cross-stitching old cat lady, minus the cat—which is probably the best part—and only thirty-four years old.

My second plan is to cross-stitch my brains out. When my mother offered to teach me to do cross-stitch a year ago as a distrac-tion after I filed for divorce, I reluctantly agreed. But with true millennial hobby energy, I took to it so fast and it became my new obsession. I think she regrets ever teaching me as she claims it's distracting me from my real life. But I find it calming and extremely satisfying. I love the quantitative and precise nature of the simple stitches that turn into a beautiful design.

And I can't seem to stop.

I even started an online shop three months ago, and have been posting on my cross-stitch social media accounts daily and tracking everything carefully. But I had zero orders until two weeks ago when

I posted one of my finished hoops online and it finally got beyond a few hundred views. The image that went viral was of my favorite cross-stitch creation which was pretty flowers in various shades of pink around the phrase: *Ask yourself: would swearing help?* I got five orders that day and another few over the following week. Luckily, I have hoops already completed and another stack with flowers stitched on them just waiting for the right phrase to be added.

I go through the rest of my shift—my last one for eight weeks, apparently—like a daydreaming zombie, then book it out to my car and head home.

Holy shit, it's happening.

I auto drive the familiar route and mentally go through my to-do list. Most importantly, I need to contact the couple I'm buying the pink RV from and see if I can pick it up this weekend.

Yup. I'm buying a pink RV.

I owe the second half of the price soon anyway, and the couple agreed to store it for me until my plans were solidified.

The problem is, Lucy leaves this weekend for a six-week trip to Europe with her hockey player boyfriend. My original idea was to head to Colorado once they got back and spend time in Fort Collins. But I can't sit around in Connecticut for that long waiting for her to return. My sabbatical will be three quarters over by then.

I groan and think about spending my eight weeks here, and how much Jacob would harass me if I weren't even at work.

He's going to be so mad about me buying an RV. That was his dream, not mine.

Maybe I'll just get in it and drive. I chuckle to myself. That is *so* not me.

I turn onto my street and realize there are two cars parked in my driveway, where there should be zero.

Oh, for fuck's sake.

Jacob and Mom.

I turn off the engine and pray for strength.

They're not even outside waiting for me like normal people. They are *inside* my house, because both of them have keys.

"I'm going to kick their asses," I mumble to myself as I stride up the walkway to my front door. I glance over and a neighbor is watching me with narrowed eyes, crouched down in front of his sprinkler. "Hi, Jack!" I wave to the older man who scrunches his face and turns back to his lawn.

Suburbia is killing me.

I have my key out, but I don't need it as the door is cracked already.

I shove the door all the way open and step inside.

"Are you kidding me?" I stand with my hands on my hips in the foyer, glaring at my mother and Jacob as they argue with each other inside *my* house. They freeze comically.

"Honey. Hi. Sorry, I let myself in," Mom says. "I brought you some takeout. I know you had a long shift today." Mom nods toward the kitchen, hands clasped and with a look on her face both defiant and loving.

I glance over at the kitchen table, where the white plastic bag filled with multiple different dishes from our favorite Chinese restaurant sits, and my stomach rumbles.

"Thanks, Mom."

Mom didn't have it easy when I was younger. Dad disappeared suddenly when I was little, and after staying home since I'd been born, she had to get a job to support us. She fell apart for a handful of years, but she went back to college, graduated at the top of her class, and got a job as a project manager. She didn't want me to make the same mistakes that she did—not that any of it was her fault. There was always a plan for me. A roadmap laid out of exactly what I needed to do and when.

The spreadsheet.

"And you?" I look at Jacob with a slight shake of my head. "I told you to leave me alone. Just this morning, as a matter of fact."

"I know. I'm sorry." There's that sad, kicked puppy dog look again.

"Have you even gone home today? Or just sat in front of my door during my entire shift?"

I've begged this man to leave me alone. I know a lot of this is my fault. I'm helping him hold on to the idea of us because I feel guilty for leaving him. I'm letting him be dependent on me.

"Raleigh." Jacob's handsome face is so hopeful. "I went home and thought about what you said. And I wanted to come back here—my actual home—to tell you—"

I groan. "Not your home."

Undeterred, Jacob continues. "—that I want to give you the space you asked for. To think. To hopefully... forgive me?"

"Sure, forgive him," Mom says sharply. "But don't you even consider taking him back."

"Clara!" Jacob gives my mother a pleading glare. She always liked Jacob, and it was hard on her, too, when we got divorced.

"She needs to focus on her career. Not a man."

"She doesn't need to focus on her career, her career is just fine." Jacob looks at me with wide eyes and desperation etched in the lines in his forehead. "Stop micromanaging. She needs to sort out her trauma from our marriage so she can give us another chance."

Does he hear himself? Someone help me.

"Jacob, Mom, please stop," I say, but no one pays attention to me.

"All that marriage trauma. That's your fault, you know," Mom snaps at him. "She's not giving you another chance. You should focus on your career as well. Or getting a job, as I'm assuming you still don't have one."

"Hello!" I shout. They both turn my way and seem surprised to see me standing there. "I'm not focusing on my career. I'm not sorting through marriage trauma. I'm definitely not dating anyone."

Jacob opens his mouth to speak and I shake my head.

"Actually, I'm going on a road trip. My sabbatical got approved." I cross my arms and freaking dare them to argue.

Jacob lets out a whimper and Mom gasps. Ah, now I've finally got their attention.

"Oh, okay, honey." Mom pauses, and I'm pretty sure I know what's going through her head. She's got a ticker tape of reasons why a road trip sabbatical is a terrible idea for my carefully planned life, the life that just imploded *again* with my second divorce. "Where are you going to go?"

Whatever. I think my multiple divorces have officially destroyed the life spreadsheet we created back in high school.

"I have some free time." Jacob has a tentative look on his face. "I can come with you—"

"No." I spit the word out. Does no one listen to me? When did I ask for either of their opinions? When did I ask for anything but space from these two humans? "I am driving cross country by myself. Alone. Just me." I throw up my hands for emphasis.

"Is that safe?" Mom cocks her head. "Driving so far by yourself?"

"You don't even like driving two hours to the beach." Jacob furrows his brow. "I always drive us."

"*Drove* us. And I'm doing it in an RV." I tilt my chin up.

"What?" A look of surprise and hurt crosses Jacob's face.

I have a flicker of regret, as I knew this would be how he reacted. Maybe I wanted him to truly hear me for once.

"You rented an RV?" Mom's face is scrunched up like she's mentally creating new potential outcomes with this information.

"I *bought* one. And I'm picking it up this weekend." I got an immediate response from the couple when I texted them from the car.

"Do you have a—"

"Yes, I organized everything in a spreadsheet, *Mom*." I might have said that sarcastically, but it's true. As soon as I got the incredible and satisfyingly petty idea to buy an RV, I opened a new Excel file and researched costs of buying versus leasing, maintenance needed, pros and cons of different manufacturers, all the things.

"Good. Because I wouldn't want you to make a rash decision. You should be—"

"I don't want to be told what I should be doing right now. What I want is for both of you to get out of here so I can finalize the sale and go pick it up. Then come home and pack."

I cross my arms again and tuck my hands into my armpits. I'm sweating. Panicking.

I'm really doing this plan, huh.

"Have you ever driven an RV before?" Mom crosses her own arms right back at me.

"As a matter of fact, I have." I don't need to tell her the only time I've driven one is when I test drove the RV I purchased, pulled behind the current owner's car. "And now it's time for you to go." I turn to my front door and push it open all the way, shooing my mother and my ex-husband out. I don't make eye contact as Jacob walks by, but I don't miss the hurt look on his face.

"Call me, honey, okay?" Mom touches my cheek and follows Jacob down the steps. I hear them start talking—arguing—again but I shut the door before I give in to the urge to shout down after them.

I need room to think. Space to figure out who I really am without the pressures of marriage, work, family, the spreadsheet. I need to not come home to this house, the one Jacob and I bought together five years ago.

I need a way out. At least for a while.

Guess I'm really going.

## CHAPTER 2

# Hello, One Third Life Crisis

ATTICUS

Saturday, June 28

I didn't get a phone call from my father to wish me a happy thirtieth birthday or to check on my recovery from the groin injury I sustained in the last game of the season.

But I did get a text message.

RICHARD

No need to reply, but I wanted to inform you that Carrie and I are getting divorced.

I didn't expect him to remember it's my birthday, nor to check on me.

And the fact that my asshole of a father is getting divorced from wife number four will be a surprise to absolutely no one. He's been married to her for six years, and my sister Lucy and I talked about the possibility at Thanksgiving last year when the wife didn't show up to dinner.

I guess being team owner of a Major League Soccer team—DC FC in Washington D.C.—means he has the money and resources to go through wives like they're new cars.

ME

congratulations

I enjoy doing exactly the opposite of what my father wants. Much like when I chose to play hockey instead of soccer starting in middle school.

Drove that man crazy.

Especially since I had been a fucking good soccer player.

RICHARD

Have you heard from Lucy? I texted her yesterday but she hasn't responded.

I could tell him she's in England with her boyfriend—my teammate, Kellen.

But she would've told him that detail if she wanted him to know.

ME

why do you think that is, Richard?

Richard doesn't respond. I imagine him clenching his jaw at the question. The only reason he's even texting me is that his favorite child—and that's not me—stopped responding to him six months ago.

Because he's a dick.

So he's debased himself by texting with his son.

Although now that Lucy's moved to Colorado to work for the Blizzard and is blissfully happy with Kellen, she's slightly less of a golden child than when she worked for our father in D.C.

I grab my gym bag and leave my apartment in downtown Fort Collins to hop in my Wrangler, which is parked in the small lot behind my building. I need to sweat this out at the team gym, which is thankfully relatively empty during the summer offseason. Fewer people to witness my sad recovery.

By now, I should be one hundred percent recovered from the

groin strain, which happened when some young asshole hotshot slammed into me after I'd made a quick cut and passed the puck to our center.

We scored. I limped off the ice. At least now I'm cleared to skate like normal again.

I used to *be* that young asshole hotshot.

Now I feel middle-aged—at least in terms of hockey.

My goal is to be top of my game at the Skate for Kids charity tournament in New York City in August, which is technically still in the offseason. It'll be six teams and two days of games, all raising money for a kids' cancer charity. We'll bring a smaller team than if it were a regular season game, based on who is available to play. Should be no pressure and all fun, but it'll be a way to show my teammates and the hockey world that I'm doing just fine.

"Happy birthday, mate," Lachlan says after I push my way through a set of double doors decorated with the Fort Collins Blizzard logo and a giant abominable snowman, and then a second propped keycard door. He's sitting on a bench, apparently doing nothing. "Thirty, aye? Old man."

"Aren't you twenty-eight?" I attempt a snappy comeback, but only manage to sound like a curmudgeon.

"Yeah. Two whole entire years from thirty." My Aussie teammate laughs and lifts a pair of heavy free weights, curling them against his biceps. A couple of our teammates are using leg machines across the room. "How's the groin?" He looks pointedly at my crotch.

"It's fine. Fucking fine." I glare at Lachlan. He's gotten way too much pleasure harassing me about my injury. Probably because it was relatively minor and the season was over, allowing me to recover the right way. But it feels like it's been a battle to get back to where I was before.

More of a mental battle than a physical one.

"I can't believe Armas is out." Lachlan shakes his head and

picks up his phone, which is sitting next to him on the bench. "But better him than you, mate."

Yeah. I'm absolutely better off than our teammate on the second line, who got injured in the same game. But his hip injury was more severe, and unfortunately it was a repeat injury. Bad enough that he'd decided that was enough for him. He hung up his skates and walked away from hockey.

"Oh—here's another message from Kellen." Lachlan taps his screen a few times and furrows his brow.

Our team captain—still in England with my sister—had texted us yesterday with the news. It hit too close to home. Armas played right wing, my position, and is only thirty-one, so he should've had a few more good years in him.

"What'd he have to say?" I focus on stretching, spending extra time on my legs and groin area. Pulling that muscle freaked me out. I took two weeks of total down time from exercising, with only light physical therapy. The downtime was okay—it was still the first part of the offseason so I tend to take it easy anyway. After that, it was a few weeks of light activity. I got on the ice a handful of times under the supervision of our skating coach, but it was basically like I was going on a stroll around the ice, like a tourist ice skating during the holidays. I'm glad not many people were around to see it.

Then it was a week of pushing myself harder.

Now I've been give the green light to act normal. But I don't feel normal. When I faced the ice yesterday, I couldn't bring myself to go full speed or trust my body. Or myself.

I look up when I realize Lachlan's gone quiet. His eyes are wide and jaw's dropped as he stares down at his phone.

"What?" I roll my eyes. Lachlan's got an inclination for the dramatic.

"Mate. They signed Barrett Steele." Lachlan looks up and lets out a shocked chuckle.

"Who signed him?" My eyes widen. Maybe he isn't being dramatic this time.

A vision of Barrett Steele forms in my head.

Basically a kid—maybe twenty-five years old—playing for Utah in the western conference, which is where we are.

"We did. The Blizzard."

It takes a second for the Aussie's words to sink in.

Barrett fucking Steele is the one responsible for my groin injury.

I growl at the memory of wanting to kick his ass when I limped off the ice. The game—and the season—was over for me.

"No fucking way."

"Yeah. They must have paid boatloads for him." Lachlan lets out a huff and looks up at me. "I wouldn't worry, though."

"Why the fuck would I worry?"

"Because he's first line in Utah? And plays your position?"

My position. Right wing.

"Fuck that." I shrug and stretch my arms out, but my stomach does a twist that I don't particularly enjoy.

"I'd be more worried about you and him fighting." I'm trying way too hard to look casual and unbothered. When I am, in fact, bothered.

"Nah. I only pick fights with the other team." Lachlan gives me a pitying look. "He won't be a bad player to have on our side, right?" Lachlan tosses his phone on the bench and picks the free weights back up.

"Can we stop talking about Barrett Steele?"

"Fine. What are you doing tonight?"

"I thought we'd get drinks?" I stand and pick out weights, pushing all thoughts of Barrett Steele out of my head, replaced by the fact that I have nothing to do on my thirtieth birthday.

Pathetic.

"Ah, damn, Atter. I'm going with Melissa to some barbecue.

Sorry." Lachlan sets the weights back down and pulls his arm across his body.

"So you fuck me over and cancel our travel plans this summer, and then can't even have drinks on my birthday?" I glare at him and he chuckles, but I'm not kidding. He's been so wrapped up in the woman he started dating a month ago. It's destined for failure. They're just too different.

"I'm happy, mate. I think she's the one."

"Who are you and what have you done with my wingman?" I scoff.

Lachlan and I are cut out of the same cloth. Or at least I thought we were. We're the players. The flirts. The fun guys at the bar. Neither of us ever date for real. We just focus on hockey and fun, which includes casually hooking up with women when we feel like it. Especially when traveling with the team, so we can get on the plane and not have to worry about running into them at Deep Roots Cafe or A Good Book or anywhere else around Fort Collins. I almost always follow that rule.

But Lachlan fucked that all up when he started dating a college professor in town.

Now he's obsessed.

To me, there's only one way this ends: in disaster. She'll dump him when she realizes how different they are and the thrill of dating a Blizzard player wears off. She's got him completely under her control and he's in way deeper than she is. He cancelled our summer plans to travel in Europe so he could stay close to her, but she cancels plans with him all the time. He's desperately in love, she's casually interested.

Between Lachlan being otherwise occupied, my injury, Kellen traveling with my sister, and Harley—my other close friend on the team—back in Maine with his long-term girlfriend, it's a weird summer.

And now I have a new thing to stress about—Barrett fucking Steele.

"How about tomorrow? Black Diamond? Seven o'clock?" Lach shoves his blond curls off his forehead. Melissa even made him cut his hair. Before her, he had a blond curly man bun we'd mercilessly make fun of him for. Now his hair is above his ears. It's like he's trying to get an office job. Shudder.

"Yeah, sure."

During the rest of his workout, I half-listen to Lachlan talk about his girlfriend's family and job and bullshit that neither of us should care about. When he finally leaves the gym, I breathe a silent sigh of relief and sink onto the bench.

My father's fourth divorce is evidence that cheating and playing around runs in my veins. It's why I've never tried to get into a real relationship. Or any relationship.

I don't want to mess someone else up like my father messed with my mother.

But with Kellen, Lachlan, and Harley all paired up, it's just me. Am I going to have to start hanging out with some of the other single guys on the team? Like Heath, Finn, and Romeo? Fuck no. That's way too much effort.

I could've traveled by myself this summer, but without my kindred spirit—Lachlan—I lost all motivation.

I *feel* lost. Like I don't quite fit in anywhere.

And that stupid New Year's Eve kiss with Raleigh Hayes is stuck in my simple little hockey brain. I haven't felt the same since. Hooking up with women has lost its allure. I haven't done it since, which is shocking, now that I think about it.

It's clear I'm going through some kind of crisis. I run my hand through my sweaty red curls. I'm probably due for a haircut, but I'm holding out so Lachlan remembers what he lost when he let Melissa bully him into cutting his hair.

My phone buzzes in my pocket, so I pull it out.

LUCY

Hey, little brother, guess who's in Fort Collins?

ME

please don't say our father is here nursing his
wounds from his divorce

LUCY

His divorce?? Oh my god

ME

yup

LUCY

I'm gonna file that away for something to talk
about in therapy

ME

also yup

aren't you in London? shouldn't you be doing
something exciting instead of texting me

LUCY

I am. We are getting ready to meet a bunch of
January's friends at a pub. A gorgeous cozy
English pub

ME

shut up

LUCY

lol. But listen, Raleigh's in Fort Collins

What? Immediate heat rushes to my face as I flash back to New Year's Eve, and not for the first time today. Or the second. Raleigh pressed up against the wall, telling me this is the only time we'd ever kiss. She was making fun of me, just like she did in college, while also making me feel wanted and seen. Not as a hockey player, but as a person, even if that person was her best friend's brother.

ME

no shit?

LUCY

Yeah—she's at an RV campsite called Lakeside Camp. Driving a pink RV

ME

a pink RV?

LUCY

Yep

Can you go check on her? I think she's going through some stuff—she took a sabbatical and bought a freaking RV—and I hate being over here and wondering if she's losing her shit

ME

yeah, sure, I think I can fit her in

LUCY

Oh, and happy birthday, Atticus. Let's celebrate when Kellen and I get back in a month

ME

thanks, Luce

Raleigh's here. In Fort Collins. Right now.

This will be the perfect distraction from my existential crisis over being the only single guy left of my close friends, my groin injury recovery, my father's fourth divorce, and the deep sense of dread at having to play on the same team as Barrett Steele next season.

I could use a friend, one who knew me before I was an NHL player. One who takes no shit from me. One who will probably laugh at my existential crisis—or maybe we can laugh about *our* existential crises together.

And my sister asked me to go check on her.

That's my motivation. Certainly not because I've been yearning to see her face again.

I'm gonna go see Raleigh.

Just to make sure she's okay.

## CHAPTER 3

# Abso-fucking-lutely Not

### RALEIGH

I struggle to back my RV into the sewage hookup area. Dragging this contraption and having to reverse it into the right spot is fucking impossible.

It's pink.

My RV is pink.

It's a light pink with two darker pink stripes.

The paint is peeling.

The windows are definitely not sealed properly anymore.

The mattress is about two inches thick and feels like sleeping on a hay bale.

It's twenty years old.

The Pink Palace seems like an appropriately sarcastic name for it. I even cross-stitched an eight-inch hoop with the name to hang above my kitchen sink.

This is my super-organized mom's nightmare for me. A poorly planned sabbatical and an impulsive RV purchase, although that last part's not really true. She just thinks it is because I never shared my planning spreadsheet with her.

But as for what to do with these eight weeks? Yeah, I don't

have a spreadsheet for that. I wanted to make one after my sabbatical got approved, but I tried to hold myself back. I'm trying to convince myself I don't need a spreadsheet for every single freaking thing in my life.

The shock on my poor mother's face when she saw the Pink Palace parked in my driveway the day before I left and she came to say goodbye? Priceless, yet also left me feeling guilty. I don't want to stress her out, but I need to get away from everything for a while.

Alas, this was Jacob's dream, not mine, and I've driven past every state park on the map instead of checking out national landmarks and beautiful scenery. What, I'm going to go for a hike by myself and fight off bears and mountain murderers?

I left Connecticut two weeks ago and I'm already done with the RV life.

I'm sleeping in a giant tin can at night and during the day, driving way slower than the speed limit, mostly because I'm terrified of high winds and changing lanes and anything else involving me and my SUV pulling the Pink Palace—a medium sized RV trailer—on highways.

Small towns are even worse. I can't park *anywhere*.

At least I belong here in the RV campsite.

And now, I'm sitting in the front seat of my car, re-reading the directions on how to dump the sewage tank. I've done it many times before. Learning how to back up this damn contraption so that the RV's sewage tank is as close to the dump hookup as possible has been hard enough.

But actually emptying the tank? Nightmare.

"Damn." I guess it's now or never. I hop out of my car and something from the edge of the treelike scatters off into the woods. A bird? A dog? A bear?

"Hello?" I peak over toward the rustle of leaves, but it falls silent.

Then the smell hits me, and all thoughts of whatever was in

the woods disappear. It's a nauseating aroma, which makes sense—this is where all of us suckers dump the literal shit from our vehicles. I almost gag, then pull it together when a couple with a dog walks by and stares at me. Judging me for my surely obvious incompetence, probably.

"Need any help?" the woman calls out with a friendly wave.

"Nope. All good here!" I infuse insane cheer into my voice, as if I'd not do anything to be staying at a hotel where I can just flush the contents of the toilet, not have to pump it out.

They move on as I connect the nasty sewer hose to my RV's drain valve. This time I *do* gag and concentrate on breathing through my mouth and keeping the cereal I ate this morning inside of my stomach.

I open the black water tank valve and let it start to flow. There are two tanks. The gray tank holds water from the sink, shower, etc. The black tank holds the nasty stuff. I watch the flow of the waste to clock when it goes clear.

New cross stitch idea: *Divorce is like emptying the sewage tank from an RV.*

Nah. Too long. Stitching all those words would take for-freaking-ever.

*Marriage is like an RV sewage tank: unpleasant and smelly?*

Still too long, and not catchy at all. I'll have to noodle on it.

Driving an RV might be better if I had company. Like a friend. Or a cat. Not a boyfriend, or, god forbid, a husband.

I'm never getting married again.

Never dating again.

The water is running clear, so I close the gross black tank valve and open the gray water tank, which flows through and rinses the pipe.

I let out a deep breath and close my eyes, careful not to breathe in through my nose. I need a shower. There's a real one in this RV park, and I can't wait to use it, as well as the real bathroom.

"Raleigh?" A male voice calls.

I scream and my eyes fly open. The sewer hose almost slips through my hands, and when I look up and see the human standing in front of me—an unshowered, twice-divorced single thirty-four year old holding a hose of shit—I wish I could disappear into the forest forever with whatever was making that noise before.

It's Atticus Knox.

Professional hockey player.

My best friend's little brother.

Old college crush.

Fucking gorgeous hunk of man.

And last time I saw him on New Year's Eve, I was letting him stick his tongue down my throat. Encouraging it, even.

Atticus is wearing a Fort Collins Blizzard t-shirt, tight against his shoulders and biceps, and a backwards gray baseball cap that can't contain the red curls that match my best friend's, who also happens to be his sister.

"Hey... what are you doing? Are you okay?" He takes a step toward me, that crooked smile on his face that got me to drag him into a dark corner on New Year's Eve.

"Hello, Atticus. I'm emptying the sewage from my RV." I try to say it casually, like I'm not probably covered in poop germs. I calmly close the drain valve on the gray tank. I need to disconnect the sewer hose next, but I'm never super confident in doing that final step, and it always smells disgusting no matter how much I let the water rinse the pipe. A vision pops in my head of me unhooking the pipe and it flying around my head like some kind of uncontrollable garden hose flinging sewage juice all over me and Atticus.

"That sounds absolutely disgusting. Do you need help?" Atticus presses his lips together and I just know he's holding back a laugh.

"You offering?" I narrow my eyes at him, daring him to say yes.

"Um, you look like you have it covered, actually." There's an adorable twinkle in his eye and I'm tempted to give him an actual lesson on emptying an RV sewage tank.

"What are you doing here? How did you know where I was?" I have to stop myself from turning my head and sniffing to see just how bad I smell.

"Lucy told me. Asked me to check on you." Atticus shifts on his feet and slips his hands into the pockets of his athletic shorts.

"Oh, for fuck's sake, Lucy." I'm gonna have words with my friend about over sharing my life with her brother.

Atticus chuckles and keeps his eyes trained on me, with a quick glance down at the pipe still in my hands.

There's no avoiding it now, so I reach over and unhook the sewage pipe, then carefully coil it into the bucket at my feet. I breathe out in relief.

Then the smell hits me, and a second later, Atticus.

"Nasty." He scrunches his nose and steps back.

"Can I help you, Atticus?" I cross my arms and try so very hard to look intimidating, but the fact that he's a solid foot taller than me makes that really hard, plus the poop pipe coiled at my feet.

"I wanted to say hi and check if you needed anything." Atticus shifts and drags a foot along the gravel-covered road, making a crunching sound.

"Well. Hi. I don't need anything, and I've gotta move the Pink Palace back to my spot." I nod my chin vaguely away from where we're standing.

"Sorry, the what?"

Shit. I'm so used to calling her by name, and RV people always do that, so sometimes I forget that it's kinda weird.

"The Pink Palace. My RV." I stand up straighter and tilt my head, but feel my entire face and neck warming.

"Ah. Okay. That's a... strong name." He raises his eyebrows. "Where are you set up?"

I point across the campsite to a shady spot next to the lake.

"Nice." He nods.

It is a nice spot, actually, I'm looking forward to that view in the morning.

"Well, goodb—"

"I'll meet you there."

"Wait, why?"

But Atticus disappears around the other side of the Pink Palace and I wonder if he was an apparition that my mind created so I could disassociate from emptying the sewage tank. But after I carefully store the nasty sewage pipe bucket, wash my hands, and pull my car and trailer out of the dump station, there he is, casually leaning against the picnic table next to my campsite.

I turn around and back in, my hands sweaty as I maneuver the RV from the driver's seat of my SUV, and am thankful that I get it on the first try and don't run into the trees or the picnic table. Or the lake.

I flip down the visor and check myself out. Hair in a skinny ponytail, a swipe of mascara, and chapstick only.

Oh well. I'm not trying to impress this man.

"Hungry?" Atticus waves me over to the table after I hop out of my car. A pizza box now sits on the picnic table along with a bottle of wine.

"One second." I hold up my hand and duck into the Pink Palace to wash my hands again. "Where'd this come from?" I say when I come back outside. He's settled in at the picnic table, so I guess he's not jumping in his car and driving away quite yet.

"Cheese sticks from a pizza place in town." Atticus shrugs. "And wine."

"Are we back at college?" A smile crosses my face at the memory of all the late nights eating cheese sticks together. One night when we were pre-partying in our apartment, he'd seen my weekly study schedule, printed out and tacked to our bulletin board. When he made fun of me for it, I pulled up his hockey stats for the last game—which were crappy so a real low blow on my part—and I offered to create a workout and practice schedule for him. He chuckled and bought cheese sticks for the group that night, and did it basically every time we all went out together.

Atticus was always tagging along with me, Lucy, and January, even though I'm sure he got invited to so many frat and hockey parties. I pretended to roll my eyes, but I enjoyed the casual flirting between us. That delicious untouchable attraction to my best friend's brother.

I slide onto the picnic table bench. He shrugs and flashes me a pearly white smile, settling down across from me.

"The wine's a bit nicer than when we were at JMU. We don't have to open it right now, since it's barely two o'clock in the afternoon."

"I'm more of a red wine drinker these days, but thank you. I'll save it for the next time I have company over."

"You have a lot of visitors?" Atticus raises his eyebrows.

"No. It's called sarcasm."

He blinks at me, a barely contained smile on his face. "And I wasn't sure about what you drank, so I brought a red as well. This one's from my mom's vineyard. I order it by the case." He pulls another bottle from the grass next to the picnic table along with a bottle opener. "I also brought you a cork screw. Just in case you didn't have one in... the Pink Palace."

"First of all, that's amazing that this is your mom's wine. Second, maybe it is okay to have a drink at two o'clock in the afternoon. I had a long drive, and you're in the offseason." I reach for the wine and the opener.

"I'm game. Have glasses?"

"I'll go grab a few." I let him open the bottle and I go grab two mismatched mugs from my mini-kitchen. "This is the best I got."

I don't tell him that I've had several bottles of wine over the past two weeks, but I've only been buying twist off, like the sophisticated lady that I am. I have no problem drinking it out of my JMU mug. "Anything else you got under the table?" I look pointedly at his reusable cloth bag.

He shakes his head and flips open the pizza box. The smell is delicious, and Atticus pushes the box toward me for first dibs.

This feels surprisingly normal. Sitting at my campsite with Lucy's brother, six months after kissing him on New Year's Eve. Seeing him is a lot less weird than I thought it would be. Because let's be honest, I knew I'd see him if I showed up in Fort Collins. Even if—especially if?—Lucy wasn't here when I arrived.

Which I knew she wouldn't be.

We bite into the cheese sticks at the same time, and I moan.

"These are so good. I forgot they even existed."

"Well, I don't get them often because the team dietician isn't the biggest fan of greasy food. But it's summer, so." He shrugs and gives me a sheepish smile.

"How's your injury?" Lucy had told us all about Atticus hurting himself in the last game of the season. She said he was recovering fine and it wouldn't affect him long-term.

He shrugs but his face tightens. "Fine. Good. Getting myself back in shape for the charity game in August." Atticus reaches for his second rectangle of cheesy bread. He shoves the entire piece into his mouth and swallows disturbingly fast.

"Oh, I actually do have one more thing for you." He jumps up and heads to his car.

"Really?" I stare at his departing back. His shoulders lift in a shrug, and he opens the back door to his red Jeep Wrangler. "Is that car even practical in the Colorado winters?" I call, watching him lean in, appreciating his t-shirt taut against his back and shoulders.

"It's great in the snow," he says when he gets back to the table, carrying an oversized rectangular box under his arm. Atticus flips it around so I can see the label and image. I crack up.

"A hammock?" I look up at him with a smile.

"Yeah. And you have the perfect two trees to set it up between." He nods next to the picnic table, where he's right—

there are two perfect hammock trees with a view of the beautiful lake. "Happy housewarming. RV warming?"

"Most people bring a plant." No one's brought me a plant. In fact, only my mother has even seen the Pink Palace.

"You're surrounded by plants. Want me to hang it?"

I nod and Atticus grabs the box and begins unpacking it. Sometimes my ex-husband would buy thoughtful things for the house. But he'd leave it in a box for months and months until I put it together myself, hired someone to do it, or shoved it in the back of a closet. There was a lot of that to donate after he moved out.

Divorcing that man broke my heart in a different way than my first husband had. Ryan had cheated on me. Leaving him was easy. Jacob lied to me, kept secrets, lost a ton of money, and kept at it until I filed for divorce a year ago. All those lies both suddenly and gradually pulled me out of love with him.

Seeing Atticus is a breath of fresh air. He reminds me of carefree, happier days, surrounded by friends and optimistic about the future.

"So your travel plans got cancelled for the summer, huh."

Atticus looks at me with raised eyebrows.

"Lucy told me." I shrug. At least it goes both ways—Lucy tells too much to both of us.

"Of course." He turns back to the pile of materials for the hammock and bends down to pick up the directions. He takes one look before crumpling it up and tossing the paper into the empty box. "Lachlan bailed on me for his new girlfriend. A university professor."

"Bummer." I pull on my skinny ponytail. "Who are you going to pick up women with then?"

"Hey, I'm not like that." He glances up and a flash of hurt crosses his face. "Not these days, anyway. And definitely not this summer. Harley's home in Maine with his girlfriend. Kellen's traveling with Lucy. Lachlan's busy being in love. And I'm here." He secures one hammock strap around the tree and pulls the material gently across to the other tree, then wraps that strap securely around the trunk.

"Sorry, didn't mean to imply anything bad."

Before leaving on her trip, Lucy had told me that Atticus hasn't really been himself the past few months, even before his injury. Kellen told her he'd not been bringing girls home when they traveled.

A flash of him kissing me against the wall in that hotel on New Year's Eve pops into my brain in full detail. Has he thought about our kiss as much as I have? No way. I pull at the neck of my t-shirt, grateful he's not still sitting at the picnic table where he would be observing me close up.

"There, perfect." Atticus steps back and admires his work, then looks at me for approval.

"Thank you." I smile at his proud expression.

"I'll just test this out." Atticus gracefully slides into the hammock and sighs happily, his body lying snugly horizontal. "Perfect. Care to join me?"

"What? No." I laugh, and so does he, but I picture climbing on top of him and snuggling up to his hard, muscled body. I shake my head and he takes it as a firm no.

Oh—new cross-stitch idea. *Hammocks: the worst place to hookup.* Or maybe something like *hammocks are a reminder being single is better.*

Okay, that one's terrible.

"How long are you staying in Fort Collins?" Atticus rolls to the side and hops out of the hammock. There's no way I'm doing that in front of anyone. I'll probably loop around like a fidget spinner. Atticus runs his hands over his clean-shaven chin. "Lucy's not due back home for another month."

"I don't know. There's a few things I want to get fixed on the Pink Palace, like touch up the paint—" I gesture toward the scraped and peeling pink paint next to the door. "—and reseal that window so the AC works better."

"That shouldn't take too long." He crosses his arms next to the picnic table.

"I've also got a side hustle to catch up on."

"Side hustle?" One eyebrow shoots up.

"Yeah. I, uh, do cross-stitch? And sell them online."

"You do cross-stitch."

"I do cross-stitch."

"Like a grandma?"

"No, not like a grandma, like a... millennial, I guess."

"Well, alright. What do you cross-stitch?"

I shrug. "Sayings. Quotes. I swear a lot."

Atticus chuckles. "Can you give me an example?"

"Sure. In the last week I've gotten four orders for one that says *Abso-fucking-lutely not.*" It's my best seller so far, which I know because of how few orders I've gotten overall, carefully tracked within my cross-stitch spreadsheet.

I have a spreadsheet problem, I know.

Atticus bursts out laughing.

"And it has some flowers on it." I love the sound of his delighted laugh. "You know, to soften the swearing."

"That is so weird, and so amazing."

"So good weird?" My face heats.

"Definitely good weird."

Weird is kind of what I'm going for these days. I want to find what makes me unique, not just be the woman with a spreadsheet plan.

"Well anyway, I need to catch up on some orders." I try to look casual. "And I might just wait for Lucy to come back from her trip. I don't have a plan." I have to kind of choke those last words out.

"Raleigh doesn't have a plan? You are the most organized person I've ever met. You've always had your shit together."

"I'm a free spirit, Atticus."

Atticus lets out a long, contagious laugh, throwing his head back and exposing the stubbly skin of his neck. "You are not."

"I am!" I practically stomp my foot. "I'm reinventing myself."

"As what?"

I shrug. "Not a boring pharmacist?" I became a pharmacist because my mother and I decided it was a stable career path that would pay well and allow me to capitalize on my strengths.

Too bad my detail-oriented nature didn't notice the fact that Jacob was gambling behind my back.

"Nothing wrong with being a pharmacist." Atticus sits back down across from me. "And reinventing yourself involves changing into something, not only changing away from something. So what are you changing into?"

"That's very deep, Atticus, but I haven't thought that far ahead." I try to keep my tone light, but his words hit me harder than they should for a throwaway comment.

He's right. What am I trying to turn into?

"You're a proper grown up." He shrugs. "You've *always* been a proper grownup."

"Driving around in a pink RV?"

"That's definitely a choice." He laughs again. "But don't be hard on yourself. Back in college, you reminded me all the time that I was a completely unserious person, unlike you. Maybe you could be a little less serious."

"I think I'm already halfway there." I glance at my crappy RV. "And I might have been kind of hard on you in college." Being hard on him was a self-defense mechanism. There was no way I was going to let myself overtly flirt with my best friend's little brother.

"Nah. You kept it real." Atticus stretches his neck to one side. "You were probably the only one besides Lucy who treated me like a normal person. January ignored me except to laugh along with you two. And most other girls threw themselves at me and were totally fake."

"You're welcome?" I press my lips together. I watched girls fawn over Atticus Knox in college, and besides the fact that he was

Lucy's brother, I was zero percent interested in crushing on someone who was given so much damn attention. I was not his type. And we couldn't be more different in our goals, ambitions, interests... I had to make sure I wasn't obvious about my attraction to him.

Atticus looks at me, a cute smirk on his face, and I'm sure that he's thinking about New Year's Eve.

"Hey, want to come to drinks tomorrow night? At a bar in town. The Black Diamond. Lachlan will be there."

I consider coming up with an excuse as being around Atticus makes me feel a bit squirrelly. I could make something up, but he'd know, and why would I want to avoid human interaction? I've been going nuts driving around by myself.

"It's my birthday. You have to come." A pained look flashes across his face, then is gone.

"It is? Happy birthday! Are you..." I do some quick math. "Thirty? Tomorrow?"

"Today."

"Today! Happy birthday!" I glance at our leftover cheese sticks. Sort of a sad birthday lunch.

"Thanks." Atticus nods. "So yes for tomorrow?"

Well. I can't say no. It's his birthday.

I think it'll be nice to be here and not drive for a bit. I can just wait for Lucy to get home.

I don't want to drive more than a few miles for a long time.

"No other plans."

Atticus smiles even wider. "Wanna give me a tour of the Pink Palace?"

I blink at him and picture the inside of my RV, where there's piles of empty hoops and half-finished designs everywhere. I basically move the pile to my bed when I'm driving and to the living area when I'm sleeping.

Also, not sure I can handle being in such a small confined space with Atticus.

"No, no I do not. I need to… clean."

"Another time, then." Atticus quirks a smile at me. "Hey, I don't think I have your number."

"Oh, okay," I say.

Then I casually give my phone number to a hot professional hockey player.

## CHAPTER 4
# Maybe Her
### ATTICUS

Sunday, June 29

I walk out of the players' gym and through the Blizzard arena to the parking lot, pushing my damp hair off my forehead. The Fort Collins sun is blazing and it's already almost ninety degrees out.

I'm antsy for drinks tonight with Lachlan and Raleigh. Seeing her yesterday brought up all sorts of feelings. I felt excited for the first time in ages. Like I have something to look forward to instead of just waiting for the offseason to pass so my regular life can start back up again.

It was shocking how fast the crush I'd had on her in college came roaring back on New Year's Eve. Especially when I finally—fucking finally—got to kiss her.

To get it out of my system, like I told her? Nah. Didn't work. I haven't been able to get her out of my head for the past six months.

And then she shows up in Fort Collins on my thirtieth birthday. On a shitty day when my father announces his fourth divorce and I find out the Blizzard acquired Barrett fucking Steele.

43

Feels like some kind of sign. An explicit sign beating me over the head that says someone's already here to replace me if I slip up.

One day, I could be like Armas and get a career-ending injury instead of one that heals with a few weeks off. Who knows what tomorrow will bring.

I shake my head and jump into my Wrangler and toss my workout bag—which I have to intentionally remember to take to the gym in the summer since during the season I can stroll in without a single thing and the team's staff takes care of everything —into the passenger seat.

Do I overflow from the seat? Yes, yes I do. Would a bigger car have made more sense for a six-foot-four hockey player? Probably. I adjust the hockey rubber duck on my dashboard so it's nestled in with the other ones.

I navigate the streets of Fort Collins back to my apartment downtown. Until a few months ago, my sister Lucy was living with me, which was weird at first but really fun in the end. We hung out and got to know each other again after a decade of living in different places. That was when she got together with Kellen. Now she's in FoCo permanently, in her own apartment with her funny little dog, Waffles.

I would say it's been quiet without her, but my kitchen is getting renovated and it's a hot mess of noise and dust and chaos most days. At least they are almost done and take weekends off, but I'm still not a fan of spending a ton of time there. I park my car and sit in the silence for a moment.

Raleigh Hayes, single and in my town.

I thought New Year's Eve was my only chance. I'd never get it again.

I should've gotten in contact with her after.

Emailed, texted, called, messaged through social media, sent an owl or a note via horseback, anything. But instead, I didn't do a thing.

I walk down the road for a coffee at Deep Roots Cafe instead of into my dusty apartment. Fort Collins is fantastic in the summertime. It's hot, but a dry heat so the ninety degrees doesn't feel as awful as where I grew up outside D.C. The sun shines three hundred days a year here.

The center of the town is lined with trees and restaurants, shops, and other retail businesses. I push my way into the coffee shop, which is cozy and crowded with people out for a leisurely Sunday morning coffee.

A pair of women whisper together as they wait for their drinks.

A toddler throws what appears to be cheerios at their older sibling at a table, the parents staring at their phones instead of intervening.

In front of me, a quiet couple holds hands.

And then there's me.

Who would I ever bring here? I imagine inviting Lachlan to get a coffee with me on a Sunday morning like this and shake my head. He'd do it, but probably talk about his girlfriend the whole time. I love him like a brother, along with my other teammates. They're my family. We even have a book club, and now that I think about it, I get to pick the October book. I haven't decided if I'm gonna go horror or thriller. Lachlan always chooses romance, the sap.

The barista hands me my latte and thoughts of book club give me another idea for an RV-warming gift for Raleigh, so I head to the connected bookstore, A Good Book.

Raleigh talked about how she wants to reinvent herself. There's gotta be books about that. I stand in the doorway and shift my baseball hat on my curls.

"Can I help you find something?"

I turn at the sound of a woman's voice. She's probably around my age, standing right inside The Good Book with a nametape pinned to her shirt. Rose, it says. Dark hair in a cute messy bun, glasses, dark eyes. Pretty.

"Oh, no, I'm just browsing."

"You more look like you're just standing there." She tilts her head.

I chuckle. "You're right. I do need some help."

"Great." Rose waits patiently for me to say more, reaching up to adjust her glasses.

"I'm looking for a few books for a friend. She's, uh, reinventing herself."

"So you want self-help?"

"Mmm, do I?"

"Or maybe memoir. I have tons that feature women reinventing themselves. After divorce?"

"Yes," I say with a nod. "That's exactly right."

"Follow me." The woman looks over her shoulder as she walks away. "I'm Rose, by the way."

"Atticus."

Rose steps down one of the narrow aisles to a bookshelf labeled *Memoir*. She runs her finger across the spines and then plucks a book from the shelf that pictures the back of a woman standing on a cliff, arms open wide. The title is *53 Stops*.

"I really like this one. She got divorced and decided to travel to fifty-three places in the year ahead of her fifty-third birthday."

I take the book from Rose. That's pretty close, even though Raleigh's twenty years younger.

"She's is in her thirties, so might not hit exactly right. But I'll hang onto it."

"Is she your girlfriend?" Rose blinks pretty dark eyes at me. "Knowing that will help me make recommendations."

"No, just a friend," I say. I'm not sure how that knowledge will help her. Rose's cheeks pinker, and I realize she thinks I'm flirting with her. Am I? I don't mean to.

But I did just tell her Raleigh's not my girlfriend. Which is a fact.

Six months ago, I'd turn up the charm a notch and obviously

flirt. But when I search for that desire inside me now, it's just not there.

"Right." She turns back to the shelf and scans a few rows of books until she finds another. "This is about one woman's sexual awakening after she split from a long-term partner and lost her job. She was thirty-five, so maybe closer to your friend's age."

I nod and take the book from her, imagining myself handing Raleigh a book with a couple—wait, no, there's three people— entwined on a bed on the front cover. *How I Found My Wild Side*, it's called.

Meh, why not.

"And here's one about a woman finding herself after her parents pass away at the age of twenty-nine. She starts her own company. It's more business focused."

I accept the book, titled *Woman Boss*, from Rose's hand. "I'll take all three," I say, trying not to overthink things.

Books for Raleigh feel like a great idea. She can read while lying in the hammock and looking out over the picturesque lake.

I follow Rose to the front.

"I'm new in town. Anything you recommend I do to get to know Fort Collins?" Rose asks too-casually as she scans the books into a tablet.

"Go to a Blizzard game," I say automatically.

She pauses in her tapping and looks up.

"Are you a hockey player?" Her eyes flit down over my body.

I nod. "It's the offseason, but we'll be back in September."

"Alright." She smiles broadly at me. "I don't know a lot about hockey, but I'll give it a shot."

Rose stares at me for another beat, and maybe I should offer her tickets or give her more suggestions or maybe even ask her out. But I don't. I don't want to make any more small talk with her, as nice as she seems.

Rose turns the tablet around so I can tap my card and sign.

"Let me know how your friend likes them." She's still got a smile on her face as I gather up the three books.

"Sure. See you around." I dash out of the bookstore.

Maybe I should follow Lachlan and Kellen's lead and get myself a girlfriend. Maybe I should try dating someone like Rose. She was obviously interested in talking to me, and I don't think it was only to help me pick out books.

But...I don't want to date Rose.

I'm more interested in hanging out with Raleigh.

Maybe Raleigh can help me figure my life out, even though her path couldn't have been more different than mine. I was skating into the unknown, pursing a professional hockey career. She was settling down in a small town with a husband and stable career right out of school.

Suddenly, her being here feels like *more* than a sign.

Raleigh is in Fort Collins.

No Lucy and Kellen to interfere.

Even Lachlan is too distracted with his girlfriend to really notice what I'm doing.

I pull out my phone.

ME

> hey, pretty lady. See you in a couple hours at black diamond, right?

RALEIGH

> Yup

> What do you think about a cross-stitch that is a giant flame and the words 'everything's fine' in the center?

ME

> I feel like maybe you should talk to a professional about that

RALEIGH

> Very funny. See you tonight

I grin and look up as I walk back to my apartment.

Raleigh's here.

This is my chance to hang out with her.

Get to know her better.

See what happens, without the prying eyes of my teammates and her friends.

No one's paying attention but me.

CHAPTER 5

## Chickens are Better than People

RALEIGH

**T**ap tap tap.

There's a sound at the door to the Pink Palace.

I sit up straight at the table. I'm not expecting anyone.

I toss my phone down next to an almost-complete hoop and small stack of packages to be dropped off at the post office today.

The smile from my text chain with Atticus fades from my face.

Maybe I imagined the sound.

*Tap tap tap.*

Nope, that's real.

Maybe I parked too close to a tree, and a branch is blowing against the door to the RV.

*Tap tap tap.*

No way. Too sharp. And it can't be someone knocking, unless they're using something sharp. Like a knife. A breath catches in my throat. I stand and peek out of the curtains. I don't see anyone. But still, I creep over and grab Fred—my trusty baseball bat—from where he leans next to the door.

Fred makes me feel better about being in the Pink Palace alone all the time. He wouldn't let anyone hurt me.

Sometimes when I close my eyes at night, my imagination starts running absolutely wild. I'm often in some kind of woods, or at the edge of the woods, and I'm a single woman in a flimsy pink RV trailer. It's not the smartest situation I've ever put myself in. But I refuse to let fear of the man—or bear?—scare me away from doing what I want to do.

Am I doing what I want to do? Is that what this is? I'm not so sure.

Wait... what if it's a bear at my door? An actual bear scraping my door with one giant claw that he sharpened on a rock deep in the woods just this morning?

*Tap tap tap.*

"Shit," I whisper and reach for the door handle. It's probably not a bear.

I must've parked too close to the tree.

*Tap tap tap.*

"Screw it." I fling the door open, Fred resting on my shoulder in a hopefully menacing way.

There's a flurry of movement jumping toward me and I basically die a thousand deaths, then stumble back until I'm leaning against the kitchen counter. Fred clatters to the floor.

Good to know I have the right instincts to protect myself.

My brain slowly adjusts to what I'm seeing standing right inside the door.

A chicken?

A white chicken, to be exact, with fluffy feathers sticking up around its head and a dark beak. She's kind of pretty.

Chicken cocks her head at me. I huff a laugh.

"What, no tapping now?" I cross my arms, my gaze flitting down to Fred, although I don't think Chicken's gonna get aggressive.

She takes a step forward.

"I mean, what are you doing in my house?" I press back against the counter and extend my foot to the top of Fred and roll him toward me.

She looks back over her shoulder.

"Are you waiting for someone? A chicken friend? Running from something? Like a bear? Need a hiding spot?"

My god, I'm talking to a chicken. I really need more human interaction.

It looks at me.

"Oh, shit, *is* it a bear?" I sigh and shake my head. "This is no place for a chicken. This campsite. The woods. Colorado, probably. How have you not gotten eaten yet?"

With a flutter of wings, the chicken half-flies further into the RV.

I scream. Then she settles at my feet and her feathers tickle my ankle. I laugh and do what any reasonable person would do in this situation. I pull out my phone and take a picture of Chicken staring up at me with my bare feet on either side of her. I cackle as I press send to Lucy and January, no caption or explanation included.

Ten minutes later, I'm heading to my SUV, Chicken secured safely inside the Pink Palace. I had some folded up cardboard boxes that I taped together to create a little corral to keep her contained. She gave me the dirtiest chicken face when I left her like that, so I promised her I'd be back soon.

What else was I supposed to do? Leave her to die in the elements?

I did some quick googling and it's a miracle this creature is even alive. There are so many predators for a chicken in a suburban backyard, let alone the woods of Colorado. Raccoons, possums, owls, bears, cats (and not the domesticated kind), snakes...the list gave me the absolute creeps. How did it survive the night? Where did it come from? Is there a chicken owner somewhere frantically searching for their lost foul?

I'll deal with finding her potential owner later.

For now, I can't leave her out there. It's a terrifying battle-ground for a chicken.

I had an intense internal battle myself when I opened a fresh spreadsheet and created tabs for supplies, feeding schedule, general information about chicken care... no.

I do not need a spreadsheet for everything.

I closed it but did not delete it.

I repeat *I do not need a spreadsheet for everything* to myself as I get into my SUV to drive to a local farm store I found online. Not something that was on my bingo card for today, but I have to go to town anyway to mail the hoop orders.

I shut my door and pull up directions just as a woman emerges from the RV in the campsite next to mine. She waves and I roll down the window.

"Morning!" She's a middle-aged woman with blonde hair streaked with gray, holding a mug that says FC Cincinnati. She's the one I saw walking her dog with her husband yesterday. The one who saw me with the poop tube. At least she understands what that's like.

"Hello," I say. "You don't happen to be looking for a chicken, are you?"

"A... chicken?" The woman's eyes widen and she pauses, then glances back at her partially open RV door. Is she wondering if I'm a crazy person?

"Yeah, never mind." I shake my head. "I'm Raleigh. Staying next to you." I nod to the Pink Palace and do my best to look sane.

"I'm Elizabeth. My husband—Darren—and I just got here yesterday with our dog. We're from Cincinnati."

"Nice to meet you." I nod. "Well. I'm off to buy chicken food! See you later!" I wave and pull away, cackling when I look in my rearview mirror and see her watching me leave with a seriously confused look on her face.

I navigate the unfamiliar roads and head to the post office first, dropping off my completed orders. This side hustle is... not very profitable. I love it, though. Maybe one day I can figure it out. Or not, and just keep it as an intense hobby.

Next to the post office is a cute little shop called Rocky Gifts. I stop in and am greeted with an adorable store filled with gifts and crafts and cards. There's a local artists section, and I pick up a postcard print of Fort Collins and a clay mug.

"These are so cute," I say to the cashier as she checks me out. The cost is way more than my total profit from the hoops I mailed out.

"Yeah, the owner loves to stock local items."

"Have any cross-stitch?"

"Huh? Oh." She purses her lips. "No, I don't think so."

"Okay. Bye!" I spin and leave the store, another confused person in my wake.

I am not a local artist. And I am not trying to stock my cross-stitch in a Colorado gift shop.

The farm store is on the outskirts of Fort Collins, and I sit in the parking lot for a second to check out responses from Lucy and January to my chicken picture.

JANUARY

Um. Why is there a chicken in your RV? On your feet?

LUCY

Are you eggs-ploring some pet options, sis?

JANUARY

She's clearly just winging it

LUCY

We egg-spect you to answer right away

I cackle and type out a response.

ME

She literally knocked on my door a little while ago. What was I supposed to do? I'm buying her food now

JANUARY

That chicken is clucky she found you, babes

LUCY

You're cracking me up

ME

Tell me you guys are googling these puns and don't just know them off the top of your head

JANUARY

Guilty

LUCY

What are you going to name her?

ME

It's not like I'm going to keep her

LUCY

Then what's your plan?

What is my plan? I don't have one. Again. I test how I feel about that. I don't hate the feeling.

Mom would be horrified.

ME

I have no plan. Any name ideas?

JANUARY

Clearly it has to be punny

LUCY

Egghead?

JANUARY

Humpty Dumpty?

ME

How about M-egg-hen

JANUARY

LOL

LUCY

Yeah. Megghen. I like it. Double pun

I slide my phone into my bag and head into the store. I don't have a good plan for Megghen, just like I didn't have a good plan for this whole RV situation. Is this progress? Or just chaos?

Inside the farm store, I'm overwhelmed. I don't go to many—any?—farm stores in Connecticut. So when an older man in worn jeans and a store branded t-shirt approaches me asking if I need help, I take him up on it.

"You want chicken supplies." He repeats my request.

Was I not clear?

"Yup. I need chicken supplies." I nod. "For my chicken."

"Right." He waves me to follow. "So you have a coop in your backyard?"

"Mmm, not exactly."

"Do you have a list of what you need?"

"I can google one if it helps?" I slide my phone out of my pocket and shake it at his back.

He glances over his shoulder and sighs. "Why don't you tell me about your situation."

"I live in an RV and I'm unexpectedly taking care of a chicken. Temporarily."

The man stops short and turns to look at me.

"That's a new one."

"Yup." I nod in encouragement of him to process this faster.

"So you need food, food bowls, water bowls?"

"Probably."

"Do you have a safe enclosure?"

"Nope. I don't have any enclosure, unless the Pink Palace counts."

He doesn't ask for clarification.

"Where is the chicken now?"

"In my RV?"

"That's also new." He runs his hand through thinning hair. "Let's get you set up with a simple, enclosed chicken run so she doesn't have to stay in your house, er, RV. Some shavings so she has a place to rest. A place to nest."

A hysterical giggle escapes me, and the man looks at me with concern.

"Sorry, sorry. This is just more involved than I thought it would be."

"Chickens aren't easy. Or cheap. And this isn't the best solution. The simple enclosures aren't the most secure. They've gotta be temporary."

"Maybe we can set up with the minimum to keep her alive while I figure out what to do with her. Like the *absolute* minimum."

The man half glares at me.

An hour later I leave the store with supplies to set up a chicken run. When I pull back into the campsite, Elizabeth is sitting out under their RV awning with her husband and dog. I wave and park my car.

"Hi, Raleigh," Elizabeth calls.

"Hey." I walk their way, stopping about ten feet from where they are seated. "I realize I might have sounded a bit unhinged before."

"Do you really have a chicken in your RV? It took me a little while to process what you said, but when I did, I was like—what."

"Yes, yes I do." I laugh.

"Okay." She nods, a wide smile on her face. "This is my husband, Darren."

"Hello," he says, his hand resting on a black lab's head. "This is Tuna."

"Nice to meet you, Tuna." I pat the happy dog's head.

"So did you get the chicken situation sorted at the store?" Elizabeth asks.

"Yeah, kind of. I got some supplies so I can care for her while I look for her real home, assuming she came from someone. I'm going to set up a little enclosed run outside so she doesn't poop all over my RV."

"That's a good idea. Need any help?" Elizabeth stands and glances at the RV. "We used to have chickens in our backyard in Ohio. So I know a thing or two about them. Plus I'd really like to meet your chicken."

"Megghen."

"Megan?"

"No, it's Megg-hen."

"Your chicken's name is Megg-hen?"

"Yes."

"Perfect."

"And I'd love the help." I shrug. "I don't know a thing about chickens."

"Let's do it." Elizabeth hands her coffee mug to her husband.

This is weird, but why not? I have literally no plans today until meeting up with Atticus later tonight, and I could use some company. She follows me back to the Pink Palace.

"I talked to a guy at the farm store. After deeply judging me, he suggested buying all sorts of crazy stuff. We argued back and forth for a bit and finally agreed to this." I pop open my trunk.

Laying across my flattened back seats is a foldable popup chicken run for outside, a wooden nest, a small tent, and various other items.

"Huh. Interesting. We had quite the extensive wooden chicken coup in our backyard. Still, the animals got to them all eventually."

"That's awful." I shudder and picture finding Megghen

ravaged by animals. I don't think she'll be sleeping outside—that tent will be going into the Pink Palace.

Elizabeth helps me unload.

"Where do you want it?"

"Maybe on the other side of the RV so no one can really see it? I'm not sure chicken coops are appreciated in the campsite."

"I think you're probably right." Elizabeth chuckles. "So what's your story, Raleigh? Why are you in Fort Collins in an RV campsite by yourself?" Elizabeth hands me a stake and I push it into the ground, securing one of the corners.

"Heh. That's a long one." I push until the stake slides into the soil. "But basically, I just got divorced—again—and needed some time off from my old life. So I bought an RV, took a sabbatical from my job, and started driving."

"That's very adventurous of you." Elizabeth watches me with her hands on her hips.

"I've never once in my life been described as adventurous. Now people are using that word but I think they really mean crazy. Or irresponsible."

"I think it fits." Elizabeth looks at me, dead serious. "Wait, I mean adventurous, not crazy or irresponsible."

"Ha." I don't want to talk about myself any more. Luckily, she lets it go. "How about you?"

"Well, we're both teachers. Our daughter just graduated college and is setting up her life in New York City, so we're spending the summer driving cross country."

"Must be nice to do it with someone." I didn't mean it to come out self-pitying, but I guess it does.

I've learned my lesson by now. Marriage isn't for me. Two divorces should be a serious red flag for any future relationships.

As in, I shouldn't have any. At least not for a long while.

I don't trust myself.

"Divorce is hard. I'm sorry you had to go through that.

Twice." Elizabeth hands me a second stake as I scoot to the next corner.

"I'm fine." I try to chuckle light-heartedly as I lean onto the stake. "One of my best friends lives here but is out of town at the moment, so I'm just going to hang out for a while. I know a few other people."

"Fort Collins is lovely." Elizabeth hands me the third stake. "The people here at the campsite seem nice, but if you need anything, you let us know."

"And I have my chicken." The third stake slides in. I rip open the food bag and pour some into a bowl, which I place inside the cage next to a water bowl.

For my chicken.

I'm ridiculous.

"I'll go grab Megghen."

I enter the Pink Palace and tentatively push the door open. I'm half afraid Megghen's going to come flying at me and attempt to frighten me to death like she did this morning.

But the trailer is dead quiet. I leave the door open and step inside.

"Chicken?"

No response. I sweep my gaze around the Pink Palace. There's a flattened pile of cardboard where her makeshift enclosure used to be.

Shit. Okay, so she's a bit of an escape artist. I can respect that.

"Megghen?"

There's a pile of chicken poop in front of my closed bedroom door. Gross.

"Come here, chicken."

There's a *boc-boc-boc* noise from a little nook underneath my sink, and I squat down. She's wedged herself in. Megghen tilts her head at me.

"Megghen. Out." I wave my hand and she flutters all at once and out the door, scaring the shit out of me. "Crap!"

I practically leap out of the RV to grab her, but Elizabeth already has Megghen in her grasp.

"Chickens are sneaky." Elizabeth gently pushes Megghen through the wire door of the chicken coop. "If you have her loose inside ever—which I'm not sure I'd recommend—watch out for eggs in weird places."

"Noted." We watch Megghen peck around at grain in her food bowl. "Thanks for your help setting this up."

"Not a problem." Elizabeth glances back at her RV. "Well, Darren and I are off to grab a bite to eat in town. Interested?"

I shake my head. "Thanks, but I'll pass for now. I'm gonna hang out here."

When Elizabeth is back in her campsite, I settle down in a flimsy captains chair—I really need to buy a better one—next to the coop and unlock my phone.

LUCY

Nice chicken coop!

JANUARY

Don't you mean eggcellent chicken coop?

LUCY

Damn. Missed opportunity

JANUARY

Do better, babes

LUCY

I clucking will

ME

My god, is this how it's going to be?

LUCY

Constant chicken puns? Yes

JANUARY

Abso-clucking-lutely

I crack up and click out of my messages to my email. There's one from my mom with a list of *ways to maximize your work sabbatical* and below that, an email from Jacob.

I sigh deeply.

Thankfully, he can't show up at my door like he would do back home. So I guess I can at least read his email.

*To: Raleigh Hayes*
*From: Jacob Ford*

*Hey, Raleigh. Just checking in with you. How's your road trip? I'm sorry our last interaction was so stressful. I was shocked that you bought an RV on your own. I always pictured us doing that together.*
*I had another therapy session yesterday. It continues to help me uncover so many truths about myself and how I acted during our marriage.*
*I hope we can start fresh when you get back. As friends. Maybe one day, we can be more.*
*I went to see your mom. We had coffee and talked about how we both want what's best for you.*
*Understandably, she's still upset you've been helping me out financially. I reassured her I will pay you back for every dollar I've borrowed. I know you sent me money before you left, and I hate to ask again, but can you help me for one more month? I have a promising second interview coming up soon.*
*I'd love to come see you. Just tell me where you are and I'll be there.*

*Love, Jacob*

I groan and drop my phone in my lap.

There is too much in that email for me to process.

I'm going to have words with my mother for spending time with Jacob. He just looks at it as support and encouragement. But really, when I told her Jacob and I were splitting up, I think she really thought *good riddance.* She's never wanted me to rely on a man in any way. It was never part of her plan for me. And she certainly never wanted a man to rely on me.

I thought it was a win at the time, but I have regrets for accepting so much in the divorce. Jacob insisted. He is so sure we'll end up back together. But he's unemployed and broke and while I love him, I'm not in love with him anymore. Maybe I'm too easy on him, but we were married for five years and it's not like he cheated on me, or worse. He just has some issues to work through, and I can't be a part of it.

I press *reply.*

*To: Jacob Ford*
*From: Raleigh Hayes*

*Jacob,*

*I left Connecticut because I need space from my life, including you. I'm glad you're figuring things out in ther-apy. I hope you continue to make progress.*
*You need to secure that job. I sent you money two weeks ago—do you really need more already? I'll transfer you some cash, but let's try to make this the last time.*

*-Raleigh*

I cringe as I press send. I'm such a sucker.

But the last thing I need is Jacob hunting me down in Colorado.

## CHAPTER 6

# Hopeless in Love
## ATTICUS

Raleigh walks through the door of The Black Diamond and a sense of relief washes over me. I'm not sure why I thought she might be a no show. This is not something I'm ever worried about when meeting up with women.

But Raleigh's here. I watch her stride toward us, a closed-lip smile on her face.

"Hello," she says. I stand and Lachlan leaps up off his chair.

"It's good to see you again, Raleigh." Lachlan pulls her into a hug first, like he's the old friend, not me.

Last fall we were all in on the fake dating scheme between my sister and Kellen. There was a fake dating committee for it and everything. It was a hard thing for me to swallow at first—my *sister* and my *teammate*—but it was clear they fell hard for each other.

We'd video call Raleigh from Connecticut along with January, their other best friend who lives in London. And they all met up here in Fort Collins for New Year's Eve.

The night Raleigh and I kissed.

Lachlan and Raleigh separate and she steps back, turning to me with a tentative smile.

Raleigh's always been the one of my sister's friends who was the most stable. She kicked ass in college and pharmacy school, got a great job right away, and got married shortly after that.

Then divorced. Then married again.

Maybe she's *not* the most stable.

Raleigh doesn't quite look like the same woman, even with her always wispy blonde hair and pretty brown eyes. There's a slightly lost look in those eyes, even more pronounced than what I noticed on New Year's Eve. Then she looked happy and free and relieved.

I realize we're all standing around awkwardly so I step forward and open my arms. She's stiff as she leans in, but her body relaxes against mine as I wrap my arms around her in the most appropriate way I can muster. It feels more than good to have her in my arms.

I swear I hear her sigh.

"Now that I'm not holding a sewage tube, you'll hug me?" Raleigh says into my shoulder.

"Exactly." I chuckle and let her go reluctantly, but before it gets weird. Weirder. "It didn't seem like the right time for a hug."

"Sorry, sewage pipe?" Lachlan gestures to an empty chair next to me and Raleigh sits.

"Yeah. I was emptying the Pink Palace's sewage tank."

"Still confused." Lachlan makes a face.

"The Pink Palace is an RV," Raleigh says with a laugh. "And emptying the sewage tank, while necessary, is my least favorite part of RV life. My second least favorite is actually driving the giant hunk of metal."

"Sounds like you need wine." Lachlan picks up an empty glass from the middle of the table and fills it generously with red wine before topping off mine. "Not sure why Atticus got all fancy on us for tonight instead of just drinking local craft beer like usual, but it's his birthday celebration."

Raleigh glances over at me, her eyes flitting down over my face briefly. I might have tried just a bit harder than usual tonight. Instead of a plain t-shirt, I'm wearing an expensive black shirt.

Instead of my backwards hat, I actually swiped some product into my curls.

I look like an asshole, and truly wish I'd just been myself.

"What've you been up to since yesterday?" I gulp the wine. I prefer beer, but this'll do the trick to relax me faster. "Any good new cross-stitch ideas?"

"Cross-stitch?" Lachlan furrows his brow in amusement. "Why am I so confused tonight?"

"Yes. I do cross-stitch and sell it online. With sarcastic or snarky quotes." Raleigh sips her wine and sighs with pleasure. "And I do have some new ideas."

"Go on," Lachlan says. "Tell us."

"It's inspired by my chicken." She pauses with a smirk.

"Sorry, your what?" I sit up straighter in my chair. "Did you say your chicken?"

"Yes, yes I did." Raleigh rolls her shoulders back and closes her eyes for a second, as if gathering the strength to tell us a story. "This morning a chicken knocked on my door, and when I opened it—carrying my baseball bat, Fred, of course—"

"—wait—" Lachlan tries to interrupt.

"Shhh, dude, let her talk." I wave at him.

"—she literally let herself into the RV. She's a white fluffy chicken."

I stare at Raleigh with my jaw dropped slightly open.

"You— you kept it?"

"Her. And yes, for now. I named her Megg-hen."

"I like it," Lachlan says with a laugh.

"You are now a chicken mom." I shake my head but can't stop grinning.

"That sounds weird, but yes, temporarily." She laughs. "Someone must have lost her—she's really pretty. Clearly a back-yard chicken. Or pet chicken. Or whatever."

"Clearly." I glance at Lachlan. "Did you know people have pet chickens?"

"Yeah. Of course." He looks at me like I'm nuts.

"Did you know chickens can be pretty?" I try again.

"Obviously." Lachlan shakes his head and turns back to Raleigh. "I bet your chicken is a silkie."

"Yeah?" Raleigh raises her eyebrows. "How would you know?"

"I watch Chicken House. It's a reality show about a family who has chickens. Melissa's really into it."

"Wow," I mutter under my breath and judge Lachlan harshly.

"Well, I went to a farm store and bought some things that she'll need. The guy who helped me thought I was nuts." She huffs a laugh.

"Careful, on Chicken House they had a really flimsy coop and it got destroyed by raccoons. Luckily, the chickens managed to escape."

"For fuck's sake, Lachlan." I roll my eyes. "Shouldn't you be working out or doing something else with your time?"

"Hush." He waves at me. "Mel and I bond over it."

"Moving on." I turn from Lachlan in disgust. He's so whipped. "So she's in a coop that you bought at the farm store?"

"Hmm. Yes? But at the moment she'll be in the Pink Palace in her tent at night and when I'm not there, since the coop is pretty flimsy. No chicken murders by raccoons on my watch."

"Smart." Lachlan nods enthusiastically.

I press my lips together. They are seriously having this conversation.

"So my new idea for a hoop is *I don't need a husband, I have chickens.*"

Lachlan laughs, and I chuckle.

"Perfect."

"But can we please stop talking about me?" Raleigh pulls at her hair and crosses one leg, then uncrosses it right away. "I haven't interacted with people this much in weeks and it's kind of freaking me out. There must be some kind of hockey gossip to catch up on."

"Sure is. We've acquired a new player from Utah." Lachlan is way too excited about this. "He's the guy that fucked up Atter's groin during our last game."

"No way." Raleigh's eyes widen and she examines me. "And you feel how about that?"

"Fine. I feel fine," I grumble. I want to punch Lachlan for bringing up Barrett fucking Steele.

"Barrett Steele." Lachlan runs his hand across the air in front of him like he's revealing something huge. "Even his name is savage."

"I don't care about Steele." I grit my teeth and know I sound too defensive. "I'm just focusing on getting myself back together for the charity tournament." I wish we were still talking about cross-stitch and chickens.

"Sure, whatever." Lachlan's phone rings loudly. He leaps up from the table. "I gotta take this."

"Ever heard of silent mode, dude?" I shake my head as Lachlan dashes away from the table, phone already nestled on his ear, a goofy smile on his face.

"That the new girlfriend?" Raleigh asks when he's gone.

"Yup. He's completely obsessed."

"Is that so bad?"

I shrug. I don't want to sound like a jealous asshole. Cause I'm not. Jealous, that is. Probably an asshole though.

"I guess not."

"Don't get me wrong—I am the most negative person in the room right now when it comes to love and relationships." She laughs with a bitter edge.

"A lot of people get divorced." See? I sound like an asshole.

"*Two* divorces by age thirty-four? It's pretty bad, Atticus."

I hate the crestfallen look on her face. Literally can't believe two men let this woman slip away.

"The way I look at it—" I lean forward and catch a whiff of a light floral scent. "You are at least a mature enough human being to be in a serious relationship—"

"And you, mate, aren't." Lachlan jumps back in the conversation as he rejoins us. "What are we talking about? How Atticus is hopeless in love?"

"Dude. Until two months ago you'd never seriously dated someone either, so shut your trap. You're not a love expert." I shoot daggers with my eyes at Lach.

"It just takes one, mate. The right place, the right time, and I was ready." Hearts spring up in Lachlan's eyeballs. "I don't think you're emotionally capable of going on a real date yet."

"I am too capable!" I'm a child. Why are we talking about my pathetic love life in front of Raleigh? "And you can fully fuck off, *mate.*"

"When's the last date you went on?" Lachlan cocks his head.

I shrug and try to look chill. "I don't know."

"Never. It's basically never."

"I go on dates." Fuck Lachlan and his insider information.

"Okay, so when's the last time you went on more than *two* dates with the same person?"

Well, shit, that answer might actually be never.

"You've never really dated someone?" Raleigh looks at me with shock.

"Hey, I met someone today that I could take on a date." It might be my imagination, but a shadow passes over Raleigh's face for just a second.

"Who?" Lachlan narrows his eyes.

"Her name is Rose. She works at the bookstore." I lean my elbows on the table and attempt to look casual and confident, like I'd actually want to take the bookstore woman out on a date. Which I do not.

"And you want to date her?" Lachlan shakes his head. "I don't believe you."

"Why not?" Because I'm lying.

"Did you ask her out?"

"No." *Fuck* no, I meant. I shake my head and plead with Lachlan to take my side. "Listen, even you just said I'm not good at this kind of thing. I wouldn't know how to act."

So that's kind of a lie. Of course I know how to ask someone out. I'm a thirty-year-old man. But I simply haven't had to do it very often. Usually women just sort of appear in front of me after I toss a charming smile and expensive drink their way.

Yup. I'm an asshole.

"Yeah." Lachlan tilts his head at me, then looks at Raleigh. "But *she* is definitely good at this kind of thing."

"Who?" I say, hoping he's not going down some ridiculous rabbit hole.

"Raleigh. Raleigh's good at dating."

Raleigh's eyes widen as Lachlan looks overly pleased with himself.

*What the fuck is he thinking?*

## CHAPTER 7

# Dating Coach

## RALEIGH

I scoff.

"I am *not* good at dating."

Lachlan could not have read me more wrong. Good at dating? Good at picking the wrong guy, yeah. Good at agreeing to bad marriages, sure.

"Really?" Lachlan raises his eyebrows. "Because you've gotten two blokes to marry you, which means you got them to date you first, and eventually propose. I'd say you're pretty good at it. This guy's never gotten someone to actually date him." He nods toward Atticus.

"By choice!" Atticus insists, his brow furrowed. I can't decide if he looks confused or offended. "If I wanted to date someone, I would've."

Offended, then?

"To be honest, I have a hard time believing that Atticus can't get someone to date him." Honestly. There's no way this is hard. There's no way this man—I let my eyes flit over his chiseled jaw, bright green eyes, deep red curls—would have a problem dating.

"Exactly. See?" Atticus practically growls at Lachlan, who is clearly just pushing his buttons.

"You need help, mate. You want to ask this Rose person out?"

Atticus pauses and I find myself holding my breath.

"Yeah." He looks at me when he says the word and I give an over-exaggerated shrug, then nod like a crazy person.

I shouldn't care in the least if Atticus dates Rose or a cute bartender or half of Fort Collins.

I'm not interested in dating *anyone*.

Definitely not him.

"Just say—can I take you on a date? Then take her on one," I say. "It would be that easy to prove Lachlan wrong."

"It's not really that easy." Atticus watches me with a blank expression that I can't read.

Of course it's that easy. What's he talking about?

I study him with narrowed eyes. I have no clue what's going on inside his head. Maybe I should text Lucy and get more information.

Or maybe I shouldn't let Lucy know how overly interested in her brother I am, because she'd see through me in about two seconds.

"Is it the actual date that's the alleged problem?" I tilt my head and take a drink, deciding I'm going to play along. Why not? But I need more alcohol to have this conversation. "Because we all know you can get women to pay attention to you without a problem. And you can ask them out—you are not shy, Atticus Knox—and they'll likely say yes."

Atticus grins at my use of his full name. "Yup." He nods. "That's it. The actual date."

"I got lucky," Lachlan says dreamily. "I didn't know what I was doing either, but Melissa took care of me. You've just gotta take a chance and then embrace it, mate."

"Christ, if I have to keep hearing about how in love you are, I'm going to walk into the Rocky Mountains and never come back." Atticus glares at his friend.

"Don't do that." I shake my head and try not to giggle. Atticus looks at me. "Listen, I did some research, and there's like all sorts of scary chicken-eating wildlife in those mountains."

"You had to research to find that out?" Atticus raises his eyebrows. I attempt to growl at him but we both burst out laughing instead.

Lachlan makes a curious sound and I turn to him. He's watching me, eyes narrowed, mouth twitched to one side.

"What?" I say. I feel like he's really seeing me. Seeing through me?

"You should be Atticus's dating coach." He looks back and forth between us and says the words slowly, as if making sure we both understand every. Single. One. Of. Them.

"Um—what?" I practically spit out the sip of wine I just took.

But Atticus is quiet, and when I look over at him, his eyes are wide as he chugs his own wine.

"Hear me out." Lachlan lifts both hands in the air. "Give my friend—your friend—some pointers. Go on a few test dates so we can make sure he doesn't totally fuck things up with this Rose person once he actually gets her out on a date."

"Raleigh, just ignore him." Atticus finds his voice and sounds oddly calm. "It's a stupid idea. Don't even look at him." His protests aren't nearly as strong as I'd think they'd be.

It's almost as if he doesn't hate the concept.

I do look at Lachlan. A hysterical laugh forms in my throat, but I beat it down.

"I mean, it might be good inspiration for new cross-stitch quotes," I say casually. "I'm trying to make enough money that I don't have to spend my savings on gas and food and campsite fees."

I really have no problem with money. Even with sending funds to my ex every month, I have plenty in the bank. Doing cross-stitch is not about money. It's about exploring a new hobby and trying to break even. Like a little game I'm playing with myself and my spreadsheet.

"Oh, come on." Again, Atticus's protest is weak. I'd think he'd be glaring at Lachlan and cutting off the conversation completely.

It is a stupid idea on so many levels.

That I am any kind of dating expert.

That I want to help Atticus Knox ask someone else out.

That Atticus needs any help at all.

That I need inspiration for new cross-stitch patterns so I can pay for my campsite fees.

"It doesn't have to be a big deal," I say, apparently on board. "I'll be in town anyway. I'll probably be here until Lucy gets back from her trip." Wait—did I decide that for sure? Yeah, I might've. "We could go over some dos and don'ts of dating."

"This is actually perfect," Lachlan says. "Atticus needs to learn how to date someone so he has something to do all summer besides whine about how much his groin hurts and how sad he is that Barrett Steele now plays for the Blizzard. And Raleigh, you need some inspiration, and unless I'm mistaken, you don't have much to do this summer either."

"I mean, you're not wrong," I say.

"Raleigh?" Atticus leans forward and touches my arm. "You don't have to be my dating coach."

I glance down at where his hand is on my arm. I like it there. He slides it off slowly, and I like that feeling, too.

"Dating coach. Mate, that's perfect." Lachlan points at Atticus and then at me with a cackle.

"Seriously, Lach?" But Atticus looks at me questioningly.

"I'd be happy to help you ask out Daisy." My voice is unnaturally squeaky.

"Rose," Atticus says her name slowly.

"Right. Rose." I clear my throat.

"Then it's settled." Lachlan drains his wine, then empties the remaining drops from the bottle into our glasses.

"I think we need more wine." Atticus glances down at his half-full glass and then locks eyes with me.

"I'll get another bottle. Least I can do for your birthday. Besides getting you a dating coach." Lachlan sings the last two words and practically skips away to the bar.

"Lachlan in love is annoying as shit," Atticus grumbles. "As if he has any idea how to be in a relationship."

"It's really not that hard," I say. Atticus chuckles and the sound rolls over me pleasantly.

"For you, maybe."

I shrug, uncomfortable under his gaze. "So you met this woman at the bookstore?"

"Yeah. Oh, I was at the bookstore buying you more presents." His eyes light up.

"More presents?" My cheeks warm as Atticus reaches down to the ground and pulls up a paper bag, pushing it across the table to me.

"Yup."

"But you already bought me the hammock."

"That was an RV-warming gift."

"And the cheese sticks."

"A simple snack."

"And the wine and corkscrew."

"Who shows up to someone's house for the first time without wine? And a way to open it?" He throws his hands up.

"RV, not house."

"Yeah, RV." His mouth twitches up on one side. "I was inspired today. Go ahead."

I accept the bag and pull out the books one by one.

*How I Found My Wild Side* has three mostly naked people entwined in a bed on the cover. I look up at Atticus with raised eyebrows, and his cheeks turn rosy.

"They're all memoirs about women reinventing themselves."

"Sexually?" I say before thinking.

He laughs. "I guess that one might be?"

The second book is called *53 Stops* and looks like a good travel memoir. The third one, *Woman Boss,* is about career reinvention. I'm struck by how thoughtful of a gift this is. He went into the bookstore—met Rose—and thoughtfully picked out these three books.

"No big deal if you don't want to read them, I just thought—"

"Thank you. They're perfect. And you're very sweet." A little knot in my chest tightens. I have the urge to hug him for the second time tonight, but god knows I'd make it awkward as shit, so I don't.

The bookish woman must have thought she hit the lottery when she met Atticus at work. I stare at him and shake my head.

"What?" His brow furrows.

"Atticus, you do not need my help learning how to date someone." The words come out sharper than I intend. "I have a feeling if you really want a girlfriend, you'll figure it out." I'm irrationally annoyed at the thought of bookstore Rose with hearts in her eyes.

"But what if I do?" He holds my gaze and doesn't crack a smile. "Want your help?"

Lachlan interrupts the moment, arriving back at the table with a fresh bottle of red wine. Atticus breaks eye contact and Lachlan spots the books as he fill our glasses.

"Oh, nice stack, Raleigh!" Lachlan tops off my wine.

"Atticus bought them for me."

"Did he?" Lachlan glances at Atticus with raised eyebrows. "And have you made plans for your first dating lesson?"

Atticus is staring into his wine, probably thinking about the bookstore woman.

First dating lesson? Just one problem.

I have a crush on this man.

If I'm totally honest, I've had one since he showed up for his freshman year of college.

And now I'm supposed to help Atticus date someone else?

But it's not like he'd date *me.*

Why would he possibly want me, a twice-divorced, thirty-four-year-old woman, when he can have someone younger and hotter and less awkward and weird?

He doesn't. We're just friends. Friends who made out that one time.

And as a friend, I'm going to help him learn how to date someone.

New cross-stitch idea: *It's fine. I'm fine. Everything is fine.* With a flaming dumpster below it.

CHAPTER 8

# Put Me In, Coach

ATTICUS

Wednesday, July 2

Today's a skating day, and it's a good distraction while I wait for my not-date tonight with Raleigh so we can start the dating lessons that I don't need.

I go through extensive stretching before I even put my skates on. My groin pull was not due to me not stretching enough, but I know I need to be extra careful because repeat injuries are common. And I'm not about to let Barrett Steele take my spot on the first line.

Barrett fucking Steele.

During that last game, he checked me so hard against the boards that all the air was knocked out of my body. I fell to the ice, which I've done a thousand times, but this time the way I landed was too awkward and I could feel the muscle yank in a way that didn't feel right.

That moment haunts me. I was terrified for a split second before I realized I could get up and limp-skate off the ice.

Was it his fault? I dunno, but I'm definitely gonna hold it against him.

I'm already sweating from the stretches, squats, high knees, lunges, and jumping jacks as I strap on my blades. No one besides me and the skating coach are in the arena. This is my last one-on-one practice with him before I start small group practices.

I meet up with the team's long-term skating coach at the entrance to the rink.

"Hey, Gerald."

"All warmed up?" He watches me intently.

I nod.

"How are you feeling today?" He looks pointedly at my groin, which would be weird in literally any other circumstance. Gerald can't be more than five years older than I am, maybe mid-thirties. He's an ex-professional figure skater and pushes all of us hard, making grown men cry even though we've all probably got fifty to one hundred pounds on him.

"I feel great. Don't go easy on me." I need the distraction. Gerald nods to the ice, and I do a half dozen warm up laps while he busies himself setting up a series of orange cones to practice quick and tight turns. He explains the drills and I get to work. I almost wipe out after a mild twinge in my groin startles me, causing me to hesitate around one of the cones.

"Knox!" Gerald shouts.

I spin to a stop and turn to him, waiting for the criticism I know is coming.

"You can't be scared of your own body," he yells across the ice. "If you get in your head, you'll never fully recover. And you are, in fact, fully recovered. So act like it." He claps three times.

I concentrate and get through all of the cone torture, and then he has me switch to practicing explosive starts and short bursts of speed. After twenty minutes of that, we move on to puck handling around cones—the fucking cones are back—and the nets, then end with shooting practice.

After an hour, I drag myself to the locker room to grab a hot shower. That felt good. I'm finally—*finally*—feeling like I can get back to where I was. And Gerald's right. I am too much in my head. In a normal summer, I'd be lazy right about now and would ramp up workouts in August as preseason got closer.

This summer I'm decidedly more nervous.

Especially about that asshole Barrett Steele.

But tonight my reward is I get to hang out with Raleigh.

As my dating coach? What the fuck. But I like her. She's funny. And pretty. And while I used to think of her as polished and put together, now she seems to have leaned in to another side of herself.

And I like that side.

I liked her before, but I might like the cross-stitching, RV-driving chicken lady even more.

* * *

After snort-laughing at the flimsy-ass chicken coup in front of the Pink Palace, I knock on the door to the RV, my knuckles making a tinny sound.

She's living in an oversized tuna can. How is this even safe?

Raleigh opens the door and I can't help the smile from widening on my face. She's wearing a sleeveless blue sundress with a low neckline that offers a hint of the swell of her breasts, and the hem stops halfway up her thighs. I try really hard not to let my eyes linger on her legs or tempting cleavage.

"Hey, I just need a few more minutes." Raleigh's curled her short hair away from her face. She gestures to an eye, like I'm supposed to know what that means, and glances over her shoulder back into the trailer. "Come on in, I guess."

"Have time for that tour?"

"Sure, and it'll take about sixty seconds." Raleigh sighs and steps back from the doorway.

I step into the RV and look around.

"Wow, it's actually roomier on the inside than I thought it would be," I lie. She lives here? This place is a closet.

"It is absolutely not." Raleigh narrows her eyes at me.

"Um, yeah, you're right." I shake my head. "This whole place would fit into my bedroom."

"Shut up." Raleigh reaches over and gently pushes me in the biceps. "It's home for now. This is the kitchen." She doesn't move but points to the sink, small refrigerator, and double cabinets. "This is the dining room."

My eyes settle on the table, where there are piles of yarn and what I'm assuming are other cross-stitch materials.

"I know, it's a mess." Raleigh tries to step between me and the table. "I basically move the pile from my bed to the table and back to my bed. There's really nowhere to store it."

It's really not a mess. Organized clutter, more like it.

The table is next to the entrance, and on the other side is a snug two-seater sofa with a pair of comfy-looking pillows and a pink fleece blanket hung across the back.

In front of the sofa is a tiny tent with mesh sides.

And a white, fluffy chicken inside.

"And this is Megghen."

"Wow." I squat down and peer at the bird.

Megghen stares at me with beady little chicken eyes.

"Wow, she's so pretty?" Raleigh suggests.

"Sure. And wow, a chicken in a tent in a pink RV is not something you see every day."

"Ah. Yes. That."

"To be sure I understand, she's inside because any creature on this big beautiful green earth could break into her flimsy chicken coup?"

"Yes, correct. She's not pleased that I shoved her inside that tent. But—oh, crap." Raleigh takes a step toward the door to the RV, where there's a pair of sneakers neatly lined up next to flip flops. "I knew it." She bends down and pulls something out of her shoe.

It's a brown egg.

I stifle a laugh.

Raleigh stands, puts a hand on her hip, and shakes a finger at the chicken. "No laying eggs in my shoes! This is the second time!"

"That is really gross." I press my lips together, but the chuckle escapes this time.

"Yeah? Well it's also really delicious." Raleigh opens her small fridge and places the egg gingerly into the built-in egg container. "Just hang out with Megghen for a minute while I finish my makeup."

Raleigh takes about three steps to her open bedroom door. I follow to peek inside and observe mostly bed, a small vanity table, and a closet with an open folded door. Her makeup is scattered over the vanity.

"Not only is my bedroom the same size as your entire RV, but my bed on its own is bigger than this room."

"Seriously, shut up," Raleigh huffs. "I'd slam the door in your face, but it sounds like a piece of cardboard."

I hold up my hands and take the few steps back to the couch to give her some privacy. Raleigh thinks I've bought her gifts so far? She hasn't seen anything. What I really want to do is buy her a bigger, better RV.

I won't, of course, because I'm pretty sure she'll think that's going a step too far.

"What are you going to do with the chick—Megghen?" I wave down at the chicken, who is watching me through the mesh with those creepy chicken eyeballs.

"I'm going to post on a few neighborhood apps," Raleigh says from inside the bedroom. "Her owner is probably looking for her."

I lean over and look at the biggest pile of finished cross-stitch. The one on top says *Abso-fucking-lutey not* in looping script and has delicate roses stitched all around it. I huff a quiet laugh. Then my eye catches on the circle above her kitchen that says *The Pink Palace* with pink swirls along the border.

I reach up to touch it and the hoop falls off the nail.

"Shit!" I fumble but catch it and re-hook it on.

"What'd you say?" Raleigh peeks her head out the door to her bedroom and my eyes flit to her red painted lips.

"Oh, nothing. Just talking to Megghen."

The chicken *boc boc bocs* accusingly when Raleigh disappears back into her room.

"What?" I whisper. "Mind your business."

Raleigh walks out of her bedroom and settles at the table to put on strappy sandals, lifting one smooth leg at a time. The whole thing feels so natural, which is the weirdest part of it all.

"You're not judging me, are you?" She looks up when she's done. "With your fancy apartment and your hotshot pro hockey player life?"

"Never." And I mean it. "You look beautiful."

She glances down at her dress and a pretty blush creeps up her neck onto her cheeks.

"Whatever. Let's go."

Fifteen minutes later, Raleigh walks through the door I'm holding open to La Dolce Vita Bistro.

"So the whole point of tonight is to teach you, a thirty-year-old man, how to act on a date." Raleigh crosses her arms and assesses me like she's searching for a lie.

"That is correct." I give my name to the woman at the hostess stand.

"Because you don't know how to do that."

"Also correct." The hostess gathers menus and waves us to follow her.

"Fine," Raleigh says. "But in exchange, I really do need some good cross-stitch inspiration."

"I can't imagine you won't get that." I don't finish the

sentence like I want to, with something like *with this ridiculous dating coach situation.*

We settle in our chairs, and I order a bottle of red from the waitress.

"So, where should we start, coach?" I ask, earning a withering look from my not-date.

"Alright. That couple over there." Raleigh nods her head to a man and woman a few tables over from us. "What do you think?"

The couple, probably in their mid-twenties, are having a conversation over drinks. Looks... fine.

"I don't know, they look like they're having an acceptable conversation." I shrug. "Maybe he looks a bit bored."

"Exactly. To me it looks like she's talking and talking and he's zoning out."

"Yeah, I see that. He's not paying attention at all."

"Like, he's just kind of staring at her with his eyes glazed over. Actually, he's staring at a spot over her shoulder, I think, not even at her. Oh—he just took out his phone and looked at it."

"Maybe he's a single dad checking on the babysitter," I suggest.

"You think that guy's a single dad?" Raleigh gives me a deeply skeptical look, then glances back over. The man is wearing a tight button-down shirt, and his hair is slicked back. He looks far too self-absorbed to be a father.

"Or maybe he's just a dick." Of course, he's just a dick. Even I know not to look at my phone while I'm on a date.

Our server approaches that table and refills the couple's wine glasses. Then she heads to the bar and the man obviously watches her ass as she walks away.

"Oh, shit." I chuckle.

Yup—he's definitely a dick.

"You saw that?" Raleigh looks at me, her voice incredulous.

"Yeah, hard to miss."

"But the woman is still talking. I think she *did* miss it."

"He's still looking. What an ass."

Raleigh squints her eyes at me.

"What? Ohhh. I meant *he's* an ass, not that the server has a nice one."

"Sure." Raleigh's mouth twitches into a smile. "So don't check out other women while you're on a date."

The server appears at our table and opens our bottle of wine, then pours a sip for Raleigh to try. Raleigh nods and the server fills our glasses. I say thank you as she leaves and make sure I don't even glance her way.

I definitely don't look at her ass.

"Is *dating tip: don't stare at the server's ass* too long to go on a cross-stitch thingy?" I swipe my hand across in front of me.

"A hoop?" Raleigh gives me an amused grin.

"The circle thing?"

"The hoop." She nods. "And yes, that's probably too long, but your head's in the right place. Another dating tip: don't get trashed."

"And no staring at your phone." I run my palm over my chin. I shaved for this date so I'm mostly smooth.

"Don't skip out on the bill."

"No woman is going to pay for her meal when she's out with me," I scoff.

"Spoken like a rich man."

I shrug. There's no use denying it. "How about always share your french fries? And dessert."

"See?" Raleigh tilts her head at me. "You don't need my help, Atticus."

"I do. I am your dedicated student, coach." A student of Raleigh Hayes for sure. "Give me a weird dating tip. One most people don't think of."

She presses her lips together.

"This is probably an anti-tip, actually, because I think any guy I asked this on a first date—or second, or third—would run screaming into the forest. But I always want to know."

"Alright, I'm intrigued."

"Ask them where they see themselves in five years. Professionally and personally."

"Wow. That's an intense question."

"I know. It's a total job interview question. But I think it comes from my mom and all her detailed planning of my life."

"So what is your ideal answer to that question?" My mind spins because she might ask me this question next. I try to focus on her answer.

"I don't know." Raleigh shrugs, color filing her cheeks. "Jacob told me he wanted to have a big house and a bunch of kids. But we never got around to the kid part, which I'm thankful for now."

I process this information, not quite sure how to respond. With my own shit answer, I suppose.

"Five years is a lifetime away. I'll probably be retired from hockey," I say, my stomach flipping uncomfortably. "And I really don't have a clear plan for after that. Professionally or personally."

"I think that's okay."

"Yeah? Because I feel like that's the exact wrong answer to give you."

"If this was a real date? Maybe." The corner of her mouth twitches up into a smile. "But this is between friends."

"Right." Isn't this a real date? It feels like one. Between friends.

"Have you really never dated anyone?" Raleigh is studying me.

"There's been women I've seen more than once, but it never felt right to keep up with them." I twist my wine glass in between two fingers. "One was too pushy about commitment. One begged me for a jersey. Mostly, they just wanted to date a Blizzard player."

"Well that's shitty."

"I guess. I don't think I've been going around breaking hearts. More like temporarily damaging egos."

"And now? Why are you wanting to date someone now?" Raleigh's brown eyes are bright, and she tucks a curled chunk of hair behind her ear. Her cheeks are lifted in the remains of a smile.

Why, indeed.

"I guess I've just been feeling really isolated lately. Everyone is partnered up."

I don't fit in with my friends who are partnered up, and I don't want to find a new group of single dudes.

And then she stumbles back into my life. The perfect summer distraction.

"Mmm." Raleigh leans back and crosses her arms, studying me with narrowed eyes.

"Also, my dad's getting divorced."

"Wow." Her face crumples. "Lucy didn't tell me that. Number four?"

I nod.

"I just told Lucy the other day. She won't pick up his texts or calls, which is gloriously savage."

"Twice divorced is bad enough. Four times? That's his whole personality now." Raleigh looks like she's thinking too hard, with her forehead remaining furrowed and her lips pressed tightly together.

"Would you want to get married again?" I slip the question right in there, making things more awkward. But she rolls with it.

"I used to think I needed to be married to be happy." Raleigh sighs and pulls at her hair with one hand. "Like, any second now, happiness will fall into my lap. I was waiting for it to all come together." She lets her eyes fall shut for a long beat. "I think my mom was probably right. Focus on myself and a career and a future, with only me in it."

Raleigh and I are so very different. She's been chasing—craving?—a stable, standard, suburban life, but is it what she really wants? Or is she working to follow her mother's wishes, and then her husband's, and maybe even society's, but ignoring what she wants from life? Does she even know?

*I* know what I want. And it's what I've been focused on for my entire life: hockey.

Maybe, for once, I'm the one who gets it. I know who I really am. Like it or not, I'm my father's son, and that's why I've never dated someone seriously. I don't want to hurt people like he has.

Especially someone like Raleigh.

So while I love hanging out with her, I need to behave myself while she's in town. I'm just getting to know her again. Hanging out. This is *nothing*. I've gotta make sure we don't fall into something that can't happen. Something where I'll hurt her.

"So, are you ready to ask out Tulip?" Raleigh breaks through my thoughts.

"Rose." I smirk and raise my eyebrows. "It's Rose."

"Right." Raleigh reaches up and runs her pointer finger over her bottom lip, then touches her neck. I watch, mesmerized at the way she touches her own skin.

"I'm not ready to ask her out yet."

Or ever, probably.

"Why not?" Raleigh blinks at me. She definitely isn't buying my bullshit.

I clear my throat and sip from my wine. "I think I need more coaching first."

Raleigh raises her eyebrows but doesn't comment.

The waitress delivers our food and Raleigh and I shift our conversation back to ways to ruin a first date. Turns out, all of them are too long to fit on a cross-stitch hoop.

See, I'm even learning her language.

And when I order the creme brûlée and she orders the cheesecake for dessert, I insist that she have the first bite of both.

"You're a good student." She smiles and takes a second bite of my creme brûlée.

A half an hour later, we're on our way back to the Pink Palace. I wanted to make the night stretch longer, but she said she needed to get back.

I pull up at Raleigh's campsite. She doesn't get out right away.

It's not like I'm nervous—I'm not going to kiss her—but there's an anticipatory tension in the car.

"Hey, what are you doing on Friday?" I say, the words out before I can really consider them.

"Hanging out with a chicken in an RV?" Raleigh says without hesitating.

A smile twitches on my lips.

"Well. I hate to mess up your plans, but it's the fourth of July, and that seems sad and lonely. Want to do something?"

"Right, good idea, we can have another dating lesson." She taps her lips with a finger. "Want to watch a movie?"

"Sure." I glance at the Pink Palace. She must mean we'll go out to the movie theater.

But she doesn't.

"We can each pick one and decide which we'll watch when you get here."

"Here?" I attempt to clarify.

"Yeah. Or we can watch both."

Raleigh wants to watch a movie with me here, in her RV, in the middle of the woods, on her tiny couch? Okay.

She nods, the sides of her mouth turning up.

"We might be able to see the fireworks across the lake. I'll check."

Raleigh blinks at me with those dark eyes before opening the passenger side door. She slips a foot out.

"Movies and fireworks," I confirm.

"That isn't a bad second date idea, to be honest." Raleigh exits the car, her dress bunched up around her thighs as she slides out of the seat.

"I'll come at seven on Friday, okay?" I lean over and let my eyes very briefly flit down her body while she's not looking.

"See you then." Raleigh slams the Wrangler's door. I roll down the window.

"Bye, coach."

Raleigh rolls her eyes and waves. I watch her unlock the Pink Palace and open the door. She calls out to Megghen and then closes the door securely behind her. She pulls aside the curtain above her couch and waves to me, and only then do I drive out of the campsite, lowering the driver's side window as well to appreciate the smell and sounds of the woods at night.

I don't love her being out here all alone, even if she did tell me about her nice Midwestern neighbors. But I wouldn't dare tell her what to do. I wouldn't dare make her think she needs a man to protect her.

But I wouldn't mind doing it.

CHAPTER 9

# I'm Not Weird, I'm Unique

RALEIGH

Friday, July 4

"Are you fucking with me, Megghen?" I stand with one hand on my hip and the other holding a warm egg that I found nestled in the hood of my hoodie on my *actual bed* while cleaning up before Atticus arrives.

Why was my chicken on my bed? There's just no excuse for that. Ever. I thought I closed the door. Can chickens open doors if they try really hard?

"It was a present," I say in what I imagine is Megghen's chicken voice. She looks up at me from the tiny square of a kitchen floor and cocks her head.

"I don't want this kind of present. I also don't want you pooping on my floor anymore." I point to the door. "It was a perfectly nice afternoon and you refused to go outside." I put the egg in the fridge with the others. "But there's still another hour and a half of daylight, so I'm sending you out."

"Because you want to be alone with the hot hockey player?" Megghen continues to mock me. "Your best friend's little broth-

91

er?" Megghen raises her chicken eyebrows and judges me. "And what are you wearing, anyway? Shorts and a tank top? Try harder."

She's so freaking judgmental. I didn't want to *look* like I was trying hard for Atticus and our not-real date, so I went with super casual.

And I really don't want to overthink why I'm having these kinds of conversation with my chicken.

I sigh as Megghen takes a cautious step toward the door.

Yesterday I'd posted in a few of the local online groups about her. I didn't mention what kind of chicken she was—which I now know is a silkie, thanks to Lachlan—or about her white coloring. I figure if someone messages that they've lost a white silkie, it'd be a safe bet they're telling the truth.

The responses I've received so far have ranged from annoying *(can you tell me what kind of chicken she is and I can check if I'm missing one?)* to creepy *(where are you located? I can come over and check if she's mine—are you single by the way?)* to hilarious *(I train chickens and have an opening in my next session, if you're interested!).*

As annoying as she is, one thing's for sure: I'm not going to give her to just anyone.

I scoop Megghen up—I had to search online for the right way to pick up a chicken, and she actually likes it when I hold her, surprisingly—and fling open the door to the Pink Palace.

Atticus Knox is standing there in a gray Blizzard hoodie, black athletic shorts, and a backwards baseball cap, wide shoulders looking like they'll barely pass through my doorway, green eyes twinkling. He's got a bottle of wine in one hand and a full reusable grocery bag in the other. The sight kinda makes a breath catch in my throat.

"Oh. Hey." I say a quick silent prayer that he didn't hear me speaking in Megghen's chicken voice.

"Going somewhere with the chicken?"

"I'm going to put her outside in her enclosure until it gets dark. She's been super grumpy all day." The chicken reaches her head aggressively toward Atticus, who retreats a few feet so I can step out of the RV.

"Does she want me to pet her?" he asks, looking like he'd really rather not.

"No, I don't think you pet chickens."

I squat down to unhook the enclosure and push Megghen inside. She spins around and glares at me with an accusatory *boc boc boc* under her breath.

"Nothing will happen to you. I swear." I close the door and hook it as she stalks back toward me. "We'll come get you when it's getting dark." I stand and step away. Who knows what an angry chicken will do?

"Good call." Atticus stands next to me, watching Megghen. "I don't want to be defending her against a bear or a mountain lion."

"Ugh, don't say stuff like that." I turn to him and nod at the goodies in his arms. "What do you got there?"

"Red wine." He holds out the bottle. "And movie snacks."

"That's a lot of snacks. Come on in."

Atticus follows me into the Pink Palace. It feels much smaller with his six-foot-four frame instead of only my five-foot-four one. He seems to take up more space than he did the other night.

And when I turn to him, he's close. Really close. I know we were alone here briefly and at the restaurant, but this is where we'll be hanging out for the night, and it's mere feet away from my bed.

"I'll grab the bottle opener." I open the drawer and pull out the corkscrew he left with me last weekend.

"I brought you a pair of real wine glasses." He pulls a box with two wine glasses out of his bag and places it on the kitchen table. "They had it at the store right next to the wine, so I thought, why not?"

"What?" I smile and shake my head. "Thank you. But that's ridiculous. Stop buying me stuff."

"I like how it makes you blush when I do."

"I'm not blushing," I lie as my face heats.

"You are. Now give me that corkscrew." Atticus holds out his hand and I pass him the device, my fingers grazing his palm. I pause at the delightful sensation of our touch.

My phone buzzes in my pocket, saving me, kind of. I pull my hand away and look at my phone. It's the text chain with Lucy and January.

> **JANUARY**
>
> Raleigh and Atticus sitting in a tree, k-i-s-s-i-n-g…
>
> **LUCY**
>
> First comes love…
>
> **JANUARY**
>
> Then comes… wait, we're not letting her get married again
>
> **LUCY**
>
> Then comes situationship?
>
> **JANUARY**
>
> I don't even know what that means
>
> **LUCY**
>
> Does anyone??

I crack up and press my phone to my chest for a second.

"Who's that?" He fills the glasses and sets the bottle down on the table.

"No one," I say too quickly and glance back down at my phone.

"No one?" Then he dumps the rest of the grocery bag on my table. Microwave popcorn, chocolate, and chips.

"Fine, it's Lucy and January. They think it's hilarious we're hanging out together."

"Of course they do." Atticus snorts. "My sister is the nosiest woman I know."

I don't mention that they're singing playground songs about us.

ME

Very busy, leave me alone

JANUARY

YEAH YOU'RE BUSY

LUCY

That's kinda gross

ME

I'm busy giving your brother a dating lesson, gotta run

JANUARY

Wait, babes… pretend you're an exciting person and do something reckless

ME

Like?

JANUARY

If I've gotta explain, then…

"You know, texting while hanging out is kind of rude. Didn't you tell me that the other night?"

I look up, and Atticus is staring at me with a smirk.

"Shit, I'm sorry, you're right. But it's with your sister and January, so forgive me?"

Atticus nods toward the loveseat, holding both glasses of wine. "What do they have to say, besides laughing at us?"

"Oh, you know. The usual."

"So harassing you about your life choices?" Atticus sinks down on one side of the couch, his body turned toward the center.

Well, okay. We will be full on touching once I sit down. I never noticed how small this couch is. I've never sat on it with anyone else.

I lower myself next to Atticus and he watches me, a slight smile on his face. Just as I expected, our knees touch when I'm fully seated.

"Cheers." He holds his glass toward me. "To hanging out with old friends."

"Cheers." I clink his and take a gigantic gulp of wine. "Damn, that's good."

"It's my mom's wine again."

"Tell her it's delicious."

"Next time I talk to her, I will." This man is staring at me and I'm not sure if I feel uncomfortable with his gaze and proximity or if I want to strip off all my clothing and mount him.

Really? Is this what it's like to be six months out of a second divorce? Ready to mount the first hot professional hockey player I run into?

I clear my throat and look away. "What movie did you pick?" I grab the remote and click the screen on. "I can project from my phone. The campsite has remarkably good wifi."

"You go first."

"Well, I picked a romance, since we're talking about dating."

"I did *not* pick a romance," he chuckles.

"Mine is *Warm Bodies*. You've probably never—"

Atticus bursts out laughing, wine almost splattering on his knee.

"You've heard of it." I bite my lip and will my face to not turn bright pink.

"Oh, I've heard of it." He stops laughing but keeps the wide grin. "And I love that movie."

"What? You do?" I let out a relieved laugh. "I thought you were going to think I was a weirdo for picking it."

"Well yeah, I kinda do, but I guess that makes me a weirdo too." Atticus takes off his baseball hat and then re-settles it on his head. "I picked *Shaun of the Dead*."

"I love that movie too!" I laugh and push his leg with my hand. "I am obsessed with zombie movies."

"Same."

"But I mostly prefer when they are light hearted or funny. *Shaun of the Dead* is one of my favorites."

"And it does have some romance in it." Atticus sips his wine and nudges his knee against mine. "It's pretty romantic how Shaun battles hordes of zombies to save the woman he loves."

"That is very true. But in *Warm Bodies*, he literally becomes un-undead for her. She brings his heart back to life." It's actually really romantic and sweet, even though it's a zombie movie with on-screen brain eating.

"Yeah, good point." Atticus rubs his chin. "Let's start with that one, and then it'll be close to fireworks time." He grabs peanut butter M&Ms from next to him and offers me the open bag.

"Um, yes, absolutely." I reach in and pull out a few, popping them in my mouth while I scroll for the movie on my phone. "Peanut butter M&Ms and red wine is perfect. Ten out of ten."

An hour and a half later, the credits roll and I lean back, eyes closed. I survived a whole movie with my leg pressed against Atticus's and didn't even die.

I might have missed half the movie though.

"Love that movie," I say wistfully.

"A serious happily ever after."

"Right?" I turn my head toward him and gulp at the intense way he's staring at me. My words stall in my throat and I forget any commentary I was saving for the end. I gulp and try to slow my heart, which has sped up uncomfortably. "Is it fireworks time yet?"

"Yeah. Let's go set up." He stands. "I'll get a few things from my car."

I follow Atticus outside and grab Megghen from her enclosure. I tuck her into her tent in the Pink Palace right outside my bedroom door and she *boc boc bocs* at me.

"Relax. You're inside so you don't get eaten. And in this tent so you don't poop everywhere and hide eggs."

When I get back out, Atticus has a picnic blanket spread out in front of two fancy captains chairs, the kind that rock back and forth. They look suspiciously new. Not like my cheap ass chair that is ripping at the side so whenever I sit it kind of leans crookedly and I wonder if today's the day it'll break and toss me onto the ground.

Atticus pours me wine from a new bottle.

"Did we really finish the bottle?"

"Yep." He hands me my refilled glass.

"You're not having one?"

"I'd love to, but I shouldn't if I'm going to drive home." He looks at me with alarm. "Which, of course, I am going to do."

I sip from my glass and know I should probably not have any more either. I'm too relaxed, too giddy, too... something.

"You can always sleep it off on the couch." I attempt to make my tone as casual as possible, but almost definitely fail. "My very tiny couch."

"I'm not sure I'd fit." Atticus chuckles and stares at me for a beat longer than is comfortable. Then the fireworks start, and he finally looks away. It takes me another few seconds to turn to the explosions of red, white, and blue light in the sky. I sneak another look at Atticus, who looks back at me right away.

"What are you thinking about, Raleigh?"

"*Warm Bodies*," I say immediately, the double entendre hitting me a second later.

He raises an eyebrow with a grin. "There's a lot to think about."

I laugh. "I'm probably thinking too deeply about a zombie movie, but it kind of represents someone completely changing who they are for someone else."

"You don't think people can change?" His voice sounds tight.

"I mean, that much? Probably not."

Definitely not. People simply don't change that much. In reality, people are who they are. And maybe they shouldn't change for someone else.

Once a compulsive liar, always a compulsive liar.

Once a player, always a player?

"That's why I don't do relationships. I'll never be good at them. It's in my blood."

I swallow and turn back to the colorful display reflecting off the lake. I want to argue with him that he could definitely be good at relationships. But what do I know?

"Do you really think that's true?" I finally say instead.

He doesn't answer and we watch the rest of the fireworks until the big finale. I expect Atticus to head out. But instead, he glances back at the Pink Palace.

"*Shaun of the Dead?*"

"Sure," I say, even though it's late and I should send him home.

This time, I don't hesitate to sit down next to Atticus. This time, our whole bodies touch. He puts his arm around the back of the couch and we watch Shaun and his friends battle zombies in England.

"I got it," Atticus says suddenly and I almost jump. He laughs and lets his arm drop around my shoulders. "Sorry, didn't mean to scare you during a zombie movie."

"No problem. What do you got?" I turn to Atticus and we are so. Close. Together.

"You can make a whole zombie cross-stitch series. Like: *I prefer zombies to people.* Or: *Don't worry, zombies only like brains.*"

"Stop it, that's amazing." I chuckle softly.

"Yeah? I'm not sure there's a big market for that though."

"People love zombies." My eyes involuntary drift to his lips.

"Mmmm, is that true?" His arm is still resting on my shoulders, like we're meant to be snuggling on the couch just like this, and I swear he tugs me just a tad closer.

"Maybe?" I push his knee with my hand and let it linger for a few more seconds. "Or is it just us?"

Just us. I like the sound of it.

Suddenly the air in the room starts buzzing. Or maybe the noise has been there all along, like the background noise of summer cicadas. I'm warm and happy and laughing with Atticus Knox, and he's looking at me like I'm his kind of weird—shit that's another good quote, but he's not moving, and I don't think he will. But the bottle of wine I've consumed gives me the courage and I lean forward to close the distance between us, pausing before our lips touch.

"Raleigh," he says, his voice raspy. It's a warning, and a question, and maybe an invitation.

"Yes." I answer all of them.

Atticus slides his hand along my jaw and into my hair. His breath is hot on my lips. We're frozen in space and time and anticipation.

I flash back to every party during college where we'd flirt and tease each other.

Every time I've insisted he's just my best friend's little brother.

I'm back to New Year's Eve when we finally got to kiss.

And now? I'm getting the chance to do it all over again.

But it's different this time.

Because we're alone.

And it's breaking the *once and never again* rule we agreed to.

Fuck it. Who cares about rules.

"Any second now, Atticus."

Atticus smiles lazily and slowly closes the remaining inches between us, touching our lips together so gently I let out a soft sigh. Holy hell, the feel of his mouth on mine. I've missed it so much. How is that possible? I've only kissed him once in my life, but I still missed him. I press my mouth onto his and let my lips fall open. His tongue meets mine, and it's exactly what I've been thinking about for six months.

Atticus wraps his hands around my waist and tugs me until I'm sitting on his lap, allowing me to melt against his chest as our mouths come together again and again. He has a hand on the skin of my waist where my tank top has ridden up and the other buried in the fine strands of my hair. A little whimper escapes my throat. Atticus pauses and then pulls me even closer, his breathing sharper. His shorts are thin and mine are ridden up so my bare thighs are pressing against his hard length. It feels so good being in his arms.

But I'm so in my head.

Is this another example of me jumping in with someone too soon after a big breakup? But this time it's Lucy's brother? And am I really jumping in or just overthinking kissing?

I shove the distracting thoughts out of my head and bury my hands in Atticus's thick curls, pushing his baseball cap off and leaning into him. I can feel him smile against my lips.

He shifts his body and gently runs his tongue along my bottom lip, then nips it between his teeth. My head spins with the pleasure of it. The teasing. I could kiss him forever.

There's so much between us. He's not just a random guy. This is Atticus. There's an encyclopedia unspoken and I want us to read every page together. Atticus's hand drifts from my waist to the outside of my bare thigh, and he strokes a single finger inside the hem of my shorts, exploring, testing, touching. I whimper again and shift on his lap, looking for more.

Is this me being a good dating coach?

The thought makes me pause. Literally and figuratively.

"Raleigh?" Atticus pulls back until he can focus on my eyes. His are hooded and turned dark green, like the color of a forest of pine trees as night falls. "You okay?" He lifts the hand from my leg and tucks a chunk of hair behind my ear, his fingertips grazing my sensitive earlobe.

I slowly slide my hands out of his hair. I stare at his lips, a deep red from kissing me.

Ohhhhh no.

I can't do this. I can't do this with *him*. I can't let myself get all wrapped up. Doesn't he like someone else? And even if that's not a good enough reason, this is Atticus.

Atticus Knox.

Not only my friend's little brother, but also the biggest player I've ever met. Not interested in relationships.

And I have no business starting something with *anyone* so soon after my second divorce.

Especially him.

I do a weird little rolling maneuver to remove myself from his lap and pretend I don't see his cock tenting his shorts. What I would do to see what's under that fabric.

"I'm not sure this is helping you learn how to date," I say with a nervous laugh, tugging the hem of my tank down to cover bare skin.

Atticus's brow furrows for the briefest of seconds, and then his face smooths out. He adjusts himself and I try not to watch.

"Right." He pushes his hair off his forehead and grabs his hat from where it's wedged between his back and the cushion. His usual flirty smile returns to his face. "Sorry about that, I got a little carried away in the moment. Inspired by your romantic zombie movie."

Words get stuck in my throat.

"I think you'll do just fine with Rose." I clear my throat but it sounds like a squeak. He blinks and it reminds me of a flinch. I know I get her name right this time.

"I've never had a problem hooking up with women. It's more the other stuff."

Now it's my turn to flinch.

"Shit, that came out wrong, Raleigh. Sorry."

And I've never had a problem getting in over my head way too fast.

"But don't worry. I understand." I nod too enthusiastically. "You're good at the other stuff, too."

Like how he's made me feel tonight. Let's call it... overwhelmed.

God, this is embarrassing. He must have women throw themselves at him all the time. Hooking up is second nature to him.

I am not special.

And I better be careful not to let myself get too wrapped up in Atticus.

He's not mine.

Not now, not ever.

"Good." I nod and turn back to the movie, which we missed a bunch of. My buzz is also gone, disappeared the second I pushed myself off Atticus's lap.

But the air is still alive between us. Charged with all that is unsaid and undone. Or maybe it's just me being incredibly awkward. I can feel his eyes on the side of my face.

"Raleigh?"

"Yeah?" I slowly turn to him. We could just talk about this. I could tell him why I'm being weird so he understands. He's already pleasantly surprised me with seeming to enjoy all my newfound quirkiness: the Pink Palace, Megghen, cross-stitch, zombie movies.

I can fix this. I open my mouth to say something, but he talks first.

"I'm good to drive home." Atticus stands and I pause the movie.

Great. So I got drunk and climbed on his lap. Wait, is that what happened?

"Okay," I say, but I don't want him to go, I want him to stay and talk to me, to make sure things aren't weird between us.

Atticus stands and walks the few feet to the door of my RV.

"You good here by yourself?" Atticus puts his hand on the doorknob.

"Yeah, of course." My stomach drops. He's really leaving. Because I fucked things up between us by initiating a kiss.

"Talk to you soon?"

I nod.

"Lock the door behind me." He pauses for a second, as if giving me a chance to say something, but I don't. He winks and shuts the tinny door behind him.

I hate being in this RV by myself. Usually I lock up and bury myself in my bed with a good book to forget where I am, Fred tucked next to me. Lately, I've been reading that memoir about the woman who has a massive sexual awakening after she got dumped and fired. Is that what Atticus is suggesting I do?

Nah. That one isn't me. Tonight I'll start the travel memoir. Maybe that's more my style. At least I know I'm not the only woman who's ever found herself lost and confused in the face of major life milestones.

But I think that maybe I am not, in fact, good here by myself.

## CHAPTER 10

# Love Language

ATTICUS

Saturday, July 5

I slept like shit last night.

I can't believe what an asshole I am.

Raleigh's trying to be nice and I fucking maul her while we were watching a movie.

She's vulnerable right now, and I took full advantage.

Well, not full advantage.

And technically, *she* kissed *me*.

Then I told her I've never had a problem hooking up with women?

*Such* an asshole.

I groan and the clerk at the farm store gives me a skeptical look.

"Can you just confirm this address?" he says, tapping on the printed receipt.

I pull out my phone and double check the address of Raleigh's campsite.

"Yes, that's right. It's a pink RV. You can't miss it."

"You know this coop is not exactly portable?" The man draws

out the last three words and furrows his brow with a deep sigh. He knows I have no clue what's going on.

"The sales guy told me." I shrug. It's possible I'm going a bit over the top with the latest gift. It's possible she is going to think I'm ridiculous.

"And I can't imagine it's allowed under the campsite rules."

I shrug again. Her current flimsy coop is pretty well hidden behind the RV, so we can tuck this away in the same spot. What's the worst that happens?

I need to make last night up to her. I know I crossed the line kissing her. But she egged me on. What'd she say, *any second now, Atticus?* Damn, that was hot. And when I pulled her onto my lap... a sheen of sweat pops onto my forehead and I get half hard at the memory.

Raleigh makes me feel like a normal human being. She rolls her eyes at me, makes fun of me, and the way she twitches her lips when she's trying to hold back a laugh? I couldn't help but kiss that mouth.

I wanted to do so much more to her.

Especially when she let that little whimper slip and wiggled against my groin. Fuck.

But she pulled away. She hesitated.

I know why.

She thinks—knows—I'm not a serious human being. Maybe I'd be good for a hookup, but not for Raleigh. She's for real. She deserves more than me taking advantage of her.

And I confirmed it last night.

"How long will you be at the campsite?" the cashier asks, jarring me out of my daydream. He taps a few buttons and the receipt prints.

"A few weeks, I think."

"Well, if you want to sell the coup when you're ready to move on—if you're not taking it with you—let me know." He raises his eyebrows, knowing that I'm not taking a giant chicken coup with me in an RV.

I picture Raleigh driving away in the Pink Palace, without the coop or the chicken, and without me.

"I have a friend who would probably buy it from you for half the original price." He flips the receipt and scribbles a name and number. "He'd also probably take the chicken."

"The chicken is not for sale." How dare he try to buy Megghen?

"Yeah. He wouldn't pay for it. He'd take it."

"Her. It's a girl." The nerve of this dude.

"Sure. Whatever."

I accept the receipt, yanking it a bit too hard from his hand.

"Someone will be there in about an hour to set it up."

I leave the farm store and make one more stop before heading to the campsite.

* * *

The Pink Palace is quiet when I pull up. I peak around the RV. Megghen's not in her flimsy coop and Raleigh's not in one of the captain's chairs I left yesterday. Maybe they're snuggling up on the couch together.

My heart pounds a bit harder as I approach the door to the RV. *Boom boom boom.* What in the actual fuck am I doing? *Boom.* I haven't even been away for twelve hours after bailing post-kiss and I show up without any notice? *BOOM.*

I tell my heart to fuck off and knock quietly.

There are footsteps inside, and then the door swings open.

"Atticus." Raleigh breathes out my name. Her hair's messy around her head and she's wearing a tight blue tank top and black leggings.

"Hey," I croak out, obsessed with the way she first looked at me, which was with raw and open happiness, no filter.

"What are you doing here?" She swallows, and I watch her throat move.

My eyes drop lower and spot the bat in her hand. "Jesus. Everything okay?"

"Oh, yeah. I get a bit jumpy." She gently leans the bat against the wall next to the door. "I can't believe you didn't meet Fred last night."

"Fred?"

"Fred." She nods to the bat. "He usually sleeps next to me in bed."

"Right. I forgot about him." I've never been jealous of a baseball bat, but here we are.

"I brought breakfast." I hold up a hand with a brown paper bag. "And, uh, another gift."

"Dude. Stop buying me things." But she smiles and puts her hands on her hips, and I can't help but let my eyes drift down to the curve of her breasts and the points of her nipples, clear through her thin tank top.

I pull off my baseball cap and slide it back on backwards. I hope she didn't notice me being an absolute creep.

"I like buying you things. Besides, breakfast is not a big deal. It's just some croissants from my favorite bak—" My sentence is cut off by the sound of a pickup truck pulling up behind my Wrangler. We both turn to watch.

"Who is that?" Raleigh's brow furrows and she crosses her arms. "And are those... kayaks strapped to the roof of your car?"

"Yeah. Kayaks. And that would be the farm store guy here to build the coop."

Saying it all out loud makes it so much worse.

Raleigh Hayes does not need some man buying her things and trying to take care of her. She's fiercely independent—obviously— and I'm just going to scare her off.

"Sorry, did you say to build the coop?" Raleigh's eyes bulge, and she looks at me with her jaw dropped. "Hold on. I need a sweatshirt." She disappears into the Pink Palace, leaving her door open and dashing into the bedroom.

"Where do you want this set up?" The farm store guy in overalls asks.

"Around the RV, next to where the other one is." I make the executive decision and really hope this doesn't backfire.

He peeks around the RV before nodding and heading back to his truck.

Raleigh pops back out of the Pink Palace in a sweatshirt. She keeps her eyes trained on the man hauling pieces of a sturdy, wooden pre-made coop to assemble around the RV.

"You really bought me an actual chicken coop."

"Probably not the most reasonable idea for a gift, but I know Megghen keeps laying eggs in random places—"

"Like in the cereal bowl I didn't put away," Raleigh grumbles.

"What?" I rub my hand on my chin. "That's actually impressive."

"I know."

"So I thought if you could feel more secure with her out here, you could reclaim the Pink Palace for yourself."

"But that—" she gestures to the stack of wood the store guy is hauling out of the truck, "—is a giant, permanent chicken coop. I'm sure it's not allowed to be built here in the RV campsite."

"That did occur to me, but they haven't complained about the current one, so maybe we can get away with this one. And worst case scenario, we bribe the campsite manager with hockey tickets or Blizzard merch."

*We.*

"Hmm. And what am I supposed to do with this when I leave?" Raleigh turns to me, hands back on her hips.

"I don't know. Don't leave?"

She huffs a laugh and shakes her head.

"You're funny. But I guess I don't have to worry about it for a while longer. Lucy's back in, what, three weeks? I can't leave before she gets home."

"How much longer is your sabbatical?"

"Five weeks."

She'll be here max five more weeks. Less, because she's gotta get herself back to Connecticut. It both seems like a long time and not nearly long enough.

Enough for what, though?

We watch the farm store guy unload the rest of the wood and grates and I let those numbers sink in.

"I'll have it taken care of. As soon as you decide to leave, I'll get it taken down and away."

Raleigh turns and I can feel her staring, so I look at her. Her eyes flit down to my lips. Remembering our kiss last night? Kisses? Now that I'm in front of her, I know I don't regret kissing her.

I do regret the way I left her last night.

"That you, Atticus. This is very thoughtful."

The feel of her in my arms, on my lap, our mouths together... it was so right.

But I can't trust myself around her.

"And the kayaks are for our afternoon activity."

"Huh?" Whatever trance she was in snaps. "Afternoon activity?"

"You've got a lake literally at your front door." I nod my chin toward the gently lapping waves on the edge of the campsite, sun reflecting against the water and forming diamonds on the surface. "Let's use it."

"I do not know how to kayak." Her eyes widen.

"What's there to know? Just sit and paddle."

"It's not that easy." Raleigh shakes her head aggressively.

"It's not?" I chuckle. "I feel like it might be."

"I... am sort of terrified of being on the water." She cringes.

"Why?" I furrow my brow, but Raleigh freezes, like an extra

terrified deer in headlights. At that moment, the farm store guy calls us over to talk about the coop.

Thirty minutes later, Megghen is settled in the coop and we're on the water in the kayaks. I'm realizing that for Raleigh, there might be slightly more to kayaking than *sit and paddle*.

"Atticus!"

I look over at Raleigh, who is floating next to me in water that's so still it's like we're gliding through ice. But she has terror in her eyes, obvious even from underneath the bill of her Blizzard baseball cap, which she dropped on her head as we were climbing into the kayaks.

"You are doing just fine."

"We are SO far away from the shore." She stares longingly at the Pink Palace.

"Raleigh? We've been out here for five minutes. Even Megghen could swim back to shore from here if she were with us. Plus, you have a life jacket on."

"You don't understand." Raleigh moans and lays her paddle across her lap. I get ready to grab it if it slips off. "I get seasick."

"On a kayak?" I suppress a snort-laugh. She's quiet for a minute, and I think she's getting ready to answer me.

"I don't think chickens can swim," she says instead.

"You're probably right." I nod to reassure her further. "But I don't think you have to worry. Seasickness usually happens with waves, an ocean, a different kind of boat, etc."

"Like a sailboat," she whispers, her eyes wide, fear dripping from every word.

"I feel like there's a story here." I press my lips together and wait patiently. Raleigh's kayak is close enough that I reach over and gently pull it toward me. The plastic bumps together and she presses her eyes shut. I keep a hand on her kayak so she doesn't drift away. It's safe out here but you should still keep your eyes open while out on a lake.

"There is."

"Go on." The sky is a bright blue, the sun warming us. Colorado is god's country. The beauty is astounding in every nook and cranny of this state. It's hot, but never humid. Mountains soar around us. The forest is lush and green, the air clear and fresh.

And I'm spending time with Raleigh.

Fleeting thoughts of my injury, Barrett Steele, and the charity tournament flit through my head, but I push the negative vibes away and they vanish in the warm air. I switch my hat to forward facing to block the sun and wait for Raleigh to continue.

"It was during pharmacy school. A bunch of my classmates were going on a sailing trip in the French Caribbean and they invited me."

"I didn't know you knew how to sail."

"I didn't. I don't." Her eyes fly open and she shakes her head.

"Okay. Continue." I press my lips together.

"My job was to stay out of the way while they did the sailing thing. But that first day? The seas were rough. I started to feel sick, so I tried hiding below deck, but... it didn't work. Made it worse. Pretty soon I was throwing up over the side of the boat."

"Ohhhh no." I try so very hard to suppress a laugh and barely succeed.

"But I wasn't the only one!" Panic crosses her face. "Another girl was puking too. So we docked at an island and god, I was so happy to have my feet on solid ground."

"I can imagine."

"They told me it was a rough day at sea. That tomorrow would be better. And the next day.... Well, the sea looked like this." She waves a hand around her. "Like glass. Clear. Smooth. Practically no waves."

"And..."

"I was just. As. Sick. Worse, even." Raleigh shakes her head. "That night we ended up stopping in French Guadeloupe. I packed my bag, got off the sailboat, and refused to get back on."

I feign shock. "Where did you go?"

"I found a hotel. But the funny thing is they don't speak a lot of English on the island. Mostly French. And my classmates just kind of laughed and left me there. I was like—good riddance. The next day I had to take a cab to the pier and hope I understood what they'd told me about getting the ferry to the mainland."

I can't stop laughing, and Raleigh gives me a dirty look, then cracks a grin, and finally laughs with me. I let go of her kayak for a second to wipe my eyes and adjust my hat.

There's a flash of movement.

Then Raleigh's kayak is upside down.

"Oh my god! Raleigh!" What the fuck happened in the two seconds I had my eyes closed?

The kayak flips back over, empty, and her head pops up from under the water one second later.

"Fuck!" She yells, water streaming off her head. She grabs her hat, which is floating next to her, and tosses it in the kayak.

"Shit, give me your hand." I reach out to her and she just freaking floats there in the water with a shocked look. I'm not sure if I should laugh or help.

"This water is freezing!" But Raleigh looks far less panicked than she did while in the kayak.

"Are you okay? Swim over to me. Wait, you know how to swim, don't you?"

"Of course I know how to swim. And I'm wearing a life vest." She sighs. "My soul kind of hurts, but I'm fine."

I snort. "What happened? How did you end up in the water?"

"Something jumped." Raleigh runs her hand down her face. "It was only a fish, and I realized that a split second too late because you decided to let go of my kayak right at that very moment and I leaned over to get away from the fish and then..."

"Wow. I guess you really don't know how to kayak."

"I told you!" Raleigh doggy paddles over to my kayak.

"Hey, just don't lean on my kayak because it'll ti—"

A split second later, I'm underwater underneath my kayak. For fuck's sake, this water *is* cold. I kick to the surface, making sure I don't bonk my head.

I spit out water and swear loudly.

"I am so sorry! See? I do not do well with boats." Raleigh treads closer to me. "Are you okay? Did you hit your head?"

"I'm fine, sailor. I was getting kind of hot anyway." I shake my head to get water out of my eyes. "Did you do that on purpose??"

"No!" She bites her bottom lip and reaches for something next to me. "Here's your hat."

I pull it out of the lake and put it on my head, the equivalent of dumping a small bucket of water on myself.

Raleigh cracks up.

"At least we left our phones at the RV." Raleigh glances to the shoreline, which does seem kind of far away now.

"It would've been great to get this on camera." I tread water and for a second, I picture pulling her toward me and kissing her in this cold lake.

"No way." She glances at her drifting kayak. "Do you think we can just swim back?"

"What?" I laugh. I gotta get this woman to shore. "No. Grab the kayak. Let's get you back in."

"How the fuck are we going to do that?" But she listens to me and pulls hers closer.

I swim to get both paddles and wedge them into my seat so they don't float away.

"Turn around and grip your kayak. One hand on the front of the seat, one on the back. You're going to pull yourself onto the seat stomach down, then do a little wiggling maneuver to get your feet back where they belong. Keep your balance or you'll end up with the kayak on your head. Again."

"I feel like this is going to be difficult," she says, but does what I say.

"I'm going to help." I glide right behind her.

"How are you going to help??"

"On the count of three." I put my hands on Raleigh's bare waist below her life vest. My hands on her skin in cold water is something else. I shake my head and focus. I'm supposed to be making up for being a creep last night, not continuing the performance. "One. Two. Three."

On three I push her up by her waist and she pulls across the kayak. Her ass ends up at just about eye level for a second, before she wiggles around like I told her to.

She's laughing so hard by the time she gets her butt back in the seat that I can't help but join her.

"This is humiliating." Raleigh takes a deep breath when she's finally situated in the kayak. I slide one of the paddles over to her. "At least it should be. Wait, how are *you* going to get up there?"

But it takes me just a quick maneuver to swing myself back into my seat, keeping my paddle secured under one hand. I've done this a million times, although I always kayak in still lakes or other calm waters so as not to violate my Blizzard contract that prohibits me from any kind of extreme sports. So even though I live in Colorado, I haven't skied since I was a teenager.

"Freaking professional athletes." She shakes her head in mock disgust.

"This has been fun." I take my hat off and wipe my hand down my face, clearing some of the water.

"At least I'm not puking."

"At least." I grin at her and she smiles back, her hair dripping onto her shoulders, looking like an adorable drowned rat.

"Let's go back to check on Megghen and have those croissants you brought."

"Sure, but we're doing this again sometime."

"Are you serious?"

"Yeah. You're in Colorado. We can go hiking too. But this is the best part of being here—the weather and all the outdoor stuff."

"Alright, Atticus Knox. Whatever you say. But can we also do indoor activities?"

"Sure. Bowling? Brewery?" I rub my chin and an idea comes to me.

"Those sound a lot safer."

"Hey, want to come to the arena tomorrow? I'm meeting Lachlan for practice." I pause. "Not that you want to sit around and watch me practice—that would be boring—but the arena is legit when it's empty of people."

"That sounds great." Raleigh presses her lips together and tilts her head. She's wet and raw and so completely herself right now, and it's the best thing ever. Our kayaks knock together.

I can be myself with Raleigh. I don't have to be someone better than I am. I don't have to impress her. I don't have to pretend to be a pretentious hockey star. I can be just me, the kid she used to make fun of back in college.

"Ready to go back?"

She hesitates for a beat and then nods. We make our way back to the shoreline, the warm sun drying our clothes along the way.

Back to what, is the question.

There's a double meaning there, and maybe her hesitation tells me she understands.

## CHAPTER 11

# Zombies Prefer Brains

## RALEIGH

Sunday, July 6

I had a high view video on social media yesterday—only like fifteen thousand views, so not even considered semi-viral, but great for me—after I posted explaining a plan for my zombie cross-stitch line. My video must have found the right people, because I got four new orders overnight. That's a record for me in one day. Luckily, I have plenty of hoops complete with flowers so I just have to stitch the quotes.

Before now, I'd posted a few images of my work, and after that one successful post early on, got a meh response. But this was my first video. And people liked it? Should I become a cross-stitch influencer?

Wow, that sounds terrible.

I calculated the profit from selling four items and then cackled. It might buy me a half a tank of gas. I'm not living some high-end lifestyle right now, but I do have to send money to my ex-husband.

Now I'm trying to figure out some quotes related to kayaking and flipping over into the lake. I bite my lip to contain the grin from the memory as I watch Lachlan and Atticus do one-on-one drills under the supervision of their skating coach. Another man—who I'm assuming is Coach Jackson as Atticus told me he'd sometimes stop by these summer sessions—walks over and stands next to the skating coach.

Atticus is right. The arena is pretty cool empty of the crowd of fans. Not that I've been to a game, so I guess I don't have much of a comparison, but the stands look packed when I catch a game streaming.

Too bad it's summer so I won't get to watch him play.

*Them* play, I mean.

I don't need to watch Atticus play hockey. Although... he looks sexy as hell on the ice right now. Yeah, okay, I can't see much of him underneath the padding and helmet, but he is like a giant graceful monster on skates.

I glance back down at my cross-stitch and complete the final few stitches. I tighten the hoop and grin at the final result, so I hold it up and snap a picture to send to Lucy and January.

LUCY

Sis—are you at the Blizzard arena??

ME

No comment on the hoop?

LUCY

Okay, I'll play your game. It's gorgeous, and I want one, but can you make mine about hockey and not zombies?

ME

Sure

LUCY

Now that we got that out of the way... What are you doing there? Are you watching Atticus practice?

Well, shit, that wasn't subtle at all. Not that I meant it to be, but I hadn't exactly planned on telling them I was coming here.

ME

It's just getting me out of the house, er, the RV

JANUARY

Perfectly reasonable to take your cross-stitch project to a professional hockey arena to watch your best friend's little brother practice

I scrunch my nose and look up from my phone. January's got a point.

ME

When you put it like that, it does sound a bit ridiculous

LUCY

Kellen just judged you hard when I told him

ME

Can't we have secrets between friends?

LUCY

Does Kellen count?

ME

Traitor

Wait—did Atticus say something to him?

I cringe and turn my phone over on my lap. My last text is giving middle school *does he like me* vibes.

On the ice, Atticus is taking slow, graceful strides toward the coaches. As if he feels my gaze, he turns and looks right at me. A smile crosses his face that turns him into a complete and utter cinnamon roll with gooey sweet icing. He lifts a hand to me, and I raise mine back. My heart basically ceases beating for a moment, then catches up when he stops in front of the coaches with Lachlan.

We just *waved* at each other.

A twinge makes me realize I'm biting my lip and smiling so wide it hurts my face.

I can't stop around this man. He makes me laugh, and I appear to have the same effect on him.

He didn't laugh at me when I told him my sailing story. I mean, he laughed, but it was *with* me, not *at* me, I'm almost positive. I admit the sailing trip wasn't my proudest moment. And these days? Boats—even if they're kayaks on a serene lake—terrify me. Maybe one day I'll get over that. Maybe Atticus will help me.

It's been about an hour, and Atticus told me the practice shouldn't be much longer than that. The skating coach leaves the ice and the boys are talking to Coach Jackson. Looks like they should be done soon.

My phone buzzes in my lap.

LUCY

Just that he's been spending some time with you to make sure you don't get yourself into any trouble in Fort Collins

JANUARY

Raleigh never gets in trouble

LUCY

Bullshit. Someone needs to make sure she doesn't accidentally get married for a third time

Damn, that hurts, but is also pretty freaking funny. And not far from the truth. Jacob and I met soon after my first divorce was final. We didn't officially date for a year, but my heart was with him from almost day one.

I definitely get too deep, too fast.

ME

Not funny

LUCY

A little funny. At least I know you're safe to not accidentally fall into a relationship with my brother

JANUARY

Um, she did make out with him on New Year's Eve. God only knows what they're doing now, babes

LUCY

Raleigh? Confirm or deny?

Oh. Yeah. Because Atticus doesn't do relationships.

I consider telling them he's interested in a girl from the bookstore but don't want to seem like I'm trying to convince them he is looking for a girlfriend, because they'll know in a split second I'm interested.

I consider telling them about how we made out on my couch in the Pink Palace while watching zombie movies. They'd lose their damn minds.

I consider telling them about kayaking, or all the presents he's brought me, or the way my chest warms when he smiles at me.

But I don't.

Because I'm only here for a few more weeks.

I'm recently twice divorced.

He's a player.

This is all some lovely interlude while I reflect on what's happened for the past decade.

## CHAPTER 12

# New Teammate, New Friend?

## ATTICUS

"How'd you feel today?" Coach Jackson crosses his arms across his purple and yellow Blizzard hoodie and examines me with too much kindness in his eyes. We've stepped off the ice onto the rubber mats—safe for the blades of our skates—that lead to the locker room.

I grind my teeth together. I don't want to be treated like I'm breakable.

"Great," I say, my voice too loud. "One hundred percent." I pull off my helmet and push my curls off my forehead.

"You don't have to shout, mate. We believe you." Lachlan snorts next to me.

"Shut your face, dude," I growl at him and turn back to Coach Jackson. "Seriously. I'm fine. I just gotta get out of my head."

That kind of weakness is not something I would admit in front of almost anybody, but Lachlan is well aware of my challenges and I know Coach Jackson is always on my side.

"Glad to hear it. And I agree. I'm seeing you hesitate for a split second when you should be going for it. That'll cost you the puck in a game." Coach Jackson reaches over to rest his hand on one of my shoulders. "But in terms of fitness, you're in better shape than you were last summer."

It's true. Last summer I spent half the time at a bougie lake resort with a couple of the guys, during which time most of us did zero working out. I paid for it when I got back to Fort Collins in August, a month before preseason.

Coach's words release some of the tension in my body. I sneak a glance at where Raleigh is sitting in the arena. She's got her feet propped up on the seat in front of her, a cross-stitch hoop resting on her thighs, and is watching me intently. She turns away with a smile when she realizes I'm looking back.

I look down and press my lips together. Last thing I need is Lachlan noticing and having more ammo to make fun of me with.

But he's already got a smirk on his face. Damn perceptive bastard. Or maybe me inviting her to practice was the more obvious clue.

"One last thing before I let you both get on with your day." Coach Jackson removes his hand from my shoulder and looks between me and Lachlan. "I've got a favor to ask."

"What do you need, Coach?" Lachlan says.

"I'm sure you've all heard that we acquired Barrett Steele."

I cannot stop a groan. Coach looks at me with raised eyebrows. "Problem, Atticus?"

"No, of course not, sorry, had something in my throat."

Lachlan chuckles.

"Anyway, he arrived in town this week. Normally I'd have Kellen reach out to make sure he's settling in and meeting every-one, but as Kellen's out of town, I was hoping you two would do it. I know it's often your group that is the welcoming committee for new players."

Wait, what?

Surely Coach isn't asking us to hang out with Barrett Steele.

"You want us to be his... friend?" I spit out the last word.

"Yes, basically. Call him, text him, get him to meet up. Make him feel welcome in Fort Collins and with the Blizzard. That kid is good—he'll be a great addition to the team."

"I dunno, I've got a lot going on." My attempt to push off the request is met by laughter from Lachlan.

"What, your dating lessons with Raleigh taking up all of your time? Your workouts too much? All that time sitting around your apartment by yourself?"

"Shut up, lover boy. Do you think your little girlfriend will let you hang out with Barrett? That kid has a worse reputation than I do."

"Don't lash out at me," he says, but some of the humor has fallen from his face.

"Well." Coach Jackson looks back and forth between us. "I don't want to know anything about any of that, but it sounds like you two have some things to work out. Atticus, I think you could be a good role model for Barrett. He's young and could use some guidance. He reminds me of you a few years ago. Lachlan, you too." He raises his eyebrows. "I'm texting you both his number now. Do your thing, okay?"

And with that, Coach turns and disappears through the arena doors leading to the locker room, where his office is.

"This is going to be fun," Lachlan says as we follow him.

I just shake my head. This is not happening. No way. I am not being friends—or even friendly—with Barrett fucking Steele.

By the time we're out of the showers, I have a text from Coach with Steele's contact details.

I flash back to that moment when I fell during that last game and felt the sharp twinge in my groin. What I really wanted to do was go after Steele and pound him, but instead, I limped off the ice, knowing the season was over for me and picking a fight would only hurt the Blizzard's chance of winning.

After he's dressed, Lachlan picks up his phone and chuckles.

"Does he really think we're going to hang out with that guy?" I say as we walk back into the arena.

Raleigh sees us and stands, sliding her cross-stitch stuff in her canvas bag and heading our way.

"That must have been so boring to watch," I say, smiling at her as she approaches us with her bag slung over her shoulder.

"No way, it was fun."

"You are clearly lying, but it's okay," Lachlan glances down at his phone. "Up for a drink? Melissa's out of town again this weekend, back tomorrow morning."

I look at Raleigh, who shrugs. "Sure. My fingers are killing me anyway." She wiggles her red digits at us.

"I'm in." More time with Raleigh is only a good thing, even if I have to share her with Lachlan.

"Let's do Horsetooth Brewing." Lachlan types into his phone. "Now?"

I nod, and so does Raleigh.

"Great, because Barrett Steele is going to meet us there." Lachlan holds up his phone for us. "He responded yes instantly."

"Oh, for fuck's sake." I groan. That was a trap. He had me—and Raleigh—agree before revealing he'd invited my nemesis.

What a smart, conniving asshole.

"Who's Barrett Steele?" Raleigh asks, looking between us with raised eyebrows.

"He's the guy who flipped Atticus over during the last game and hurt his—" Lachlan looks pointedly at my groin.

"Ohhhh, no." Raleigh covers her mouth with her hand.

"Also the player who the Blizzard just acquired." Lachlan practically giggles with glee.

"No!" Raleigh's eyes widen.

"And why are we going to get a drink with him?" My voice is tight. Can I bail? Shit. But Raleigh would probably still go and I'd be leaving her alone with Lachlan and Barrett.

"Because we're supposed to be nice to him. Coach Jackson asked. Also, Kellen already texted us saying we should take him out."

"Fuck that."

Raleigh laughs. "How bad can he be?"

I give her a look.

It's gonna be bad.

* * *

Barrett Steele is charming the shit out of Raleigh.

Not hitting on her, exactly, but he's smiling and witty and I fucking detest him with every bone in my body.

He looks fit. Like, ripped. Taller than I am. Bright blue eyes. Straight blond hair sticking out from underneath a baseball cap.

A backwards baseball cap.

Is that what I look like? Fuck.

I want to punch him.

And he still hasn't apologized for that last game. Not that it would help. Not that I'd accept his apology.

"I'm the second of four kids." Barrett leans back and links his hands behind his head, his triceps popping out.

Well fuck you, Barrett, I have impressive triceps too.

"My older sister plays pro soccer and my younger twin brothers are playing hockey in college."

"So there's going to be another couple Barrett Steeles in the NHL soon?" Lachlan is captivated by the kid. He should be making fun of him with me, not starting some kind of bromance.

"Before I know it." Barrett adjusts his baseball cap and Raleigh watches him do it.

I really, really want to punch him.

I excuse myself for a second and head to the bathroom to throw some water on my face. Leaning on the porcelain sink, I stare at myself in the mirror.

*Pull it the fuck together, dude.*

This isn't about Barrett Steele. Not really. It's about me getting in my own head about so many things. The fact that I suddenly don't feel as confident as I have my entire life. With hockey and with women.

With Raleigh.

I walk back out and stop at the bar for another round of drinks. The brewery has open, tall ceilings and wooden paneling on the walls. One side of the room has a mural painted on it that I haven't noticed before, depicting Colorado mountains and blue skies. Raleigh's RV needs a paint job, so I ask the bartender about it and she gives me a business card of the artist.

I feel much calmer, but I walk back to the table and sit just as Barrett asks Raleigh a question.

"What about you, Raleigh? What's your story?" Barrett leans back in his chair, hands folded on his stomach.

I imagine he was talking about himself the entire time I was gone. But now? Asking Raleigh about herself? Fuck me. He is really risking his life right now.

Women must see through him. There's no way Raleigh will be interested in him.

"Well," Raleigh says, her cheeks rosy. From the alcohol? Or Barrett's attention? It better be the first one. "I'm on sabbatical from my job and driving an RV around."

"That's amazing. I've always wanted to do that." Barrett reaches for his beer and takes a long swig, and we all watch him.

He sure as fuck has not always wanted to do that.

"Yeah?" Raleigh says. I don't like the interested look on her face.

"Maybe next summer in the offseason I'll rent some ridiculously luxurious camper. Visit all the national parks. Star gaze, hike, you know." Barrett winks at Raleigh.

*Winks* at her. I clench my hand around my glass of beer.

"My RV is definitely not luxurious." Raleigh chuckles.

Lachlan snorts softly and I whip my head to him. He's looking back and forth between Raleigh, Barrett, and me with the biggest shit-eating grin on his face.

"You alright, mate?" he says to me.

Barrett and Raleigh stop talking and look over.

"Of course. Why would I not be alright, *mate*?"

"No reason." But Lachlan smirks and turns his attention to Barrett. Thankfully, my friend does something useful and asks Barrett a series of boring questions about how he's settling in.

Raleigh leans over to me and places a hand on my forearm.

"Hey," she says in a low voice, only for me. "I had an idea."

I lean in, loving her attention on me. Loving her hand on my arm.

God, I'm such a brat.

"Tell me."

She holds up her other hand. "A hockey cross-stitch series. Starting with something like *hockey is the only love I need* or *boyfriend requirements: hockey player*."

I chuckle. "Sure, but can you can handle an onslaught of more orders? Aren't you still buried underneath zombies?"

"Is that an undead joke?" Raleigh twitches her mouth to the side.

"An unintentional one."

"And you're cute in assuming I'd get a slew of orders." She cocks her head at me. "Or something like *I only date hockey players*."

"Do you?"

"Clearly not." Raleigh laughs and leans back, regrettably removing her hand from my arm. "As I've never dated a hockey player."

"We can fix that," Barrett says, butting his big fucking head into our conversation.

Honestly, I am going to body slam this guy.

"Raleigh is on a dating ban." I immediately regret the words as everyone at the table turns to me, Lachlan with a smirk, Barrett with raised eyebrows, Raleigh with narrowed eyes. "Self-imposed," I rush to add. "Right, Raleigh?"

"I wouldn't say that exactly, but..." She turns to Barrett. "I recently got divorced."

"Oh, sorry to hear that." His face crumples in manufactured empathy. His fingers twitch on the table and I picture him reaching over and squeezing her hand.

He better fucking not.

I curls my toes. I shouldn't care if he touches her, laughs with her, dates her, etc. I shouldn't care what she thinks of him. Or of me, for that matter.

But I do.

For fuck's sake, I do.

I want to spend more time with Raleigh.

I'm gonna ask her to hang out again. And again. And again.

That feeling of this being a big deal—spending time with her this summer—is heavy on my shoulders.

## CHAPTER 13

# Outdated Millennial

### RALEIGH

Saturday, July 12

Impressive social media engagement and new orders proves that people like quotes about hockey players. And zombies.

I wonder if I should combine them?

But my fingers are sore, and I need a break from doing cross-stitch. That last video I posted racked up more views after last weekend, and I got two new orders. That might not sound like a lot, but it takes a few hours to stitch each quote. My pile of hoops with flowers already stitched on them is getting lower, so my next goal is to get ahead in case I keep getting steady orders.

But for now, I'm caught up, so I'm going to take a break and continue reading the travel memoir Atticus got me.

I carefully approach the hammock, like it's a wild animal I'm trying not to startle. I've tried to get into this thing multiple times but each time I chicken out—no offense, Megghen—because I'm terrified of spinning around and landing face down in the grass. But I googled it. I've gotta start with my butt in the center of the hammock, then get a hand on both sides of the contraption before slowly swinging my legs up and around. And then the key is to lie diagonally, not straight, to keep stable.

I can do this. I wasn't an athlete when I was young, but I'm not as clumsy as Lucy. She'd end up on the ground for sure. But I haven't gotten in yet, and I feel bad that Atticus spent all this money on me and it's just sitting—er, hanging?—here.

I tuck the book under my arm and slide my butt onto the hammock very slowly.

So far so good.

Megghen *boc boc bocs* at me from her sturdy chicken coop.

"Don't watch me!" I hiss and give her the dirtiest look.

She keeps staring, cocking her chicken head.

"I'm a chicken, not you," I say in her chicken voice. "Just get in the stupid hammock."

I roll my eyes. Why is she always so judgmental?

"Fine. I'm not trying to impress you anyway." I grip the sides of the hammock like it's the floating door next to a sinking ship in the middle of the ocean. "I can do this," I whisper. Then I look around and crack up.

What on earth am I doing?

Like right now, this very second, but also with my life?

Why do I dream about never going back to my pharmacy job again?

I really, really need to explore what that's about. I thought my dream was to take a break from my life in Connecticut, have a few adventures on the road, get some space from the small town where both my ex-husbands and my mother live.

Now that I'm out, I kinda never want to go back.

But what, exactly, do I never want to go back to? My job? That town? Any small suburban environment? Proximity to my exes?

It's not clear.

And then what would I do? Cross-stitch? Even if I did it twelve hours a day, I don't think I could make enough to pay rent or a mortgage.

I love not being trapped in the pharmacy all day.

I love letting my mind wander and taking care of Megghen.

Fort Collins is growing on me, which is amusing because over the past year, January and I had to listen to Lucy gradually fall in love with this place without even realizing it.

It's different with me, of course. One hundred percent different. Lucy ran away from her old life to try to prove something to them.

I'm doing it to prove something to myself.

To prove I'm choosing the right life, not just staying in it because I'm an object in motion on a certain path and I'll stay that way unless something stops me.

I slowly swing my legs up and slide them onto the hammock, sighing with relief. I lean back—diagonally—and smile up into the trees.

Hell yeah!

I set the memoir on my belly and carefully pull out my phone to take a picture to send to Atticus.

ME

I finally got my ass into the hammock!

His response is immediate, which is how it is with us these days.

ATTICUS

it took you this long? I could've given you a lesson

how's the book?

We've hung out multiple times since going for a drink with Lachlan and Barrett Steele after practice last weekend. It's like we've given up dating lessons and just let ourselves fall into our... friendship?

That's what this is.

It feels like more. But it's not.

Besides the kissing during zombie movie night.

Oh, and the kiss on New Year's Eve.

And that's it.

Otherwise, just friends.

Two days ago we had lunch in downtown Fort Collins and walked the streets after. When we approached the street with the coffee shop and A Good Book, I suggested going in. He simply said no.

Then I asked him when he was going to ask out Rose the bookstore employee, but he just gave me a funny look.

Thinking about our kisses?

Because I'm *always* thinking of our kisses.

ME

Haven't started it yet. If I follow her path, I'll only have to visit 35 places before my next birthday, not 53. Doable, yeah?

ATTICUS

that your plan?

ME

Sure is not

Atticus sends a laughing emoji and I look back up into the trees. Traveling sounds great, but I'm not the person that January is, flitting around the globe and living in a bunch of different countries, traveling, exploring.

My phone buzzes on my chest.

ATTICUS

do you have time to save me? Lachlan is dragging me out again with Barrett Steele tonight

ME

That kid is your nemesis

ATTICUS

I just don't like him

I chuckle. It hadn't escaped my notice that Atticus was a bit off last weekend when we were out with Barrett. I can kind of understand it. He's a hockey star coming onto the team to replace their friend. He's also the player who is responsible for Atticus's injury.

But I think if Atticus gives him a chance, Barrett might fit right in with him and Lachlan. The three of them could charm the pants off the entire state of Colorado.

I don't think I imagined it that Atticus was getting particularly annoyed when Barrett turned his attention to me. It was innocent, though, and Atticus must see that. Barrett is good-looking and entertaining, but I'm zero percent interested in a twenty-five-year-old professional hockey player.

I pick up my phone again.

ME

So what's the plan?

* * *

I am not a huge drinker.

And from what Lucy tells me, during the season, neither are most of the hockey boys. Their bodies are their jobs and they are hyper focused on staying fit.

We are not in hockey season, but Atticus hasn't drank a ton tonight.

I've had two glasses of wine, but that's it for me. I don't want to get sloppy—or sweaty, as it's hot tonight—and I plan to drive home at some point.

Although that ship might have sailed. Will a ride service take

134

me to the campsite? Probably, but it feels extra uncomfortable to take a hired car into the woods.

"It's too bad Melissa's out of town this weekend again. I would've loved for you two to meet her." Lachlan looks between me and Barrett.

"And here we go." Atticus sighs deeply and raises his eyes to the sky.

I watch the conversation with a grin on my face.

"She's the love of my life, mate," Lachlan says.

"Amazing." Barrett drains his beer and slams it on the table. "And the kind of sappy, whipped love that I hope never finds me."

"What?" Lachlan furrows his brow.

We're sitting outside on Main Street in downtown Fort Collins, the bar is crowded, and the night is beautiful. I'm in a cute graphic t-shirt that has a mountain and *Colorado* on it, and a pair of straight jeans with a hole in the right knee. I did some shopping in town this week and am working on getting out of the *I'm a pharmacist* look. My usual go-to has been black pants or skinny jeans and a boring, work appropriate short-sleeved shirt. I have very reluctantly put my skinny jeans in the back of a drawer in the Pink Palace.

I haven't been to bars regularly in years.

A lot of years.

And I don't want to look like some outdated Millennial.

The fact that I'm even thinking about this kind of thing means I am, in fact, an outdated Millennial.

"I'm happy for you, but relationships are not for me. They're just a big distraction. And I like being free. Especially as a hockey player—women basically line up to be with me." Barrett slides a glance to me, seeming to remember I'm there. "Sorry."

"Don't worry about me. I'm not lining up to be with anyone." I'm definitely not. And that feels good. The thing is, I loved the idea of relationships. I loved the idea of marriage. That must be true, given I got married twice before the age of thirty.

But I'm not sure if it's meant to be for me.

I think this adventure I'm going on is the right thing. I think letting myself discover all my hidden layers—the ones I've missed over the past thirty-four years while I've been following my spreadsheet—is right.

"Don't be a dick, man." Atticus shakes his head at Barrett.

Being around these pro hockey players is wild. Apparently, all they've been doing is sleeping with the women who throw themselves at them.

I've only had sex with two men in my entire life, and I married both of them.

My cheeks heat just thinking about how sheltered I am in that category.

"Are you telling me you don't enjoy when girls line up for you? I've heard the rumors about you two." Barrett looks pointedly at Lachlan and then Atticus.

"Yeah, we used to be like that." Atticus's face tightens. "But once I saw thirty bearing down on me, things changed."

"And when Melissa found me a few months ago..." Lachlan says in a dreamy voice.

"Lordy." Atticus groans and looks down into his half-full pint. "Please, spare us."

Barrett chuckles and Atticus joins in a beat later. Aw, are they bonding?

"Hey." Lachlan narrows his eyes at them.

"Seriously though," Atticus says to Barrett when their laughter fades. "At some point you gotta realize there's more to it then hooking up with a ton of women."

My breath catches in my throat. Did Atticus Knox really just say that?

"Do I really gotta?" Barrett snorts.

I glance around the table. Lachlan's wide-eyed staring at Atticus, who has a contemplative expression on his face. Barrett's shaking his head and looking disgusted.

Then Lachlan side eyes me and smirks.

"What?" I blink as my cheeks heat. Lachlan holds up his hands like *what?* back at me.

Atticus jolts out of whatever thoughts had him trapped, then drains his pint.

"I think it's time for another round." Barrett looks around the table.

"No thanks." I shake my head and look at my almost empty wine glass. Last time I drank more than two glasses of wine, I ended up on Atticus's lap in the Pink Palace.

Barrett and Lachlan stand.

"I'm good," Atticus says. "I'm gonna need to drive Raleigh home later."

I press my lips together. He is, huh?

"Suit yourself, mate." The boys disappear into the crowd.

And even though we're surrounded by people, I suddenly feel like Atticus and I are all alone.

"I'm not ready to go home yet." I turn to Atticus, suddenly aware of how close his chair is.

"I didn't say you were." He doesn't look at me, but his thigh shifts so it's gently leaning against mine.

"And you don't have to drive me home." I'm insisting on something and I don't even know what it is.

Atticus looks at me and his lips fall slightly open. A tingle runs up my spine when I let my eyes rest on his mouth. The mouth that was on mine only a week ago. The mouth that kissed me like he both wanted to and needed to. The one that I fantasize about—

"So you're going to drive yourself?"

My eyes jerk up to meet his and he slowly smirks. He definitely caught me gazing at his mouth. But who would blame me? Probably half the women in Fort Collins have drooled over Atticus Knox's mouth at one point or another.

"Maybe not." Thank god he doesn't know what I was thinking.

"I'm not one to judge how much someone's drunk, but there's no need to drive if you don't have to."

"Right." I scrunch my face and glance down at my empty wine glass. "Well, guess I'm not going anywhere for a while."

"I'm not ready to drive yet either. But do you want to go for a walk?" His green eyes envelop me like a deep, dark forest.

"What about—" My voice is low and I nod toward where Lachlan and Barrett disappeared.

"Let's ditch 'em." Atticus huffs. "I can't hear another word about Lachlan's girlfriend and I'm not sure how long I can hold myself back from punching Barrett in the face."

I laugh and Atticus pushes his leg against mine.

"Aren't you worried that Barrett will replace you as Lachlan's best friend?"

"No, no I'm not." Atticus turns his body so that now our knees are knocking fully against each other. He leans his forearm across the back of my chair. The man is watching me like I'm the only person in the room.

"I'm ready when you are." I curl my toes. Yup. Atticus and I are ditching the others so we can be by ourselves. That—whatever it is—is definitely happening.

"Let's not fight through the bar. We can leave this way." Atticus nods to the street.

"Should we tell them we're going?"

"Nope. I'll text Lach."

I nod and follow Atticus when he stands and squeezes through a few tables. He looks over his shoulder at me to make sure I'm there, then holds out his hand behind him. I stare at it for a second and then reach my hand into his. His is cool, and he lightly captures my fingers against his palm.

I breathe deeply even as my heartbeat accelerates. What's going on here? Atticus looks over his shoulder again as he pulls me through the tables.

When we get past the tables and onto the sidewalk, another thought crashes into my consciousness.

Atticus likes me.

Like really likes me.

I know he had a thing for me during college. But that was light flirting and banter and making fun of each other. We both knew nothing would ever happen between us for at least two reasons: my boyfriend and the fact that he was Lucy's brother.

Now I wonder—did that crush on me ever go away?

He's not just being friendly.

There's something more here.

He's been kind and helpful since the day I got here. He's brought me gifts and planned things for us to do. He goes out of his way to see me, invite me places, spend time with me.

But didn't I just think about how relationships aren't for me? That I need to figure myself out, crush or not?

There's people lingering in groups on the sidewalk and Atticus continues to hold onto my hand as we make our way through the crowds. We get to the corner and I stand next to him as we wait for the light to change. He firmly grips my hand, weaving his fingers with mine.

Who is talking about relationships though? I've spent a decade trapped in a version of myself that I'm not sure is true anymore. Living in small town Connecticut, married (to two different men), working a well-paying, reliable job, planning a suburban mom future.

That's all over now, and I think I might be lucky to have escaped.

Lucky that Jacob fucked up so royally.

Because if he hadn't, I would probably have ended up pregnant and tethered to Jacob and that town forever. There would be no driving the Pink Palace across the country—because if I'm honest, Jacob was never going to plan that trip—or quitting my job to do cross-stitch.

Did I say quit? I meant taking a *sabbatical* to do cross-stitch.

One day, I'd like to consider having kids... but it would have to be the right situation. And I'm about as far from that as one could possibly be.

I shake my head as Atticus tugs my hand to cross the street. Music drifts toward us from the next block and there are groups of people walking around the well-lit street. One group is comprised of laughing twenty-something women, wearing way less clothing than I am. Another is an older couple. Then a pair of young men.

I wonder what they think of me and Atticus.

It doesn't matter, not just because they're strangers, but because whatever this is between us has nowhere to go.

It's not like I'm *not* going back to Connecticut or my job eventually, right? But maybe... A shiver runs down my spine. I need to shelve that thought for now. Shove it onto a deep, dark, hidden bookshelf in the library next to the encyclopedias.

"You okay, coach?" Atticus squeezes my hand and I turn to him.

"Of course. But where are we going?"

"There's a band in the square. I thought we could watch for a while." He glances at me, and the look is so raw and needy.

"Sounds fun." We walk on in silence.

And what about Atticus?

I need to be careful.

Not just because he's my best friend's little brother.

But because there's something about him that is vulnerable. I can't believe I'm even thinking that about the hulking, tough, six-foot-four hockey player holding my hand.

It's true, though.

Between Lucy telling me he's not been hooking up with women recently, his injury, his kind and cautious way with me, and how he initially reacted toward Barrett Steele. Plus, his father's fourth divorce.

He's going through some shit.

And no one is really around for him right now.

Except me.

I need someone, too. And my friends are all otherwise occupied.

Except Atticus.

This is definitely more dangerous that chasing a casual college crush.

He asked me to be his dating coach so he could go out with a bookstore girl he likes, and here we are walking through Fort Collins hand-in-hand.

But I'm not ready to call bullshit on the dating coach thing yet.

As we round the corner toward the square, the music gets louder and the crowd gets thicker. Atticus moves me behind his back and pulls me through the crowd until we're standing against a retail store window with a side view of the band. It's indie folk rock with acoustic guitars and an earthy feel to the raspy voice of the lead singer, who is singing about the one who got away.

I don't think Raleigh from a year ago would recognize this person. Raleigh who hadn't yet discovered there was a reason her husband had been pulling away from her. That there was an insurmountable canyon between us that wouldn't be fixable, no matter what he thinks now.

I always thought of myself as boring and predictable. Is this who I am now? Am I someone completely different yet?

I'm not sure.

I shut my eyes and appreciate the cool glass through my shirt.

"Isn't your place not far from here?" The words come out of my mouth before I even know they're there. I open my eyes and Atticus turns to me sharply.

"Yeah."

"Is it still under construction? I need to use the bathroom."

"Nah, they actually wrapped up last week so things are still a little dusty, but it's all usable."

I push off the glass.

"And I'm kind of in the mood for zombies." I cock my head. "Up for part two of our movie night?"

*What am I doing?*

"I don't think we finished Shaun of the Dead, which is a fucking crime. Let's go."

I laugh airily and keep my eyes locked on Atticus.

Are either of us unclear on what is happening here? I don't even mean between us in general, I mean what we are going to do tonight. Right now.

Because he is too eager to take me back to his place, and I was too eager to ask.

Atticus tugs my hand and I follow him through the crowd.

Actually, I think we both know what's going to happen, even though the words haven't been spoken. I've never had a one-night stand. Would hooking up with Atticus be considered a one-night stand? Am I really planning to do that?

I push away the thought that I need to be careful of my heart and whatever Atticus is going through right now. I'm not gonna think about any of that anymore, at least not tonight.

But as Atticus leads me away from the town square and toward his apartment, which I'd only previously seen on video calls when Lucy was living there, I come to a realization.

I need this thing with Atticus, whatever it is.

I need to let myself fall for him, just a little.

Not all the way.

Just enough for him to help me figure out who I am these days.

## CHAPTER 14

# Is this Helping?

### ATTICUS

You would never know that prior to kissing Raleigh Hayes last New Year's Eve, I haven't had a case of nerves around women since my college days.

Which was also related to Raleigh Hayes.

I can't believe she suggested coming back to my place, but I'm not sure what it means. Does she really just have to use the bathroom and want to finish the movie?

Nah. There's more to this.

My fucking hand is wobbling as I fit the key into the outside lock to my building. Embarrassing. I can't even sneak a look at Raleigh standing next to me, because I'm afraid I'd drop the keys altogether, but I know she's watching.

The key finally goes in and I turn it before pushing the door open for her, doing my best to be as casual as possible.

Raleigh clears her throat and walks through. "So your construction is all done?"

"Yup." I nod and touch her back as we head toward the elevator. Small talk? Not sure I can handle that right now.

I've never been insecure around women. Just like I've never been unsure of my hockey abilities.

But here I've been, questioning my fitness level and being intimidated by the idea of Barrett fucking Steele, the one who is responsible for my injury to begin with.

Which, by the way, he STILL hasn't apologized for yet.

After kissing Raleigh—twice—there's some kind of storm brewing inside of me. Maybe it has to do with my father's fourth divorce. How that truly sealed my own fate as a player and a rake. How could the son of someone like that ever be taken seriously as a romantic partner? It's impossible. If I was different, I would've shown those differences by now.

Lucy is. She's kinder. Sweeter. An authentic person in relationships, even when she got walked over by her ex-fiancé.

But me?

I'm hopeless.

I was still a baby when Mom divorced my father after finding him cheating with a twenty-five-year-old woman, who he later married. And later divorced.

I played along with seeing Richard with my sister on 'his' weekends, but he mostly ignored us when we were there. Lucy would make excuses for him. I was always pissed off about it. So when Lucy went off to college, I was done.

I had no interest in a relationship with that man.

I was worried if I was around him, he'd rub off on me. In case it was nurture over nature. But it was hopeless—I was already a player by the end of high school.

Lucy got our mom's genes, and I got our father's.

That's why I haven't ever cared to try to date someone.

Until now.

Wait—until now? Do I really want to date Raleigh? For real?

There's no one else in the elevator, and the muted quiet envelops us as the doors slide closed. Both of us stare at the floor ticker as we ascend.

"Where did we stop the movie last time?" Raleigh asks as the doors slide open to the long hallway leading to my fifth-floor apartment.

"I think we stopped around when they hunkered down in that pub, surrounded by zombies." I hold my hand over the elevator door sensors as she steps off.

"Ah, right."

And now I'm thinking about what interrupted the movie last time. Her ass wiggling on my lap, her mouth on mine, the feel of the soft skin of her waist beneath my fingers.

Raleigh slides her hand around my elbow for the walk to my door. Is her heart beating as fast as mine? I don't know what to do with my body right now. If this was a woman I was taking home for the night—and it would never be to my own apartment—I'd be all over her, anxious to get started and done so I could sneak away.

But I seem to have lost all game when it comes to Raleigh.

Because it's not a game with her.

My apartment renovation *is* basically finished, the new kitchen appliances all installed and the granite countertop secured. But as we walk in, I watch Raleigh note the plastic sheet still covering the couch to protect from construction dust.

"I can pull that off real quick," I say. "They're coming back next week to finish cleaning."

"Don't you have a TV in your room?"

I turn to Raleigh, who crosses her arms and looks at me with wide, brown eyes. Dark eyes I could drown in. I've never been that guy who loves girls with blue or green eyes. It's the dark brown ones that really draw me in with their depth and richness.

Like hers.

"Yeah, I do."

I throw my keys on the side table and lead Raleigh down the hallway, past the guest room where my sister stayed last year. I gesture to the hallway bathroom. Raleigh disappears through the door.

I step into my bedroom and take it in. King-sized bed carefully made. Freshly-vacuumed carpeting thanks to the cleaners, who were here two days ago. Next time I'll get them to deep clean the living room of all the dust. The entrance to my large walk-in closet is cracked open, revealing carefully hung clothes. I'm a mostly neat and organized person, so I don't have to dart around straightening things up now.

A deep-set comfortable loveseat is against the wall next to my bed, facing a large television mounted on the wall. I don't use it much in here since I live alone and have a bigger TV in the living room, but it's come in handy during the construction.

"You are such a neat freak," Raleigh says from behind, startling me. "I usually am too, but the Pink Palace is so small it feels cluttered and out of control."

I turn and drink her in, t-shirt snug against her chest, arms hanging by her side, her expression uncertain. "Want some popcorn?" I hand her the remote control. "Just search for the movie and buy it if it's not on streaming."

I escape down the hallway and stick the popcorn bag in the microwave, leaning against the counter to ground myself.

This is Raleigh.

This is my chance with her.

I can't let her slip through my fingers.

Three minutes later, I sink into the couch next to Raleigh, handing her the big plastic bowl of popcorn and throwing a few pieces into my mouth. She's got the movie paused at the scene in the pub where the group is surrounded by zombies. Our thighs are a few inches apart, and I regret the fact that my loveseat is much bigger than the one she has in her RV.

"Where would you go?" Raleigh asks.

"Huh?" I turn to her.

"In a zombie apocalypse. Where would you go to hunker down?" She looks at me with her eyebrows raised.

I chuckle before reaching in and grabbing more popcorn.

"Maybe the Blizzard arena, because it's pretty secure. We could get the whole team there. There's plenty of food at concessions and in catering, and we could fight off zombies with hockey sticks and skates."

She laughs. "That's perfect. I'm screwed in the Pink Palace. Can I join you guys?"

"Eh, not sure there's room."

"Hey!" She tosses a piece of popcorn at my face and it bounces off my nose. "But I have cross-stitch needles that I can stab zombies with. I'd be useful."

"They're pretty short, so you'd have to get really close." I take a handful of popcorn and casually lift my hand over her head. "But you *could* toss Megghen at them as a distraction."

"How dare you." She glances up and I drop the handful of popcorn. Pieces bounce off her head onto her lap and the couch. "Seriously? You want to have a popcorn fight?"

Raleigh reaches for popcorn and throws it at me point blank before I can even flinch.

"Hey, you got popcorn in my eyeball," I say, giving her a sad look while I fist another pile of popcorn and come in from below to toss it up like confetti.

She giggles and reaches again for the bowl, but I grab her wrist and shake out the popcorn she's got in her clutches.

"No you don't. You're making a mess in my clean room."

"Not fair," she says, her voice airy and breathless. "And you started it."

Both of us stare at where my hand surrounds her narrow wrist. There's a tingling shooting up my arm from the site of our connection, and she visibly shudders.

It's not just me.

She feels it too.

"I have a confession." I slide my hand down her wrist and onto her palm to stroke her fingers with mine.

"What's your confession?" Raleigh turns her body toward me, her knee nudging against mine. She meets my gaze.

I pick a piece of popcorn from her hair and drop it back into the bowl. Her mouth twitches and she waits for my answer.

In the background, there's a battle against the undead. We ignore it—both of us know how it ends, and it's happily ever after for Shaun and his girlfriend.

"I lied about needing a dating coach."

Raleigh snorts a laugh and it should break the growing tension between us right now, but it just doesn't. "What do you mean?"

"I don't want to ask anyone else out." I pluck a few more pieces of popcorn from her lap, the couch, and one perched on her shoulder.

Her laugh is easy and light, just like it was back in college when she'd make fun of me as I tried to flirt with her.

"Anyone else?" She repeats my words.

"Yeah." I reach over and tuck a strand of her wispy hair behind her ear, letting my fingers linger against her earlobe. "It was an excuse to spend time with you."

"With me?"

"You keep asking me questions." I can't help but lick my lips, tasting a hint of butter. I glance down at her mouth, plump and pink. "I'm in a weird place."

"With your injury?"

"That, and more. But then you show up in town in that pink contraption." I swallow hard and lean toward her, closing the distance by half. "Looking at me like this. How am I supposed to resist you?" Desire roars through my veins.

She makes a *mmm* sound.

Does she want this as much as I do? I don't know. Maybe. Because I want her so bad right now that my whole body aches.

But this isn't only about wanting to hook up with her.

I want *her*.

"Why did you come here, Raleigh? When you knew Lucy was gone?"

"I don't know." She shifts her body but doesn't drop eye contact.

"What was your plan? I know you had one, even if you say you didn't, because I know you, Raleigh. What was going on—"

"Atticus," Raleigh interrupts with a strangled sigh. "Stop over-thinking things. That's *my* job, remember? And even I don't want it anymore."

I blink. That's what she said to me on New Year's Eve. She's right, but there's more I want to say. I'm realizing things in this very moment—how much I want to see where this goes with Raleigh. Even though she's already halfway through her eight-week sabbatical.

I want to try to *be* with her.

Without my sister watching over us or my teammates paying close attention.

"Okay. Then what do we do now?" I ask.

She leans forward and I can feel her hot breath on my mouth.

"Let's start with kissing." And then she brings her lips to mine.

Her mouth is soft and she opens it up to me, letting me wrap my tongue around hers in a move that is sensual and sweet. All overthinking—all thoughts, actually—leave my head and it's only the press of our lips together, the taste of her mouth, her skin beneath my fingers.

And then she's up on her knees and swings one leg over so she's straddling me, her hands resting on my shoulders. My hands fall instinctively to her waist.

She pulls back and looks at me, her expression heated but also unsure.

"Too much?"

"Fuck no, Raleigh." I shake my head. "Not enough."

She watches my face as I move my thumbs on her waist, loving the feel of the soft skin of her curves. I want to pull her hips down flush against me, but I force myself to behave as she works out whatever's in her head.

"You know, you're the first guy I've kissed since before I married Jacob."

"First of all, I absolutely hate the fact that you just named your ex while you're sitting on my lap." I drop my hands and squeeze her ass playfully. She yelps and scoots forward away from my hands, almost exactly where I want her. Some of the tension fades from her face when I half groan, half sigh. "Never do that again."

"Fine. What's the second point?" she asks, leaning back in for a brief, soft kiss, swiping her tongue slowly and sensually in my mouth.

"Second of all, this is technically the *third* time we've kissed since your divorce." I am so fucking hard right now and I reach down to adjust my cock against the unforgiving denim.

A little satisfied sound comes from her throat, half moan, half sigh. Fuck me. I slide my hands back onto her ass, and this time, I press her forward all the way. This time, she definitely moans.

"Believe it or not, I haven't kissed anyone else since your divorce either," I whisper.

"Really?" Raleigh leans back, her forehead crinkled.

"Yeah," I say, shifting my groin against her pelvis. Her eyes shut briefly.

She opens her eyes and rocks gently against my groin, her arms resting on my shoulders.

This woman.

She's mine.

I need her to be mine.

I'm gonna let this happen. I'm gonna let myself go with her— not completely, of course, just a little bit—and try to forget all my issues with dating someone or falling in love.

Not that this is love. Of course it's not.

"I have something else to tell you," Raleigh says. "Before this goes any further."

"Tell me." My voice cracks as she continues to gently, slowly rock. Doing this fully clothed is almost more of a turn-on then being naked. Who knew dry humping was so good?

She squeezes her eyes shut for a beat. "I've only slept with two people in my entire life."

Holy shit. I've slept with... I definitely stopped counting a long, long, time ago.

"Raleigh—" I start, but what am I going to say to her? I don't want to talk her out of this, but I want to be sure she really wants it. I don't want to fuck this woman over. She's so good.

Too good for me.

Raleigh crashes her lips on mine and her breath quickens as she grinds against me. I kiss her again and again, and soon our tongues are intertwined and her chest is pressed up against me. The little noises she's making have me on the edge. I want more, but kissing her, her rubbing against me fully clothed, almost has me coming through two layers of clothing.

I can't help but reach between us and press my hand between her legs. Her jeans are too thick but she writhes against me.

Fuuuuck. I flick the top button of her jeans open and unzip, giving me access to her soft underwear, such a thin layer between my fingers and her pussy. Fuck me—she's soaked already.

"Raleigh, tell me how bad you want this. I need to hear it." I breathe into her neck while I stroke her over the thin layer of fabric.

But this summer—for the remaining time Raleigh is here—I'll pretend to be the man Raleigh deserves. If she allows me to. I'll let myself imagine being the kind of guy who could commit to a woman like Raleigh. A woman who men *should* commit to, not fuck and flee.

"Yes, I'm sure. I need you—this—to help me move on. To help me change."

"What the fuck would you want to change?" I growl and reach behind her with my free hand so I can run my hand up her back, unhooking her bra and setting her breasts free. They're at mouth level and I push up her shirt and bra to take one rosy nipple in my mouth. It pebbles under the swipes of my tongue.

With my other hand, I push aside her underwear and gently stroke her wet entrance.

I echo her moan as she presses down on my hand.

"I don't know." She's breathing heavy now, and I need her wearing less clothing. "Just trying out a new me."

I let go of her breast and look up, my fingers still swiping her pussy, spreading the wetness, rubbing and creating friction. "I like the old you. And the new one. I like all versions of you."

Emotions cross her face so fast, I can't identify them.

"Thanks," she whispers, then pulls off her shirt and shakes out of her bra before gently removing my hand and standing.

I wiggle my jeans off and collapse back on the couch in my boxer briefs, leaning my head back to watch her push her jeans all the way off. When she tries to climb back on my lap with her underwear on, I shake my head.

"No. Take those off." My voice is husky and I reach in to rub my hand on my cock as she slides out of her underwear. "Hey. I'm clear, by the way. I got tested earlier this year and haven't been with anyone since."

"Me too," Raleigh says with a breathy voice. "And on the pill."

She pauses before stepping forward, and I drink her in, smooth bare shoulders, the generous curve of her breasts leading to peaked nipples from my tongue, her chest flushed, her pussy glistening between thighs the perfect size to wrap around my waist. She's made for me.

I don't think I realized what my type was until this very second.

Then again, maybe I don't have a type.

Maybe I just have a thing for Raleigh.

I sit up and reach for her bare hips, pulling her forward while kissing her belly, a hand moving back between her legs, my access now unencumbered. When I look up, she's staring down at me with her mouth partially open, her chest heaving.

I stand without stopping my hand and pull her face to mine to kiss her again. She slides her hands up and down my chest, over the bumps of my ab muscles.

"Jesus, Atticus," she pulls away and huffs a laugh. "You spend way too much time in the gym."

"Are you complaining?" My thumb rubs her clit and she gasps and holds onto my arms.

"No. No complaining."

I love the way her breath catches when I walk her backwards to my bed, only taking my hand from between her legs so I can cup her ass with two hands and wrap her legs around my waist.

She buries her hands in my curls and wiggles against me.

"Atticus," she says under her breath and kisses me again. "I need more of you."

I kiss her again. And again. And again until the world starts to spin gently and I lower her down, peeling her legs off me so I can step out of my boxer briefs.

I pause and admire her laid out and waiting for me, my heart bursting in my chest. This feeling—the anticipation of making love to her—is unlike any I've ever had before sex.

It's different with her.

It's different because it's Raleigh.

"You know, I think I'm okay with being your rebound," I murmur.

Raleigh throws her head back and laughs, and when she looks back at me, I lean in and nuzzle into her neck.

"I'm glad you think I'm funny," I say before sucking gently. My cock presses against her abdomen.

"You are not my rebound," Raleigh breathes.

"Mmm." I lay a line of kisses down the valley of her neck to her right nipple. "I'm your rebound, and you're my dating coach. It's okay."

She huffs another laugh, but then I arrange my cock between her legs and press my throbbing length against her center, pushing gently against her entrance. Raleigh gasps, the intake of air turning into a soft moan as she shifts down to increase the pressure.

I watch her expression morph as I reach down to drag my cock along her.

"God, Atticus, I love the feel of you against me." Raleigh closes her eyes and throws her head back, exposing her gorgeous neck. "Just you."

"Me too." I push my cock until I'm halfway in, unable to contain my own moan. "I can still get a condom." I've never prayed harder for anything than for her to say no.

I'd do it, of course.

"No. I want to feel you."

Thank fuck.

"So you like this?" I press further and my cock slides all the way into her, the perfect fit, her pussy tight and wet and more than I'd dreamed of. I pause and take in the moment. Her lips parted slightly, eyes closed, bliss etched into her face.

My cock naked inside of Raleigh is more than I can handle. I haven't slept with someone without a condom in years. Not since I was young and dumb and took too many risks.

"Atticus," she moans. "Stop torturing me."

I roll my hips and press forward to get even deeper inside her. But I don't thrust. I wait. I stare at this beautiful woman, a perfect fit.

"I'm gonna need you to look at me and tell me exactly what you want me to do."

"Oh come on," she groans and her eyes flutter open. "You know what I want." She attempts to buck against me but I hold her hips still.

"Say it." Then my mouth twists into a wicked smirk. "Beg."

She bucks again, and I almost forget about my hot little game.

"Please, Atticus." Her eyes are half closed and she lays back and reaches her hands above her head, scooting and pressing down on me. "Please."

"That'll do." I hold back a moan as I press in and slowly glide out, savoring the feel of her. God, the look on her face right now.

So much flashes through my head as I move slowly inside Raleigh, her sounds escalating my pleasure. I watch the pleasure building on her face, and she meets my gaze, eyes heavy with need.

Raleigh's the only one I've ever really wanted. I was afraid to admit it, because I was never going to get her.

And here she is.

Raleigh whimpers and I focus only on her.

"Atticus." Raleigh rolls her hips to meet mine, taking all of me deeper and deeper.

"Right here, baby." I reach my hand between us and rub her clit, watching her face to see how it changes with my touch.

"I'm going to come," Raleigh whispers. Her hands grip my ass and she wraps her legs tightly around my waist.

I pump harder and faster until she screams out and her pussy clenches around my cock, and only when her orgasm is coming down do I let myself go, wave after wave of pleasure causing black spots on the edge of my vision.

When it's over, I roll off Raleigh and lie on my back for a moment, breathing heavily.

"You okay?" I turn my head to Raleigh. She's staring at the ceiling, a ghost of a smile on her face.

"Yeah." She turns to me and smiles. "That was amazing."

"It was." I reach for the box of tissues on my nightstand.

"You're a great rebound."

"Fuck off." I reach over and tickle her waist. "Take that back or I'm gonna do it again."

"I definitely want to do it again," Raleigh says, but closes her eyes. "In a bit."

I grab a few tissues and reach between Raleigh's thighs to clean her up, then head to the bathroom. When I get back, she's standing next to a pile of her clothing.

My stomach drops in disappointment, even as I take in the sight of her standing naked in my bedroom.

No part of me wants her to leave right now.

"Tell me you're not going?" I know I sound desperate.

"No. I'm just not a sit-around-naked kind of woman." She scrunches her face.

"Well that's unfortunate, because I'd definitely like to sit around naked with you."

She picks up her t-shirt.

"Wait." I stride over to my dresser. "I have a shirt for you."

Do I have t-shirts? Yup, drawers full. Am I going to give her one? Nope, I'm sure not.

If she's gotta put on clothing, it needs to be something that shows she's mine.

She holds out her hand and I toss her the item, drinking in the sight of her breasts as she examines what I threw to her.

"Your jersey?" She looks over at me, a smirk on her face, and turns to show me the back of the purple and yellow jersey. It shows the number eight plus Knox.

"Yup."

"And you want me to wear it right now." She pulls it in to her chest.

"I'd prefer you wear nothing else."

"Alright." She pulls the shirt over her head and lets it fall to just below her ass. She looks down at the jersey and then up at me.

The sight of Raleigh Hayes standing in my bedroom wearing my hockey jersey? I think I'm getting hard again just looking at her.

I close the distance between us and wrap my hands around her waist, pulling her flush against me.

"You look hot in my jersey."

Something flashes across her face. Does she know I don't give just any woman my jersey to wear?

As a matter of fact, she's the only one.

I've spent years sleeping with women who only saw me as a hockey player—which, to be fair, is how I see myself—and knew I was never gonna commit to them.

A few tried to get me to agree to be their boyfriend, but I hardly ever slept with the same woman more than a few times. I never wanted them to catch feelings.

I certainly wasn't going to.

Sleeping with them was only physical. I was never in my head. I was an animal, fucking fast and hard and then when it was over, ready to leave. Yeah, I always made sure the woman was satisfied, I'm not a complete asshole.

But it was *physical* satisfaction, not emotional.

I reach down and cup Raleigh's ass in my hands, pulling her up and against me.

"Yeah?" Raleigh says, breathing hard, her arms around my neck. She hops up and swings her thighs around my waist, linking her ankles at the small of my back. I moan as her pussy presses against the length of my hard, bare cock.

"I have something to say to you." I press her against me and her breathing gets faster.

"What?" Raleigh's eyes flutter as she moves her hips.

"You're fired."

She stops moving and her eyes fly open.

"Fired from what?"

"As my dating coach." I lean down and press a soft kiss to her lips. "You were a fucking awful coach."

She huffs a laugh. "Was I?"

"I mean, you're currently grinding your bare pussy against your student's cock, so yeah, I'd say you were pretty bad."

"Fine. I'll look for a new student."

"Like fuck you will." I growl and walk her over to the bed,

pressing her down against the comforter and reaching down to rub her clit.

She half laughs, half moans.

I don't know how long Raleigh is going to let me touch her like this, but I'm sure going to find out.

## CHAPTER 15

# Everything is Fine

RALEIGH

Oh, holy mother of god.

We just finished having sex—again—and Atticus is passed out. It's still the middle of the night. My mind races and I can't get myself to fall asleep.

He snores lightly behind me, his arm draped across my waist, his whole body pressed against mine as the big spoon. He's like a warm blanket that I want to snuggle up with forever.

Well, not forever.

Obviously.

This is a one-night stand.

Also, obviously.

But... I'm not a one-night stand kind of girl. Doing things like this is not like me. Things being sleeping with a gorgeous professional hockey player.

Not like the old me, anyway.

And while he *is* probably a one-night stand kind of guy, I have a feeling this was not one. Or am I wrong about that? I desperately want to talk to my friends about this.

Oh no. Lucy.

Have I made things permanently weird with my best friend's little brother and therefore my best friend?

I shift and Atticus's breath hitches and his arm shifts on my waist. I stay frozen until he settles back into steady breathing.

There's been no casual dating in my life. No hooking up with random guys in college or at bars in my twenties.

Just Raleigh Hayes (then Monroe then Hayes then Ford then Hayes again) doing exactly what she's supposed to do in life, following the spreadsheet, over-planning her entire life.

Although two divorces are probably not in anyone's spreadsheet.

I move again and Atticus rolls over onto his back, so I scoot closer to the edge. I think I need to get out of his bed and find some space to think without his warm, hard body touching me.

Do all one-night stands include such amazing sex? Like the best sex of my life?

Maybe that's the whole point. No inhibitions, no predictability, freedom from the expectations of marriage or anything serious.

Careful not to shake the bed too much, I slowly wiggle my body until my toes are hanging off, then swing my legs over until I can sit up and place my feet firmly onto Atticus's bedroom floor.

I sneak a look at the gorgeous man sleeping lightly in bed behind me. He's probably going to be unhappy that I'm sneaking out. But I can't sleep. I need to go. I stand and hunt around the dark room for my belongings. My clothes are in a messy pile in front of the bed.

A delightful shiver runs up and down my body when I think of the way he talked to me last night. The way he made me beg. I cover my mouth with a hand and tiptoe out of the room, grabbing my things from the floor next to his bedroom door and pulling the door mostly shut behind me.

I duck into the hallway bathroom and pull on my jeans. I have one arm half out of Atticus's jersey when I change my mind.

Nah. I'll wear it home. I can return it later.

I catch myself in the mirror and breathe out in a huff.

My hair's sticking up everywhere—sex hair if I've ever seen it. I have mascara smudged beneath my eyes and remnants of foundation on my cheeks. My contacts feel like burlap on my eyeballs.

I'm way too old to be sleeping in makeup or my contacts.

I am a hot mess. Yet... I find myself smiling.

It's gonna take me hours to process all of this. Days. Months? Years? But I can drive myself home and start that thinking tonight, since I'm sober now.

I open the bathroom door. Across the hall, Atticus's bedroom door is wide open.

"You aren't trying to sneak out, are you?" Atticus appears in the hallway from the kitchen, two water bottles in his hands.

The man is standing there like some kind of greek god in his boxer briefs, his ab muscles ready to cut steel, arms strong and screaming to be touched, thighs thick. Heat flushes through my entire body.

"Uhh—" I'm fully dressed—in his jersey, no less—with my bag in hand. No denying my intentions. "Kinda."

Atticus's face falls.

"It's one o'clock in the morning. You're really gonna walk through the streets of Fort Collins to your car, then drive into the forest by yourself in the middle of the night?"

Yikes. That sounds terrible.

"Guess I hadn't really thought it through."

"What if there's a bear lying in the hammock, Raleigh?"

"Do bears... sleep in hammocks?" I'm half horrified and half entertained. I hadn't really considered middle-of-the-night wildlife, which is shameful, because I'm sure Megghen thinks about bears all the time.

"Not the point, coach."

I press my lips together. "I gotta get home and feed Megghen. She's probably terrified by herself."

"Is she inside?" Atticus looks adorably concerned.

"Of course."

"Phew." He breathes out pointedly, still clutching the two bottles of water, still looking gorgeous. "Fine. We'll go to the Pink Palace. But I'm gonna bet a year's salary that my bed—" he nods into his open bedroom door. "—is a lot more comfortable than yours. Let me get dressed."

My jaw drops as he dips into his room.

This was not the development I expected.

Twenty minutes later, I'm pulling up to the Pink Palace in my car with Atticus in his Wrangler right behind me. He wanted to drive me but I wasn't feeling awesome about being stuck at the campsite dependent on someone else. Even Atticus.

It's pitch dark as the gravel crunches under my tires and I am very, very grateful that Atticus insisted he come with me.

I get out of my car and gently close the door. The sounds of the middle of the night on the edge of Colorado wilderness blanket me. The rhythmic chirping of crickets and croaking of frogs. An owl hoots. Rustling in the woods—thankfully, Atticus appears by my side.

"Think there's a bear in the hammock?" I whisper. "Or right there in the woods?" I point to the pitch-dark treeline.

Atticus lays his arm across my shoulders.

"There are definitely bears in the woods, but probably not in the hammock," he whispers back. "But to avoid me having to fight one of them, let's get inside."

I giggle and unlock the door to the Pink Palace. Megghen *boc boc bocs* as soon as we walk in, then seems to stare at us, looking back and forth between me and Atticus. I've managed to securely trap her in her tent, so there probably aren't any surprise eggs.

"I don't think she likes me touching you," Atticus says, but leaves his arm on my shoulders.

"Maybe not." I look up at him and he immediately leans down and kisses me, letting his lips linger on mine.

"Let's get you to bed." Atticus kisses my forehead. "I'll feed Megghen. Maybe she'll like me better then."

"She just needs a scoop of that." I point out the container with her food. "And needs is a strong word. This is more like her bedtime snack."

"Obviously she needs a snack." Atticus flashes me a crooked grin as I step into my bedroom.

Do I put on pajamas? Are we snuggling or getting naked?

But I don't have to decide, as Atticus appears behind me, wrapping his arms around my waist and nuzzling into my neck. I lean back and sigh.

"Let's get you comfortable," he says. "What do you usually sleep in?"

"A tank top and shorts."

"Still devastated you don't sleep naked." Atticus sighs. "Personally, I prefer to be naked, but I'll wear my briefs until you get used to me." He slides off his joggers and then reaches behind his neck to pulls his shirt off in one swift motion, revealing those cut abs.

Heaven help me.

Wait... until I get used to him?

I pull my comfy but decidedly unsexy pajama shorts and tank top from my closet. Atticus watches me as I strip down, most interested when I peel his jersey off. I hold it out for him.

He reaches for my wrist and tugs me to him instead.

"You hold onto that for now." He pushes the jersey out of my hand and wraps his hands around my waist, pulling me in for a long kiss.

Our plan to go to bed is immediately sidetracked as his hands slide into my underwear and onto my bare ass. I moan into his mouth.

"Maybe we can go to bed in a little bit instead," I say when he moves his mouth to my neck, then trails kisses down my chest to my nipple. I reach my hand into his boxer briefs and grasp his long, hard length. Suddenly we're both naked again.

Atticus kicks the door shut and lowers himself onto the bed, pulling me on top of him.

"I don't want to traumatize Megghen," he says, and I laugh, then stop when he pushes against my wet entrance. He slides right in and I writhe and rock on top of him, riding his cock as waves of pleasure build.

We come at the same time, and minutes later he clicks the light off and sweeps me into my bed, which is much too small to be sharing with a six-foot-four man, and—Atticus was right—much less comfortable than his. I scoot until my head is resting on his bare chest, the sound of his heartbeat lulling me to sleep.

"Good night, Raleigh," he says, one hand tucked beneath his head, the other lazily rubbing my back.

This is definitely not a normal one-night stand.

What is it, then?

* * *

I wake up alone in my bed to the sound of a cabinet closing in the kitchen, and it takes a second to remember last night.

Out with Atticus and Lachlan and Barrett.

Home with Atticus.

The best sex of my life. Then back here after I tried to escape alone. Sex again. Then sleeping wrapped up with each other.

I chuckle and shake my head.

And I guess he's still here.

I pull on some thin fleece pants and sneak into the bathroom. Obviously Atticus sees me. It's a freaking RV, after all.

"Coffee?" he calls.

"Sure," I respond through the door, biting back a smile.

"How do you like it?"

"Uh, cream and one sugar." This is so weird. I clean my teeth and run a brush through my hair. I hear the coffee machine spitting out a fresh cup and I take a deep breath before leaving the bathroom.

"Morning," Atticus says when I emerge. He offers me a steaming mug and adjusts the hat that sits backwards on his head. I don't even remember him grabbing that at his apartment when we left last night.

"Hey." I accept the mug and sip the perfect coffee.

"I put Megghen outside in her coop." He looks right at home in the Pink Palace, but also completely and utterly out of place.

"Thank you." Is this awkward? Or amazing?

"What do you want to do today?" Atticus's green eyes are locked on me.

"I dunno." I shrug. "Cross-stitch?"

"Can you teach me?"

"I'm sorry, what?" I snort, because I heard him, but, what?

"Teach me to do cross-stitch."

"You want to learn to do cross-stitch."

"Yes."

"You, Atticus Knox, professional hockey player, want me to teach you to do cross-stitch."

"Correct." He lowers his mug to the counter. "I'm getting the impression you don't think I can do it."

I laugh. "I don't think it's an ability thing." I glance down at his hands. "Although you might struggle to thread the needle."

"Let's do it."

"Alright. Let me get dressed."

Twenty minutes later, we're seated at the table with supplies spread out in front of us.

"I've been wanting to do a how-to for my social media," I say. "But haven't gotten around to it."

"Perfect. Let's make a video together. You can promote it by saying you taught a hockey player to cross-stitch."

"That is actually hilarious." I cock my head. "Would your PR person approve?"

"You mean my sister?" Atticus smirks because yeah, Lucy is the Blizzard's head of PR. "Yeah, she'd be okay with it."

I chuckle as I set up my phone.

"Ready?"

"Yep."

I click record.

"Alright." I turn to Atticus to start the video's introduction. "I'm Raleigh Hayes, and today we're going to teach my friend to do cross-stitch. Want to introduce yourself?"

Atticus lifts an eyebrow.

"I'm Atticus Knox, first line right wing on the Fort Collins' Blizzard NHL team. And I'm very excited to learn cross-stitch."

"Great. So here's your hoop with fabric already inserted and a pattern attached." I push a six-inch hoop toward Atticus with white fabric hooked in and a pattern pinned on top.

"Excellent." He picks up the hoop. "I'm ready, coach. Teach me all you know."

"I'll do my best." I crack a smile. "You can make some flowers and I'll work on stitching a quote."

"What quote are you working on?"

"One that you inspired, actually." I hold up a half finished hoop.

"So far it just says *zombies prefer brains*," Atticus says. He adjusts his baseball cap and smiles at me.

This might be really, *really* good for views and sales.

"You didn't let me finish." I touch the empty space beneath the first words. "I'm going to add: *so you're good.*"

Atticus laughs with a bright white beautiful smile.

Damn, he is charming. And good looking. And a lot of fun. And takes an interest in me and my life.

"What's next?"

I show Atticus how to pull apart the yarn and start a simple stitch with some red thread for roses.

"Like this?" Atticus hold up his hoop after five minutes. There's a completely uneven row of five cross stitches.

"Um." I press my lips together and touch the hoop. "You are learning, that's for sure."

"You're not impressed." Atticus looks devastated, but there's a twinkle in his eyes.

"Everyone has to start somewhere, chicken."

"Did you just call me chicken?" Atticus's jaw drops. "I thought I was rebound?"

"Okay, I'm stopping the video." I tap the red button and crack up. "I need to know where to edit out the inappropriate bits."

"Why ever would you want to do that?" Atticus lays his hoop down and leans over to me, touching my chin with his pointer finger and bringing his lips to mine. "I need a break anyway," he says against my mouth.

"We've only been doing this for like ten minutes." But the breath is quickly escaping my lungs as he moves his lips to my neck —he's so damn good at that—and slides a hand under my shirt up my back.

"More like five." Atticus tugs me by my waist until I'm firmly on his lap. "You are so hot when you're doing cross-stitch."

"Words I never thought I'd hear," I say with a breathy voice. I shift on his lap and can feel how hot he thinks I am. There's an ache between my legs and I wiggle on him. He groans and brings his lips back to mine, swiping his tongue inside rhythmically.

Somehow he gets us off the bench and onto the loveseat where we first watched the zombie movies together, and I'm on my back with him tugging my leggings off. My underwear comes too, and I close my knees as cool air hits my pussy.

"Last night was too fast. All three times," he says, nudging my legs open and looking down at my center. He swipes a finger along my slit, causing a gasp to escape my throat, and moans when he finds me wet. "So ready for me."

And I am. I'm ready for him, more than I have ever been for a man.

Physically, of course.

Do I like him? Yeah, I do.

I've known Atticus for more than a decade. But watching him kneel over me, his green eyes greedily watching as he rubs my most sensitive spot and I grind down on his hand, I wonder how I managed to suffer through sex before Atticus. God, that is dramatic, and I know it, but this is something else.

I'm going to come too fast, and it's embarrassing. I close my eyes and try to slow down the ripples of pleasure that are starting, a precursor to the waves that are building in the distance. My eyes fly open when I feel Atticus's rough cheeks on the inside of my thighs working their way up to my center, and then his tongue is doing all the work.

"Oh my god, Atticus." I arch my back as he slides his hands under my ass and presses his face into me.

I can't help it. I come so fast and hard that I reach back and grip the armrest behind me for stability.

"That's my girl," Atticus rasps, coming up for air after all the waves have subsided.

"That was embarrassing," I whisper.

"Why?" Atticus stands and chuckles as he grabs a tissue from the table to wipe up his face.

"I'm so easy to please." I watch him as he adjusts his erection in his athletic shorts and close my legs, wiggling to ease the ache that is still there. Or there again, I'm not sure. "At least with you."

"Good. Want to go back to doing cross-stitch?" He nods back to the kitchen table and our abandoned cross-stitch materials.

"Definitely not yet." I push up onto my elbows. "Do I need to beg again?" But then I laugh, the sound deep and suggestive, as his eyes darken and he pulls his shirt off so fast I hardly see it happen.

"We're going to an actual bed, Raleigh Hayes." And then Atticus swoops me up into his arms like a bride on her wedding night and whisks me to my bed.

"Any way you want me," I say as he lowers me onto the bed ten steps later and is magically naked. I pull off my sweatshirt and watch him swallow as he takes in my loose breasts.

"Turn around." He licks his lips. "On all fours, Raleigh."

I pulse between my legs and comply, getting on my knees and already breathing hard as I stick my ass in the air toward him.

"Fuck, Raleigh, your ass is so good." He gives me a light slap on one of my cheeks and I startle, but then lean into it. "You like that?"

"Yes." I let my head hang. I guess he's got a kink, and maybe I do too. Only one way to find out. "Do it again."

Atticus chuckles and lightly slaps my ass again, then sinks his finger inside my pussy from behind. I lean back into him and whimper.

"You want this so bad, baby, don't you?"

I nod my head.

He grips my ass in his hands and pokes his cock gently into my entrance. I cry out and press back into him, and he thrusts inside me in one swift gesture.

"I know I said I wanted to go slow this time," Atticus pants behind me. "But I can't help myself with you."

"Don't stop, please." I feel like I'm a different person but also exactly me right now. This is all about pleasure and fun and going after what I want. And with Atticus? It's exactly what I want. And need.

He doesn't need any other encouragement and pumps into me hard, sneaking one hand around to rub my clit. This time the orgasm builds differently. Slowly. Giving me enough time to soak in what is happening.

I don't really want to think too deeply about what this all means.

Not right now.

I don't want to *over*think.

I do my best to focus on the feeling of Atticus inside me, the way I'm already clenching around him. But I can't help but notice the way he's whispering my name, so sweetly. Does he even know he's saying it?

What is he thinking?

The waves of pleasure sneak up on me and then knock me down at once, and Atticus is moaning behind me as he comes, holding himself tight against my hips.

We collapse on the bed together a minute later. He smiles and lies on his side facing me. I turn to him.

"Why are you smiling?" I ask.

"Why are *you* smiling?" he retorts.

"Am I?" I touch my face with a finger and, yup, there it is. We both burst out laughing and he keeps his gaze locked on me.

"Should we finish that video?" I finally say, but he's playing with my nipple and doesn't look like he's ready to leave this bed.

An hour later, I kick Atticus out of the Pink Palace as I know he needs to go work out and I need to edit the video we finally finished. And I need a freaking minute to process everything that's happening.

Also, I have a whole shitload of texts from my friends checking in on me. I stopped responding to the group last night after telling them I was out with some of the hockey boys.

I settle down outside the Pink Palace facing the lake in one of the captain's chairs, Megghen happily pecking away at seeds next to me, the peaceful view of the water soothing my soul. The video is freaking adorable almost just as it is. I just cut out the part where he called me *coach* and I called him *rebound* before he started kissing me. He's so cute and smiley in the video and *oh my god*.

Then there's the gap where we paused the video and—my cheeks heat when I realize we came back looking subtly different. Hair mussed, cheeks pink.

Now it's time to face my friends.

To confess what I've done. I bite my lip. *Who* I've done.

"Do I have to tell them?" I ask my chicken. Megghen looks up for a second and I swear she nods before going back to pecking.

"Yup, no secrets with your best friends," I warn myself in Megghen's chicken voice.

"I hate that you're right."

I also realize I really need to start talking to people more so I don't morph completely into a chicken lady.

I open the group text chain with Lucy and January.

ME

Hey

LUCY

SIS WHERE HAVE YOU BEEN?? I almost sent a search party after you. Atticus left me unread as well

Her response is immediate. I can't lie to these women about what I was doing last night.

And for the past few weeks.

ME

I have something to tell you, Lulu

I hope you're not going to be mad

They know all about New Year's Eve. I didn't tell my friends right away, but could only hold it in for a few days into the new year before I confessed. They squealed.

JANUARY

I bet I can guess

LUCY

Waiting patiently

JANUARY

Hold on—I'm gonna go make popcorn

ME

It's about Atticus

JANUARY

YOU HOOKED UP WITH HIM, BABES.
ADMIT IT

ME

...

LUCY

We knew it!

The phone immediately lights up with a video call from Lucy, and when I press accept, she and January pop up in the screen together.

"I can't believe you guys are still hanging out together without me." I moan.

"Yeah, well, I would say I wish you'd have come, but then you wouldn't have done whatever the fuck you've done with my brother." Lucy's mouth is cracked into a huge grin.

"Did you sleep with him?" January leans into the camera, her big dark eyes comically large on my screen.

"I mean, yes?"

The both absolutely freak out. Lucy gasps and covers her face. January jumps up and spins around with the phone, doing a funny little dance before collapsing back on the couch next to Lucy.

"Was it good?" January asks with a wide grin.

"Do NOT answer that!" Lucy shakes her head violently and makes a retching sound.

I press my lips together and don't say a word.

"But sis, I feel like this was inevitable." Lucy cocks her head. "Don't you?"

"No?" This was the least inevitable thing I could imagine

when I left for my road trip in the Pink Palace. I was just trying to get away from my ex-husband and my mother and my job.

Speaking of, I need to call my mom.

"Babes, you drove an RV cross-country to Fort Collins when Lucy wasn't even there. What did you plan to do while you were in Colorado? Because you're not hiking all the mountains or taking advantage of the great outdoors."

"Hey, we went kayaking the other day."

"You went kayaking? With Atticus?" Lucy mutters something to January. "You, terrified of water ever since your doomed sailing experience?"

"Hmm, yeah. And we ended up in the lake." I can't keep the grin from my face.

"You are smiling." January narrows her eyes at me. "About capsizing off a boat."

"I mean, it was a kayak, not a sailboat or a cruise ship."

"So was this a one-night thing?" January probes. Lucy is quiet next to her, lips pressed together and brow furrowed like she's deeply contemplating something.

I think about her question. I've already wondered this myself. It could've been a one-night stand. Until he came back to the campsite with me in the middle of the night and cuddled in my crappy RV bed, then made me coffee, recorded a cross-stitch video, and took me from behind after slapping my ass.

My god, who am I?

I think it's safe to say this is *not* a one-night stand.

"I don't know." I sigh. I do know, but I can't vocalize it. "He recorded a cross-stitch video with me." I offer that detail instead. "I'll send it to you guys. I posted it on my socials."

"Hang on, my brother cross-stitched?"

"Yeah. I taught him a simple stitch. It's a beginner how-to video."

"That sounds very not one-night stand like." January laughs. "So is it friends with benefits?"

"I have no label to share with you." I shrug, and there's a few beats of silence.

"Lucy?" I ask. "You okay with all this?"

"Raleigh Durham," Lucy says, using my old college nickname. "I've never been more okay with something in my life."

I let out a huge sigh of relief.

"I don't even know what it is. I don't even know if it is a thing. I don't know if it'll happen again." To me, I sound desperate. For what? Approval? A repeat?

January laughs and shakes her head. She's got her phone in her hand.

"Oh, it's a thing. You see how he's looking at her in the video?" January shows her phone to Lucy.

Was he looking at me in a certain way? He was definitely charming, and smiley. I need to watch it again.

"Wow." Lucy smiles at me. "Do you know I've never met a girl that Atticus has dated? I realize he and I haven't lived in the same place for over a decade, but still. Never once has he introduced me to someone." She taps her chin with her pointer finger. "Or even mentioned anyone. It's been ridiculous."

"We are not dating," I say firmly.

I think about how sensitive Atticus is about his father. About his terrible relationship with him. About how he desperately doesn't want to be like him.

"Alternatively, he's just been having fun banging a lot of girls." January throws up her hands.

"That could also be true." Lucy shrugs.

"You already got a few comments on the video," January says, looking back down at her phone.

"I do? I don't think I've ever gotten a single comment on a post or video."

"You've also never featured a Blizzard player in one." January squints her eyes. "You have ten comments."

"What?" My phone buzzes and a text preview shows up over the video.

ATTICUS

I just shared your video on my socials

I huff out a laugh, but there's also a weird pit of dread in my stomach. I have a feeling things are spiraling out of control. This thing with Atticus—whatever it is—needs time to settle. And putting us in the public eye is the last thing I need.

Who knows, maybe no one will watch it.

## CHAPTER 16

# Apparently, It's a Lot



Wednesday, July 16

"Two hundred thousand views? Is that a lot?"

"Seriously?" Raleigh asks, her jaw dropping open.

I chuckle, happily swaying in the hammock next to the Pink Palace, arms stretched above my head. Raleigh is sitting in a captain's chair next to me. I guess I know two hundred thousand views is a solid amount.

"Come on, get in here with me." I hold out my hand, palm up.

"Atticus, I've gotten *twenty-one orders* in the past three days. That's almost as much as I've had in total before the video." She glances down at my extended hand and appears to consider.

"Well, congratulations."

"How am I going to fulfill so many orders?" Raleigh pulls at her hair and it sticks out on one side. She points at me. "It's all because of that video and you sharing it so casually on your social media. You have a few hundred thousand followers. Or more?" Raleigh stands, tosses her phone on the chair, and takes a tentative step toward me, hands on her hips.

"I have no idea how many followers I have. I'm so sorry. Let me make it up to you." I crook my finger at her.

She rolls her eyes but places her hand in mine anyway. Warmth cascades through her fingers onto my skin.

I guess I didn't really think it through when I shared the painfully adorable video of Raleigh teaching me how to do cross-stitch. The video immediately got hundreds of likes and many comments. I'm not in the habit of reading my comments, or even posting very much. I only do it when the team PR person—my sister—harasses the team to put ourselves out there in a positive light.

But I am loving the wondrous look on Raleigh's face as orders pile up. Like the look she has right now as she stands next to the hammock, hand in mine.

The past few days with Raleigh have been everything. I've adored every moment with her.

Even hockey is going better. I've been meeting with Lachlan and Barrett to skate and scrimmage and I don't hate Barrett as much as I did before. It's like exposure therapy. He's still cocky and insufferable. Loud and obnoxious. A partier. A player.

And he sort of reminds me of myself from five years ago.

Probably why I—strongly dislike?—him.

Nah, it's probably still hate.

"I'm going to have to temporarily close my shop while I catch up."

"No way. Don't do that." I tug her closer and she steps so she's hovering right over me.

"Or I guess I could put a note in my confirmation email saying the time to shipping is longer than usual." Raleigh purses her lips to one side. "Like weeks more."

Contemplative Raleigh is so hot. My eyes drift down to her gray tank top, tight against her breasts, and her pink short shorts with the white stripe down the side.

"Lean down on my chest and then very slowly lift your legs

up." I adjust my body so I'm diagonal on the hammock. I haven't been able to keep my hands off of this woman, and today is no exception.

Raleigh leans over and places her hands on either side of my neck onto the fabric of the hammock. I breathe out at her closeness. I slip my hands around her waist and tug her up, but the hammock swings precariously and she gasps and freezes.

"We're good, I won't let you fall." I chuckle and pull her up until she's laying flush on top of me, her legs securely on the hammock.

"This is the worst possible idea. And position," she says, her hair hanging on either side of her face.

"Don't worry." I cup her ass—so accessible through the soft fabric of her shorts—and press her down gently. "The best position. I bet we could slip these shorts off you and christen this hammock right here, right now."

"Oh my god." She shakes her head, violently at first, then stops when the hammock swings. "My neighbors are right there. They're probably watching us from their window." But she relaxes onto me, her body molding to mine.

"Let's give them a show, then." I slip my hands into her shorts and start to shift one hand to her front. She gasps.

"Atticus! Get your hands out of there and help me get down." Raleigh's cheeks pinken and I think I could convince her to carry on, but I'm not going to push her with this kind of thing, because I'm not an asshole.

I mean, I am an asshole, but not with this.

"Alright." I withdraw my hands. "But I told you, we'll be fi—"

Then her neighbor's RV door slams shut. Raleigh startles, the movement causing the hammock to abruptly swing, shifting Raleigh's weight from on top of me to next to me and then—

"Fuck!" I manage to hold her against my chest as we twist around and off of the hammock, flying into the air and falling the (luckily) very short distance to the ground.

We land with a hard thump on my back, her hands on either side of my head. I'm lucky there's no rocks or hard tree roots around the hammock. But between the impact and the gorgeous woman on top of me, the air whooshes out of my body and I can't breathe.

It wouldn't be a bad way to die, I suppose.

"Holy shit, are you okay?" She shoots up until she's sitting up straddling me, head touching the bottom of the hammock. She pats my chest and then my neck as if to check for cracks. "Did I just break you??? I'm going to get in so much trouble!"

I wiggle my shoulders, then my legs, then push my groin gently up into her. She huffs and puts her hands on her hips.

"I think I'm just fine. I was sacrificing myself for you, did you see that?"

"I did," Raleigh chuckles, then starts to laugh, and I catch it next.

Both of us are cracking up and she tries to hop off me, but the hammock gets in the way and I hold her in place by her hips.

"Atticus." Raleigh's posed on top of me, her wispy hair like a halo around her head. Sun beams in between the leafy green trees, illuminating the air around her.

"But I like this view." I take my hands off her hips anyway.

She sighs and leans down to kiss me, a smile still on her lips.

"You're going to have to help me cross-stitch, you know. I have no hope of catching up on these orders."

"Or, and hear me out—" I kiss her. "—we make another video and get a shit ton more orders."

"No way!" Raleigh rolls off and sits up, and I do the same next to her. She turns to me and sighs. "You have grass and dirt all over you." Raleigh wipes my back and picks a large leaf out of my curls.

I am fully smitten with Raleigh Hayes.

And that might be a problem.

Monday she announced she's halfway through her eight-week sabbatical. And while that aligns pretty well with when I'll have to be back in hockey mode starting with the Skate for Kids charity tournament next month in New York City, it feels like the summer will be gone in the blink of one of Megghen's creepy chicken eyes.

And then I'll immerse myself in hockey, like I always do.

And she goes back to Connecticut and her old life, as has been her plan all along.

Hopefully not *all* of her old life.

Earlier this week she told me how her ex-husband continues to text and email her. She told him she needs space, and that they're not getting back together.

Still, I can't fully read her on that.

Yeah, she's sleeping with me. Spending all her time with me. But we're temporary.

He was her permanent.

I hope it stays in the past tense.

I hop up and reach my hand down to Raleigh to help her up.

"You all right over there?" Her RV neighbor calls from in front of her RV.

"Hey Elizabeth." Raleigh—cheeks pinker by the second—takes a few steps toward her.

I jump to my feet and wince at the twinge in my groin, taking a second to confirm that it is all in my head. I feel one hundred percent on the ice, but once in a while I'll get a phantom pain that seems to be my body freaking out that I'll hurt myself again.

I need to be careful I don't mess myself up before hockey season, especially not doing something stupid like flipping off a hammock.

I pull out my phone to check the time—almost noon—so I need to run home and get my stuff together to meet the skating coach, Lachlan, and Barrett.

Raleigh disappears into the Pink Palace and re-emerges with a pair of eggs in her hand.

"Oh, lovely." The neighbor accepts the eggs while I respond to a text message chain with Lucy.

LUCY

I can't believe Raleigh is in Fort Collins and I'm
not there

ME

I'm taking care of her

LUCY

You better be. Not being sleazy, are you?

ME

I'm offended you're even asking

And I am. I get why my sister is protective of Raleigh, and I've actually been surprised at how positive she reacted when Raleigh told her we're doing more than hanging out as friends.

Personally, I would've kept that detail from Lucy, for the same reason I'm glad most people are out of town while I figure things out with Raleigh. I can't imagine trying to be with her in front of so many witnesses, like how Lucy and Kellen got together last season.

Then again, two hundred thousand views on our cross-stitch video might contradict that idea.

I'm watching Lucy respond when a colorful delivery van pulls up in front of the Pink Palace. A guy jumps out of the driver's side and slides open the back of his van, emerging with a large bouquet of red roses.

Raleigh turns at the sound and her eyes widen at the flowers. She turns to me with a sweet smile on her face.

Only one problem.

They're not from me.

"One of you Raleigh Ford?" the man asks, looking between Raleigh and her neighbor.

"It's Hayes, not Ford." Raleigh's brow furrows as the man hands her a tablet to sign before handing over the bouquet.

"Enjoy!" He jumps back in his van and pulls away, his tires spinning gravel as he departs.

Raleigh glances at me, eyebrows raised. I stand here like an asshole, phone in hand, and shrug.

Who the fuck sent Raleigh flowers?

Raleigh plucks the card from the bouquet and opens the little envelope.

Her eyes widen and she mouths *fuck*.

Oh, but I do know.

I slip my phone in my pocket and stroll over, doing my best to project casual nonchalance, not the chaos of my insides as my mind fixates on Raleigh's ex-husband. Nothing like another man sending flowers to the woman I just spent the night with.

"You okay, dear?" Elizabeth asks, resting a hand on Raleigh's forearm.

"No." Raleigh shakes her head, still staring at the card.

"Not okay," the neighbor says, glancing at me. "But the roses are gorgeous."

I stop a few feet from Raleigh and she raises her brown eyes to mine.

"Jacob," she answers the question I didn't ask.

And with that one word, I feel like everything shifts.

"I'll catch you later, Raleigh, okay?" Elizabeth says, her eyes darting between the two of us. "Let me know if you need anything." She disappears back into her RV.

I don't know what to say to Raleigh.

"I thought he didn't know where you were?" My heart thumps loudly in my chest, like a cadence to my own funeral. Or at least back to my singledom.

Raleigh hands me the card. I accept it and skim over the words.

*Raleigh, I hope you're not giving up on us. I'd love for you to teach me cross-stitch. Love, Jacob*

For fuck's sake. Fury rushes through my veins and my stomach clenches.

"I guess he saw the video." I want to crumple up the card and shove it in my pocket so I can burn it or trash it later, but instead I hand it back.

"I'm gonna go put these in water." Raleigh disappears with the flowers and the card and I stand there like a complete outsider.

Water? I would've preferred she throw the roses to the ground and stomp on them. To have laughed and said I'm her only cross-stitch student. Maybe I should've made a joke about how he probably couldn't have helped her go viral like I did.

But instead, she suddenly seems far away from me.

Why didn't she throw them out?

I'm terrified Raleigh's just using the summer as a brief intermission to her normal life, the one she's chosen every day since college. Married life as a pharmacist living in suburban Connecticut.

A future with me is so not Raleigh Hayes.

And I don't want to hurt her.

Shit. I can't just stand here.

I gently knock on the door to the Pink Palace and Raleigh calls for me to come in. The flowers are in a tall plastic container, one that takeout soup might have come in, and it looks like it's going to fall over. Guess she doesn't have a fancy vase for flowers in the RV.

I might love giving Raleigh gifts, but I'm not going to buy one for her so she can put roses from her ex-husband in it.

"It's not like I'm hiding from him," she says, and my heart clenches. "I was just sick of him showing up at our house, or my job, or waiting for me in my parking lot."

"Sounds like a stalker." But I don't miss her slip calling it *our house*.

"Nah." Raleigh shakes her head. "He's harmless."

Harmless? Hardly. He's not giving her the space to move on with her life. He's pressuring her to stay in constant touch.

He's trying to take my place in her cross-stitch videos.

"I have skating practice, but I can stick around if you want me to—"

"No, it's okay." Raleigh stares sightlessly into the giant bunch of flowers. "I have a few things to do."

She won't even look at me.

I want to pull her into my arms and kiss her goodbye. But I don't think that would be welcome at this moment.

So I slip out of the RV and jump into my Wrangler, flooring it to get out of the campsite. My phone buzzes in the cupholder, so I slow to a stop before turning onto the main road. Maybe it's Raleigh asking me to come back.

Nope. It's a text from an artist who I contacted recently, the one whose card I got at Horsetooth Brewery the other week.

MATT - ARTIST FROM BREWERY

I have availability a week from Sunday

ME

great

MATT - ARTIST FROM BREWERY

I'll send you a sketch of what I have in
mind soon

I open my text chain with Raleigh, filled with flirty texts and images of cross-stitches and screen shots of comments from our viral video, and tap out a message.

ME

I would like to take care of the paint job repair
for the Pink Palace. But I'll need your
permission to be, ah, a little creative

RALEIGH

That is totally not necessary

ME

you won't regret it. well, you might, but time
will tell

RALEIGH

lol. Okay, you've got me interested

This has gotta be better than a boring bouquet of roses.

Shit, am I really competing with Raleigh's loser ex-husband? I've never been one to fight for a woman. If one of my teammates hits on someone, I'm out. I just haven't ever cared that much.

But Raleigh?

I think she's worth fighting for.

## CHAPTER 17

# Oh, Come On

## RALEIGH

Jacob answers the phone right away.

"Raleigh, I'm so glad you called," he says without waiting for me to say anything.

"Why are you sending me flowers?" I push back one of the curtains and watch the back of Atticus's Wrangler depart the campsite.

"Do you like them?" He sounds so excited. I want to kick him. How dare he?

"They're roses, of course I like them, but I don't want them from you."

Jacob has the audacity to make a sad little sound.

"It feels like so long since we talked. Since I saw you. I miss you, Ral."

I sink onto the couch and lean my head back, closing my eyes and wishing for strength.

"It's only been a month. And you ask for money, and then you spend a ton to get roses delivered. So really, I bought myself those flowers."

The sickly sweet smell of the roses fills the Pink Palace, and my stomach clenches in objection.

"I have a job interview tomorrow, so I wanted to celebrate."

It's like we're having two entirely different conversations.

"That's great, Jacob." I guess I'll join *his* conversation, because otherwise we'll talk in circles for eternity. "Where is the interview?"

I don't know why I bothered to ask, but Jacob launches into a description of the company he's interviewing with. I mostly block him out. Him getting a job would be amazing. I've already said I'm not giving him any more money, but I still feel so damn bad he's struggling. Because while I'm having some kind of existential crisis, I'm at least not financially destitute.

Probably because I'm not a gambler. Or a compulsive liar.

I don't *not* care about him. In other words... I still care about him. But I'm realizing it might be a real problem to continue this kind of relationship. Have I been enabling Jacob by giving him money and not cutting him off completely?

And I'm only now processing the look on Atticus's face when he saw the flowers. It was surprise, bewilderment, then understanding. I truly thought they were from him until the delivery guy called out my married last name.

Then Atticus fled.

And I didn't stop him.

It takes me a minute to realize Jacob's gone quiet.

"Raleigh?"

"Sorry, what did you ask?"

"I asked when you're coming home." His voice sounds so hopeful.

"I don't know." I sit up and stiffen my back. There's a sharp edge to my voice, and a pregnant pause follows.

The answer is, of course, in four weeks when my sabbatical is over. But he knows that. He just wants me to confirm I'm coming home to *him*.

I'm not, though.

"I saw the video of you and that hockey player."

"Mmm-hmm. I figured that from your note." If he thinks I'm

offering any information or insight as to what I was doing with Atticus, he's gotta be freaking delusional.

"You don't have to do this, you know," Jacob says softly.

"Do what?" I grind my teeth together. I tap my phone to put him on speaker and lay it next to me so I can drop my head in my hands.

"You're trying to be someone you're not." He pauses, and I consider hanging up on him, because I don't want to hear whatever he's going to say next. "I loved you exactly as you were. As you *are*. There's no need to buy an RV and drive across the country and do whatever it is you're doing with that hockey player to prove something."

"I don't know what you're talking about." I want to sound confident, nonchalant, angry, even. But I feel insecure. Upset. Defensive. My phone buzzes. "Wait, are you trying to video call me??"

"Yeah. I want to see your face."

"No." My voice cracks. Because the thing is—he's kind of right. I'm trying to be someone different. I don't want to be the same person I was when I married him. I want to evolve. But what if that's just not possible? What if we are who we are and there is no changing a person at their core?

"Okay, I understand." Jacob makes a squeaking sound. "Ral, I'm sorry if I upset you, now or with the flowers."

I don't want his apologies, and I don't want to be having this conversation anymore, because it's making me feel unmoored instead of adventurous.

"Where'd you get my address?"

"I met your mother for coffee and she gave it to me," Jacob said simply, as if he'd been waiting for me to ask.

"She *gave* it to you?" My head jerks up.

There's no way. *Mom.*

"Well," he draws out the word. "She might have accidentally told me."

I stand, snatch my phone from the couch, and step outside to do laps around the RV. Megghen *boc boc bocs* as I walk by each time.

"Please stop calling me. And don't send me anything else."

Jacob ignores my protests and launches into another long apology and recap of his latest therapy appointment.

I've got so much unresolved shit. With myself and with my ex.

I'm not sure why I thought buying an RV and driving cross country would make me a different person. He's right. I'm the same Raleigh that got here four weeks ago.

Just because Atticus Knox is paying attention to me, doesn't make me different.

I end the call with Jacob and immediately call my mother.

"Mom."

"Hi sweetheart!"

"Tell me you didn't tell Jacob where I am."

"No, of course not! I mean, crap, I kind of did." She gasps. "Is he there?"

"Mom!"

"He showed up outside my office—I guess he missed stalking you so decided to start stalking me—and I took him for coffee. He was freaking out about you not being in town."

"Oh, for fuck's sake."

"That boy is not stable."

"Yeah? Well he seems to think he's the most stable he's ever been."

"Dammit." Mom sighs. "He wanted to know where you were. He asked if you'd seen Lucy yet. I said no, she was traveling for the summer... and then he got this look on his face."

"So you gave him my exact address??"

"No! But he threatened to go to Fort Collins and go to all the RV campsites until he found you. He said he just wanted to send you something."

"Well, he did. He sent flowers."

"Sorry I didn't warn you. I meant to, then forgot." Mom huffs. "You dodged a bullet by divorcing him."

I snort, then sink into a captain's chair and let my eyes settle on the peaceful lake. Maybe I'll live here at the campsite forever.

It doesn't really matter how he found out.

What matters is that my ex-husband now has my exact location.

CHAPTER 18

## *Just Hanging Out*

ATTICUS

Saturday, July 18

Something's shifted with Raleigh.

We've both settled into spending most of our days and nights with each other, acting as if we're dating even though we haven't labeled it.

But there's also the unspoken.

Less than four weeks left in her sabbatical.

The fact that I'm a professional hockey player in the offseason.

Her ex-husband.

*Especially* that.

I asked her how she felt about the flowers the day after she received them, and she just shrugged it off, like it wasn't a big deal that her ex keeps trying to win her back and that he knows exactly where she is.

I didn't push it. I should've stayed and talked to her about it when it happened. It was too late the day after.

"Want to get a drink or ice cream?" I ask, my arm slung over her shoulders. Raleigh's leaning into me and we're walking perfectly in step. We just finished eating Thai food and are walking through the streets of Fort Collins. "Or skip those options and head back to my place?"

"How about both and then your place?" She looks up at me and I lean down to kiss her lips.

"Whatever you want, coach."

Raleigh laughs and elbows me in the side, which is normally her reaction when I pull out the *coach* nickname.

Even though I fired her from that role last week.

I picked her up from the Pink Palace a few hours ago and made sure Megghen was fed and settled in her tent inside the RV so Raleigh would feel comfortable coming back to my place for the night.

This all feels like we're living in some kind of fantasy world. I have to remind myself this is basically a vacation fling.

At least for Raleigh. She thinks I'm fun, but I can't help but think that she sees me the same way that I think Lachlan's girlfriend sees him.

A bit of fun. Nothing serious.

And I'm definitely not going to ask her if that's true.

"Black Diamond?" I suggest, pointing ahead of us to the bar where we first met up with Lachlan. There are groups of people standing outside the bar around a few high tables.

"Sure."

I hold open the heavy wooden door to Black Diamond and Raleigh steps inside. I follow, grabbing her hand and approaching the bar. There's a ring of people waiting for drinks, and we stop right behind a man and a woman.

I'm busy focusing on the feel of Raleigh's hand in mine when the woman turns around.

*Oh, fuck.*

I know her.

Long blonde hair, freckles, bright blue eyes. I hooked up with her... last fall, maybe? Zoey? Susan? Laura? Fuck, I forget her name.

She was a perfectly nice woman. Beautiful, even. Still, it was not a great decision, because I'd met her at Horsetooth Brewing, and I knew she was local. I normally try to avoid local women because then there's the risk of running into them when we least want to.

Like right now.

We hooked up the first night but didn't sleep together. So we met up another night and went back to her place.

Then I ghosted her.

And now she's back to haunt me.

Mary? Maria? Fuck, I really wish I remembered her name, if only to convince myself I'm not such a sleaze ball. She hasn't turned around and spotted me, so I'm safe so far.

I gotta get out of here. I take a step away and tug Raleigh's hand to follow. We'll move to another spot to wait for drinks.

"Atticus?"

But it's too late.

I turn my head toward Zoey-Susan-Laura-Mary-Maria. I was so close. So close to avoiding this situation. But now, with long blonde hair draped over her shoulders, she's facing me, and so is the dude with her. Raleigh is looking her way curiously.

Shit.

"Oh, hey..." I almost call her Zoey-Susan-Laura-Mary-Maria, which is definitely not right.

"Marcy." She spits out the word with a hard *M* as if she hoped it contained daggers or poison. Marcy crosses her arms and twists her mouth.

"How are you? It's been a long time."

"Yeah. A long time." She turns to the dude she's with, a big guy with tattoos and a beard, but I'm also a big guy, so. "Can you get us drinks, please?" Marcy flutters her lashes at the man and he shrugs and turns back to the bartender. Then she steps forward and narrows her eyes, practically hissing. "A long time since you completely blew me off." She ignores Raleigh.

"Sorry about that," I mumble, my gaze sliding to Raleigh. Her eyebrows are pinched and she's watching the woman carefully.

Marcy looks sharply at Raleigh, as if just noticing she's standing there.

"Hi," Raleigh says, her voice steady but guarded.

"Well, hello." Marcy's expression softens just a tad, then hardens again. "Are you Atticus's latest?"

Ouch. This is going just as badly as I'd imagined.

"Latest?"

"Latest fling. Did you just meet him tonight?"

"No—" Raleigh starts, but Marcy cuts back in right away.

"Just be aware, it doesn't last long with him. He'll lose interest in about thirty seconds. Definitely after you sleep with him." She turns to me and spits the last words out. Literally, I feel a few drops of saliva hit my face. I try really hard not to wipe them off dramatically.

"Uh, thanks for the warning." Raleigh slides her eyes to me. Her mouth is now partially turned up into an amused smile, but her eyes are still worried.

I'm not sure what to say right now. Luckily, Marcy's dude saves us by stepping back over with her mixed drink.

"Good to see you." I take the escape opportunity and pull Raleigh away and into the empty slot at the bar. I sense Marcy behind me for another few seconds, then she walks away.

"She is not a fan of yours," Raleigh whispers.

"No, she's not." I don't blame her. I don't like who I've been with women for the past decade.

"What happened between you two?"

The bartender looks my way and I order two beers, forgetting for a second that Raleigh prefers wine.

What happened? Nothing. The usual. She's hot, I hooked up with her, but I didn't want anything more. I didn't even feel bad about it at the time.

Do I now?

No, I don't. I try to feel something. Regret, shame, pity, any kind of negative feeling for how I treated Marcy.

But I can't do it.

"We hung out a few times," I say lamely. "She might've wanted more, I didn't."

"Guess my dating lessons came too late for you and Marcy." Raleigh accepts a bottle of beer and elbows me in the arm.

I chuckle.

"I told you, I don't want to date anyone. I just want to hang out with you."

That sounds far too serious for who I am as a human being, but also far too casual for what I really feel for Raleigh. Which is what, exactly? I don't know.

But she's not a fling.

She's not someone I've just hung out with a few times.

## CHAPTER 19

# Should I Cross-Stitch It?

## RALEIGH

Friday, July 25

Sweet baby Jesus.

The cross-stitch orders have gone out of control. It's been almost two weeks since I posted the video teaching Atticus to cross-stitch and we're at almost *five hundred thousand* views and a lot more orders. That's huge for me.

I've had to close the shop temporarily.

I drop the zombie cross-stitch I'm working on—*Zombies prefer brains, so you're good*—onto the table and click open my email. That one is by far my biggest seller, clearly because of the video. I really wish I'd picked a shorter quote as my fingers are about to fall off.

There's another message from my online post looking for Megghen's owner. *Is she a silkie?* At that my heart lurches. But then: *if she's a brown one, that's my chicken!* I respond quickly and then delete. The inquiries from my online post have significantly slowed down. Today's message was the first in days. I mean, I want to find her owner, I do, but I also like having her around. I recently figured out that chickens like to snuggle. Seriously. I saw a video online and tried it out. I picked her up and brought her slowly against my chest. I was a little afraid she'd peck a hole in my neck but instead she laid her little chicken head against my shoulder.

I don't think I'm ever going to eat poultry again.

She's like my therapy. My ex might go to a human counselor, but I go to Dr. Megghen. She's also my encouragement when I low-level panic about my overwhelming cross-stitch orders. I messaged all my customers and told them it would be a a few weeks —or longer—until I could ship the orders and they could cancel if they wanted.

Only a handful took me up on it.

I had the idea to create a cross-stitch kit with the zombie quote I was working on with Atticus. I added a note on my online storefront about shipping delays and the quicker availability of kits. I can get those put together and shipped in no time at all.

Except I'm spending a lot of time with Atticus, so I don't have as much free time as I should, considering I'm on sabbatical and have no other responsibilities.

Atticus.

We've spent every night together for the past two weeks. Sometimes at his place, which, admittedly, has a much more comfortable bed than the Pink Palace, and about twice as big. But we stay at the campsite sometimes anyway. I think Atticus likes waking up and watching the sun rise over the lake. He even convinced me to go out on the kayaks again. It was on a day that a repairman came to reseal the windows. This time we stayed closer to shore and my panic levels were much lower. I didn't even capsize—myself or Atticus. It was *almost* enjoyable. Probably because Atticus did it shirtless this time, and he doesn't wear a life vest like I do.

Fine. It was fun.

He left a few hours ago to workout.

This thing is our little secret, kind of, since multiple people know about it.

But none of them are in Fort Collins.

Lachlan is so wrapped up in his girlfriend and Barrett is so wrapped up in, well, himself, that Atticus has managed to keep it quiet from them.

And the others are too far away to be able to truly interfere. Not that Lucy and January aren't trying.

I glance down at the jersey I'm wearing. Not only did he leave it here after that first night, but he wants me to wear it. He wants to lay claim to me... I get the feeling he hasn't done that with women often. Ever? I suck in a breath at the thought that what we have is special, not only to me, but to him as well.

The thing weighing heavy on me every day is Jacob.

He's texting me way too much. I told him he can't call me, and I muted our text chain. But it's always there with new messages. I flip over my phone and tap through to check out his latest from this morning.

JACOB

Good morning, beautiful

My favorite days with you were lazy Sunday mornings when we snuggled on the couch with our coffees

I scoff and shake my head. I literally have no recollection of that ever happening. Maybe we sat at the kitchen table and scrolled our phones? But I don't think we were snuggling on the couch. I think he's completely re-writing our marriage in his brain so he can hyper focus on something during his therapy.

I should tell him to back off once and for all. Block him. It's been a month since my last payment to him. When will he ask again? Maybe he won't. Once he's financially stable, then I'll cut him off emotionally as well.

I let those beautiful roses remain in The Pink Palace for twenty-four hours before I walked them over to Elizabeth. She accepted them with raised eyebrows when I told her that the smell in the small space was making me nauseous. It wasn't a lie. Every time I looked at them, I felt sick.

Does Jacob really still love me? He's been drowning in the ocean of his gambling addiction and compulsive lying, and he needs some way to survive the raging sea.

I think I'm a life boat for him. I'm calm waters.

But he's not the way for me. I don't even like the water.

I consider what to type back, but I can't think of anything appropriate. I don't want to argue with him. I don't want to casually respond as if his texts are welcome.

While I think, Atticus buzzes in.

ATTICUS

up for a kayak?

I let out a short laugh as his message breaks the building tension inside me. This man cracks me up every time we're together.

ME

I almost died kayaking and you want me to go again? Like, again again?

ATTICUS

that is categorically false

ME

You flipped me

ATTICUS

also false. you flipped me, and that was the first time we went. last time, we both stayed completely dry and it was a delightful afternoon on the water

ME

Hmm. Maybe. Either way, at some point I was in a lake filled with probably electric eels and crocodiles

ATTICUS

so many things wrong with that sentence,
coach

A knock at the Pink Palace door startles me. Is it Atticus? Texting me as he walks up to the door, probably with the kayaks already set up? I snort. Because even though the water still scares the shit out of me, I'll get back on it with Atticus. He'd save me from drowning (along with the life vest) and scary Colorado wildlife.

I drop my phone onto the counter and stride over to the door. Fred leans against the wall in the corner, but I haven't even thought about touching him for weeks.

I don't need Fred when I have Atticus.

I pull the door open, a huge smile on my face.

But it's not Atticus.

It's Jacob.

Oh, for fuck's sake.

"Raleigh," he says with a sigh. "It's so good to see your face."

My jaw drops as I take in my ex-husband standing in front of me. Crisp white polo shirt and khaki pants, blond wavy hair in a perfect swoop across his forehead. He looks young and fresh, and his big blue eyes drink me in: Blizzard jersey, shorts and bare feet, hair tucked behind my ears.

But his eyes linger on the jersey.

"What are you doing here?" I cross my arms tightly across my chest.

"Do you have a minute?"

"My god, Jacob, couldn't this have been an email? A text? Even a video call?"

He has the courtesy to dip his chin to his chest and cringe.

"But you don't want me to call you anymore."

"Showing up is not better!" The nerve of this guy. My shoulders tense as I block the door to the Pink Palace.

"Yeah, maybe not." Jacob blushes and runs his hand over his face. "Sorry."

Instead of meeting my gaze, he looks around the campsite, his eyes landing on the two new captain's chairs.

"Jacob. What are you doing here?"

"Can we talk?" Jacob nods his head toward the lake and the chairs. The same chairs that Atticus and I sit in and have coffee the mornings we are here.

"We can stand." I step outside of the RV, keeping my arms crossed to protect myself. There's no way I'm inviting him in. The Pink Palace is sacred, especially now that Atticus's mark is in so many little corners. A Blizzard sweatshirt he left the other night on top of my dresser. Two coffee mugs drying on the small counter next to the sink. His bookmark in the spicy memoir he bought for me and decided to read after I finished. He's inserted purple tabs marking the sections he said he wants to discuss with me.

"I got that job," Jacob says, a shy smile settling on his face. "The one I've been talking about."

"Good for you." I breathe out. It's a relief, really. He's been unemployed for so long. And it'll help me to stop supplementing his life out of guilt. This will be the final cord to sever between us, and I can do it without guilt now that he'll be making money of his own.

Although him showing up here points in another direction.

He starts to ramble about the company, but I block him out. He's told me all of this in texts and emails over the past week. I know he had his third and final interview three days ago. That things went really well and he liked the interviewers. That this job would give him health insurance, a 401K, and a salary that can pay rent and buy food.

"It's a lower level than my last job, but I can work my way up," he says as I zone back in.

"Congratulations. Because, Jacob? I can't keep supporting you," I say, my voice softer than I mean it to be.

His face falls. "I know. I was hoping for one more month—" Jacob stops at the look on my face, which must be one of pained resignation.

Of course he needs more.

One more month.

It'll never end.

He'll track me down wherever I go. He'll never let me out of his life. After he has enough money, it'll be something else. He'll need someone to talk to about his investments, or ideas for a Christmas gift for his mother, or a reminder on what lawn mowing company we used.

"—but that's it. And then I'll have my first paycheck and be all settled. By the time you get back home, I'll be a different man."

"I don't know, Jacob." My stomach turns.

By the time you get back home.

"Hey." He steps forward and swipes a finger on my cheek. "You okay?"

I flinch, surprised to realize my cheeks are wet. Am I crying over this man? *What* am I crying over?

His words repeat in my head: *by the time you get back home.*

That's what he said.

Because the truth is, my sabbatical ends in less than three weeks. I'm supposed to go back to Connecticut and return to my pharmacy job and my old life.

But I don't want to.

"I don't know when I'm coming back."

"But your sabbatical is almost over?" His crinkles his nose in a way I once found charming.

I shake my head too aggressively. "Maybe I'm not coming back."

Jacob breathes in sharply.

What am I talking about? Of course I'm going back. I'm just sad because I don't see a way that I'll truly be rid of Jacob and that part of my old life.

He's right—I'm not the kind of woman who travels in an RV and reinvents myself.

I'm just playing a part here.

And the show is almost over.

The look on Jacob's face breaks my heart. Or does something to my heart. More like stabs it with a kitchen knife. It's like he's desperate for my attention. My approval. Have I left that kind of impression on him? That he needs to fix himself for me? If so, I really screwed up.

I think I might have screwed up in a lot of ways.

Divorcing him was not one of them. But staying in such close contact—who did that really help? Instead of giving both of us a clean break, I've been sending him money. Emailing him. Texting him back. Taking his phone calls.

I've been enabling Jacob.

I'm an enabler.

All he's doing is thinking about himself and his own problems instead of actually getting out there and solving any of them. Therapy's done wonders for his self-awareness—I think at this point he's more in touch with his own issues than most people are—but it's time he live his life.

"Your mom's been kind and supportive to me while you've been gone," Jacob says.

"My mom?" I snort. I've talked to my mom multiple times about this. She's been firm with Jacob, not encouraging.

She's even started a spreadsheet for him to try to push him to get his life together so he'll leave me alone.

My phone starts buzzing with a call, but I ignore it in my pocket. Then it buzzes a few short beats. Text messages. I sigh and pull it out.

MOM

Raleigh, I think Jacob is on his way to see you. I'm so sorry, I've been trying to talk sense into him, but he sent me a text this morning that makes me think he's in Colorado.

I groan.

"Everything okay?"

I ignore Jacob and tap out a text.

ME

Thanks. He's here

The three little dots dance around with her response, but I put my phone away.

"That was my mom, warning me you might be showing up."

"Was this the wrong thing to do, Raleigh?"

"Yeah, it was." I squint my eyes shut. I have to get through to Jacob that he needs to live his own life without me.

And then my eyes fly open at the sound of a Jeep Wrangler on the gravel drive of the campsite.

## CHAPTER 20

# *Unexpected but Inevitable*

## ATTICUS

an hour earlier

The Aussie is sobbing in the penalty box.

"For fuck's sake," Barrett says, paused next to me on the ice, staring at Lachlan.

For once, I agree with the sentiments from the young hotshot. I don't even mind that he's standing next to me, matching my posture with crossed arms and helmet tucked in an armpit.

"I don't think he's ever been dumped before." I shake my head. I *know* he hasn't. He's got a slightly stronger dating history then I do, but not by much. I suspect Lachlan's a giant softie inside and just pretends to be a player to protect himself.

Whereas I'm an asshole, through and through.

"This is why dating is a bad idea." Barrett scoffs. "Giving women that kind of control? Falling in *love*? The fucking worst. Just punch me if I ever try to do that."

"What, are we fucking friends now?" I turn to look at Barrett.

"Why not?" He smirks and shrugs.

"Because you fucked up my fucking groin, dipshit." I shove him in the arm, not *not* aggressively.

"Ow!" He rubs his shoulder, looking hurt. Emotionally.

I'd rather have punched him. He's like the incredibly annoying pain-in-the-ass little brother I'm thankful I never had.

Barrett's face turns red and he scrunches his face and groans dramatically.

"Yeah. I know." He's got the common courtesy to cringe. Or maybe that's a pout.

I grind my teeth together. I'm actually going to punch him.

"Listen." Barrett clasps his hands together. "I really am sorry about that. I've been meaning to apologize but didn't want to sound like a dick."

"So you thought *not* apologizing was the way to handle it?"

"Is this our first fight?"

I'm gonna kill him. I growl.

"Okay, okay. I should've apologized right away." Barrett rubs a hand behind his neck and stares down at the ice. "But you and Lachlan... I don't want to look like a loser in front of you two. You're like, my big brothers."

For fuck's sake.

I shake my head, words escaping me. Barrett looks up at me with wide eyes, and I almost feel bad.

"I— I get in the zone on the ice and feel like I can bust through walls, like the Hulk on ice."

I grunt. I know the feeling. And it's what makes him so damn good. I'm finally starting to accept that we're probably lucky to have him on the team.

"But you look good now? Aren't you all healed?" Barrett looks at me like a wounded puppy.

I'm back to wanting to kick him.

Not that I'd ever kick a puppy.

*Is* this what it's like to have a little brother?

"Yeah," I hiss. "I'm fine. Whatever. You're forgiven. Let's never speak of it again."

Barrett smiles broadly and I turn back to the penalty box with a roll of my eyes.

Shit, when did I become the old curmudgeon? Barrett is me five years ago. Hell, he's me *one* year ago.

And when I look at Lachlan, I feel like he's future me, when Raleigh leaves Fort Collins.

Two. Weeks.

I shake my head to get the image out of her driving the Pink Palace out of that campsite and onto the highway back to Connecticut. It'll take her at least a week to get back to the East Coast. Will she leave in a week? A few days?

We haven't talked about it at all. Like we're pretending there's no expiration date to our relationships.

When she goes, I'll be the one crying in the penalty box. Fucking pathetic.

This is why I've never let myself date.

Wait, no, that's not true. I've never been afraid of being the one devastated. I've been afraid of being the asshole, hurting women along the way.

But it's different with Raleigh.

* * *

I turn into the campsite and let my eyes land on the RV. Lachlan's breakup is throwing me off. I couldn't even get details from him on what exactly happened with Melissa, just that she broke up with him and it was very much one sided. He said he was going to her house after practice to beg her to work it out. We tried to talk him out of it—and I cannot believe I'm referring to me and Barrett as 'we'—but he couldn't be reasoned with.

I even texted Kellen in England and Harley in Maine to see if they would reach out to him.

The whole this-will-inevitably-crash-and-burn vibe is spot on to me and Raleigh.

I'm so lost in my thoughts that I don't notice what is happening in front of the Pink Palace until I pull up and find the spot next to Raleigh's car already taken by a shitty compact car.

And then my eyes land on Raleigh.

She's standing in front of her RV with a dude. A dude who looks like he belongs in a tiny cubicle at some soulless corporation that make something dumb like door knobs or garden hoses.

It's gotta be her ex-husband.

But what the *fuck* is he doing here?

Raleigh's eyes are wide as she watches me pull to a stop.

A primal instinct takes over and I wrench the door to the Wrangler open and hop out. I clench my fists as I stride over to them. Raleigh's watching, and his gaze swivels to me. It seems to take a million years to walk the handful of feet to where they are standing.

"Who's this?" The guy says and turns back to Raleigh, as if I'm just some annoying neighbor or a fucking flower delivery driver.

"It's Lucy's brother. Who lives in Fort Collins." Raleigh throws one hand up in the air. She's clearly annoyed at him. And at me? She didn't toss me a smile, exasperated or otherwise. "You know who Atticus is."

Jacob stares at me with narrowed eyes. I've got at least five inches and seventy pounds on this guy, and his confident look only lasts a split second before he flinches and breaks eye contact.

"Yeah, from the ridiculous cross-stitch video," he mumbles.

Does this dude have a death wish? How dare he talk shit about our video. That was pure art. The best thing I've ever posted on social media.

"Yup. That's me." I enunciate each word carefully.

"I'm Jacob," he says in a voice that he probably thinks is strong, but reveals his uncertainty with a slight wobble. "Raleigh's husband."

I'm going to end this asshole.

"Very much *ex*-husband," she says quickly and glares at him.

"Atticus Knox." I pause. "Raleigh's boyfriend."

Both of them drop their jaws at the last word.

"Boyfriend?" Jacob darts a look at Raleigh, but she keeps staring at me, the spot between her eyebrows crinkled into double lines. Her eyes are wide and the corners of her lovely pink lips turned down.

Well, shit. That was the wrong thing to say, I guess, especially before we even talked about what we are. Not that we were ever going to do that. There was no need since our end date is both close and clear.

"I'm not sure there needs to be labels," Raleigh says carefully, looking at me with a blank stare and then at Jacob with a withering expression. He looks down and kicks a pile of gravel like a chastised child.

"Jacob arrived a little while ago. I didn't know he was in town. I didn't realize he was coming to see me," Raleigh says, her words to me but her current glare directed at her ex-husband. He meets her gaze, his expression much softer and filled with tenderness. "He wasn't invited."

"But I know you like surprises," he says.

Does she? Shit, I don't even know. But given the look on her face, maybe he doesn't know either.

I don't like the tension between them. Right now it's negative, but I think any kind of tension between two people could turn into something. Hate could turn into passion. Anger into ecstasy.

Especially given their history.

They were married.

Husband and wife.

Now we're all standing around staring at each other. I want to send this asshole away. I want to do more than send him away, actually, but that would have to do. It's up to Raleigh, and she's just standing here, not saying a damn thing.

"Raleigh and I have some really important things to talk about." Jacob turns to Raleigh as he speaks. He's probably too chicken to hold my gaze.

I let out a low growl and Raleigh's eyes widen as she looks between us.

Why does she look so confused?

"Raleigh?" I say, and she finally seems to see me.

"Um." Raleigh clasps her hands together like she doesn't know what to say.

Um? That is not the response I want from her. It feels clear what should happen right now, and it's Jacob getting the fuck out of this campground.

"I just need to think for a second." She squeezes her eyes shut.

What is she thinking? She doesn't want to be with her ex-husband. I know that. He's had boundary issues from the moment they got divorced.

So what's going on here?

But I have a feeling I know.

It's me.

She's not unsure about her feelings about Jacob. She's unsure about her feelings about *me*.

Insecurity roars over my head and I can't catch a breath.

This is why I don't date.

It's too complicated. Too messy. I don't want to be insecure about anything.

Something aches in the pit of my belly. I take a deep breath.

"Well. I'll give you two some time to... catch up." I pause for a second, hoping she insists I stay, hoping her ex-husband leaves instead, but nobody moves. Nobody says a thing.

Fuck.

I spin around and stride quickly back to my car, jumping in and throwing the Wrangler into reverse.

"Atticus!" Raleigh calls, but it's too late and I don't even turn around.

This thing with Raleigh has gotten out of control.
*I'm* out of control.
And it's going to end badly, just like Lachlan and Melissa.

## CHAPTER 21

# You're My Kind of Weird



"I can't accept that you really feel that way." Jacob dips his head into his hands. I finally gave in and led him to the captain's chairs facing the lake. There was no way I was letting him in the RV.

"You need to." I have no idea what I'm doing on so many levels, but I do know that I need to make Jacob accept what I'm telling him.

That it's over. That we need space.

Permanent space.

Maybe we can't even be friends.

But I can't say those things directly quite yet as he can't even comprehend me telling him we're never getting back together.

"I've never stopped loving you, Ral," he says, looking up at me, still hunched over.

My instinct is to reassure him that I love him too, but I resist. I care about him deeply, but that's where it stops.

"I'm not in love with you." My voice is firm but gentle.

We've been at this for an hour and I'm burnt out. He sighs and shuts his eyes.

"And I'm exhausted." I stand. "I need you to leave now. Leave the campsite and Fort Collins."

"No." Jacob looks up, his expression panicky. "Can we meet up once more?"

I shake my head.

"Tomorrow? Please? Then I promise I'll get out of your way. I'll get out of your... life."

I'm not sure I believe him, but I desperately need him to leave me alone right now.

Jacob departs the campsite when I agree to meet up with him tomorrow evening, and I head back inside. To do what? I'm exhausted, but I won't be able to nap. I'm wired, but don't have the focus to cross-stitch.

I collapse on the loveseat and lean my head back.

My heart hurts on so many levels.

Watching Atticus drive away upset was the worst feeling I've had since I found out that Jacob had been secretly losing money.

But I feel like I owe Jacob one last time to talk.

Or maybe I don't *owe* him that, but I want to give him one more chance to accept what's not going to happen between us.

Even though it's upsetting to me. Even though it was clearly upsetting to Atticus.

Jacob was my husband for five years and I've done a shit job establishing boundaries and enabling his recovery post-divorce. I see that now.

This is all my fault.

I don't think—I just get in my car and drive.

It's late by the time I get to Atticus's apartment complex. I text him from outside his building's door.

ME

I'm at your door. Can we talk?

A few seconds later, Atticus buzzes me in and is waiting outside the elevator on his floor. I take in his messy hair sans hat, tight gray t-shirt, loose athletic shorts over thick thighs. Those intense green eyes are locked on me.

"You okay, coach?" he asks. "It's late."

"As if I could be anyone's dating coach." I moan, then I walk right into his arms, pressing my face against his chest. Atticus wraps himself around me and kisses the top of my head. He feels so good. All the emotions of today rush through my body and settle while I'm in Atticus's arms. This feels right in every single way.

Even if it's not.

But tonight, I'm not going to let guilt or what's right or wrong stop me.

I turn my head up and Atticus is waiting. He places a slow, sweet kiss on my lips and my chest fills with warmth.

"Hey." He pulls back and looks at me intently. "I'm sorry about before. I was an asshole."

"So was I."

"Never." Atticus slides a hand along my jaw, onto my neck, and into my hair.

I let myself smile.

"You really used the 'she's my girlfriend' line on my ex-husband, didn't you?" I was pissed at the time but my heart still leaped when he said the words.

"Shit. Yeah. But you didn't seem to think it was funny at the time." Atticus's brow furrows. "I was so fucking jealous."

"Of what?" I run my hands up Atticus's chest and link them around the back of his neck.

"He had you for a long time. He married you."

"And I divorced him."

Atticus grunts and pulls my body against his.

"Let's go inside."

I nod and let him take my hand and lead me into his apartment. Instead of bringing me to his bedroom, he takes us to his couch in the family room.

"I'm going to pour us wine," he says and heads to the kitchen.

"It looks good in here." The mess is cleaned up and almost all traces of the construction gone.

It's only the end of July, but it feels like the summer is wrapping up. Things are being finished off. His offseason is winding down. I'm getting ready to go back to Connecticut.

Things are ending.

"Want to talk about it?" Atticus returns to the couch and sinks down, handing me a wine glass.

I take a sip and consider. Do I want to discuss things with Atticus? I can't possibly explain or justify my relationship with Jacob. Why we stay in touch, why I send him money, and why I feel some kind of guilty loyalty to him. Atticus wouldn't understand.

*I was so fucking jealous,* he said just now.

I'm afraid to ask what he even means by that. It doesn't matter anyway.

I sip my wine and slide the glass onto the coffee table, then lean my head in the nook of Atticus's arm and close my eyes.

"I don't want to." I breathe in and out of my nose, appreciating the scent of Atticus. I run my hand up his thigh, muscles thick and taut under his long athletic shorts. His breathing quickens as my hand gets higher and I turn my face up to him, wanting to taste his kiss.

He doesn't deny me.

I don't know exactly why I came here tonight, but it wasn't to talk. It was to feel something, and being in Atticus's arms is a safe space for me to feel all the things.

We kiss softly until I swipe my tongue along his bottom lip, and when he makes a sound in his throat that resembles a growl, the ache between my legs intensifies. I move the hand on his thigh up to the hard length of him, rubbing up and down slowly over his clothing.

"I love when you put your hands on me, Raleigh," Atticus says between quickening breaths. He lifts his hips to meet my hand, increasing the pressure. I love having this kind of control over him. I love how much he wants me. I love how much I want him.

That's a lot of loves.

I slide off the couch onto my knees and slip between his legs. His eyes darken as he understands.

"I want to take you in my mouth," I say. It's not the first time I've done it with him. It's a huge turn-on to watch him lose control over my touch. My mouth.

And right now, all I want is him. His body. I don't want to feel anything in my heart. I want to feel it in the rest of my body.

"Raleigh," he says as I tug down his shorts and boxer briefs to free his cock. His dick springs up in front of my face and oh my god, it's gorgeous. Terrifying, but gorgeous. All thick and veiny and fucking throbbing. I wrap my hand around the base and run it up to the tip, where a drop of precum is resting. I lean over and lick it, swirling my tongue around his head.

What alien creature has taken over my body? I don't know, but I don't want to be Raleigh Hayes any more. Or Raleigh Ford, or Raleigh Monroe. I just want to be whoever this is. Someone who is passionate. A lover.

Who just so happens to be with the hottest, sweetest man ever.

A man who, it turns out, is a huge softie on the inside.

A man who hugs my chicken. Makes me coffee. Brings me gifts all the time.

Atticus.

This guy.

The man who called me his girlfriend to my ex-husband.

I can't even begin to process that.

I roll my lips onto the tip of his cock and take as much of it in my mouth as I can. It reaches the back of my throat and I almost gag. Atticus moans and buries his hands in my hair, setting the pace of my sucking.

I'm having a really hard time thinking about leaving. Or not leaving. Or anything. And I think he's just as fucked up about this whole thing as I am.

His cock hitting the back of my throat means I can't think about my ex-husband or my job or anything that isn't this. That isn't making Atticus Knox lose control.

I've never known it like this with any other man—neither of my exes had caused desire to pool between my legs while I went down on them.

Atticus gently but firmly slides my mouth off of his cock and then stands, pulling me up with him and tugging his shorts up.

"Let's take our time, Raleigh." His voice is a husky whisper and I can only nod.

I almost ask him not to say my name. Because I don't want to be Raleigh anymore.

At least not tonight.

I don't want to be taken advantage of by my ex-husband.

I don't want to feel bad about talking to him or not talking to him or about liking hanging out with Atticus or about more than liking hanging out with Atticus.

Because this is definitely more than like.

I don't want to go any further down that line of thinking.

Atticus tugs my shirt up and over my head, his heated eyes only leaving mine for a split second when the fabric is over my face. He leans down and kisses my shoulders, my neck, and the soft, sensitive spot at the base of my throat. His hands work to unhook my bra and he deftly slides it off my body, moving to cover my breasts with long, slow tongue swipes and kisses.

I close my eyes and grip his shoulders.

My heart is breaking because I'm afraid this is the beginning of goodbye. This whole summer was a long goodbye. We started something that we can't finish. That we're not capable of finishing because of space and time and who we are as people.

Atticus reaches down and pushes my shorts and underwear down over my hips, his mouth on mine as he strips me naked.

When he's done, he leans over and picks me up in his arms. I can't help but giggle.

"What are you doing?"

"Trying to make you smile." Atticus turns and heads down his hallway, carrying my naked body to his bedroom.

"Well, it worked."

In his room, he deposits me on his bed, where I watch him strip down, starting by removing his t-shirt with one swipe of his hand behind his neck, ending with a quick ditch of his shorts and boxer briefs. Then he's on me, kissing every inch of my skin, his mouth making its way down my abdomen until it's between my legs, sucking on my clit and making me cry out in pleasure. The man is painting me with his tongue, and every nerve on my body responds to his artistry.

When he knows I'm close, Atticus moves his mouth back to mine and kisses me as he teases my entrance with his incredibly hard cock. Finally, he's inside me, thrusting inside with long, slow, maddening moves.

"Atticus," I whisper into his neck when I can hardly take it anymore.

"Yes?" he asks, but I don't respond, focusing on the sensations gripping my body, a building of pleasure that brings us higher and higher. We come together a minute later and then he collapses next to me.

"That was perfect," I murmur. I didn't mean to say it out loud.

"What were you going to say?" he asks, turning his head to me.

"Hmm?"

"Before you came. You said my name."

"I don't remember." I shake my head and nestle into his side. "But we forgot about our wine."

He shrugs and closes his eyes. When he dozes off, I stare up at his sharp jawline, the air moving in and out of his nose, and the way his eyelids move like he's dreaming of something.

What was I going to say? I'm not sure, but I'm glad I didn't get a chance to find out. I don't understand the feelings that are rushing through me. It's too intense. Too much.

I could live here in his bed forever. With Atticus. In his arms.

But the timing is all wrong.

There were no rules for what we've been doing this summer, but any second now, he will also realize how wrong we are for each other. How different our lives are.

I've already figured that out.

I have too much baggage. Too many things I still need to sort out about my past. About myself.

Can Atticus be patient? Would he wait?

No way.

This pro hockey player—and a self-proclaimed player with women—is not going to wait around for some nobody to deal with her issues.

Too many thoughts rush through my head.

Like how I told Jacob *maybe I'm not coming back.* Those were just words meant to freak him out though, right? I might be trying to test out a different version of myself, but let's be honest, people don't really change.

And how I have only two weeks left on my sabbatical.

How I ignored yesterday's voicemail from my manager checking in.

I'm just some entertainment for Atticus during the offseason. He's testing out having a girlfriend-shaped person in his life.

Not a real one.

Maybe I'll leave and he'll ask out Rose from the bookstore.

This thing is destined to end, and it'd be best if I started acting like I understand that fact.

## CHAPTER 22

# *Fucking Disaster*

## ATTICUS

Saturday, July 26

"Can I bring you home?" I'm in my kitchen pouring coffee into a to-go cup for Raleigh. I desperately want to come back to the RV with her, but she's having none of it.

"No." Raleigh shakes her head definitively. "I have a busy day and I can't handle your, uh, distractions." She gives me a small smile. I wish she'd step around the island and wrap her arms around me, but she stays put behind the granite barrier.

Something changed since her ex-husband showed up yesterday. It's like she's put on an extra layer of armor on. She's not the same open, free woman I've been spending time with. Or she is, but guarded. Worse even than after the flower delivery.

I think she's slipping through my fingers.

At least she came to me last night. I was a mess in the hours after I fled the campground like a petulant child. I should've stayed to help Raleigh in whatever way she needed. Instead, I ran.

"You sure you don't want to hang out?" I hand her the coffee, wincing at my neediness.

"I gotta run. I need to feed Megghen and make sure she's not escaped her tent to lay eggs everywhere."

I force a chuckle. "Tonight then?"

It's like I'm begging her to spend time with me. I hate it.

"Can't today." Raleigh shakes her head and rejects me yet again. My stomach drops. "I have to catch up on cross-stitch orders, then clean up my RV, then this evening I have video calls scheduled with my mom, and also Lucy and January...." She ticks off a list of tasks that I feel like could be done in two hours, tops, not stretch the rest of the day.

But she clearly doesn't want me around.

"Alright. Barrett and Lachlan want to get drinks tonight, so I'll go do that. Lach's still a mess."

"I can't believe his girlfriend dumped him." Raleigh looks almost relieved at the change of conversation, her face relaxing a tad.

"I can." There's never been a relationship more predictable to blow up.

"Really?" Raleigh cocks her head. "Why?"

The reasons tick off in my head. Because he's not meant to be in a serious relationship. Because they're simply too different from each other. Because she probably realized he's not the guy you settle down with.

I'm definitely not going to say those things. They sound like all the reasons Raleigh and I shouldn't be together.

"I saw them together. The chemistry just wasn't there." I did see them together earlier this summer, but they had chemistry. *That* wasn't the reason they were destined to break up.

Raleigh's phone buzzes in her pocket, ending the conversation. Her eyes widen for a split second.

"Everything okay?" I ask, fishing for information.

"Yup." She takes a few steps around the counter and leans up for a kiss. I press our lips together, but it only lasts a beat as she pulls back too fast. "Talk to you later."

And then she's gone.

* * *

Lachlan is absolutely trashed.

And Barrett is egging him on.

"I'm coming back with shots and beers," Barrett announces, seemingly unaffected by the alcohol. Damn twenty-five year olds and their superior livers. He weaves his way through the crowds at Black Diamond and steps next to a short blonde woman at the bar, smiling down at her.

I have a feeling he'll be a while.

"So what happened, dude?" I turn back to my destitute friend. "You ready to talk about it yet?"

"Fuck." Lachlan groans and drops his head in his hands. I shoot my hand out and still the wobbling beer bottle that he bumps with his elbow.

"I thought everything was going great?"

"I thought it was too." He looks up with glassy eyes. "But then I showed up for another one of her stupid faculty barbecues. It was going fine—boring as shit and filled with her judgmental colleagues—and I made an awkward joke. No one laughed. Then she walked over just as one of them asked where I went to college. I said I didn't and they all gave each other this look. Like I was the scum of the earth. But I went straight to the NHL, mate?"

"They sound like assholes."

"Yeah." He nods. "She didn't defend me. Went all cold and distant. Afterwards, I drove her home, and before she got out of the car, she said she has to focus on her research. And she doesn't want to be in a serious relationship. With me."

"It sounds like what you usually tell women, but swap in hockey instead." I say it more to myself then to my friend, but he jerks his head up to look at me.

"That's fucked up, mate."

"I know, I'm sorry. But isn't it true?"

He groans. "Yeah."

"And I didn't mean to offend. I was more thinking about me." *Oops*. Hadn't meant to say that out loud.

"You? Raleigh?" He perks up.

"Uh—" Oh, shit. But I forget why I'm even hiding this from one of my closest friends.

"Oh come on, mate." Lachlan lifts his eyebrows. "It's obvious you're fucking her. I might be distracted with Melissa—" his voice hitches. "—but I'm not an idiot."

I run a hand roughly over my face. Might as well talk through this. For his sake, at least. It might help distract him from the breakup.

"Yeah, things have happened with Raleigh."

"Things?" Lachlan cracks a smile for the first time all night. I glance over at Barrett, who looks like he has no intention of moving from the spot next to the blonde woman. He even got himself a drink, but I don't see shots or beers for the rest of us.

"We've spent a lot of time together." That's an understatement. Every day. Almost every night. "We're not official. And she's leaving in a few weeks."

"How much time together?" Lachlan narrows his eyes, studying me.

"I don't want to talk about it." It's one thing telling him that Raleigh and I have been hooking up, it's a different story to talk about how things are getting more out of control.

"Love is worth it, mate, even if you get your heart broken into a million pieces." Lachlan's voice squeaks at the end like a pubescent boy, and his eyes fill with tears.

Fuck.

I do not want to end up like Lachlan. He's a fucking mess. A *pathetic* mess.

"It's not love."

But as I say that, my gut clenches and a lump forms in my throat.

It better not be love.

I'm not equipped for love.

I don't *want* to be equipped for love.

I scoff and cast an annoyed glance at Barrett. I could use a fresh beer right about now. And that shot.

If by some stupid chance this is love, I need to squash it. Suffocate it. Hide it. Beat it down until it goes away, because there is no future for me and Raleigh.

Fuck. Maybe it is love.

* * *

An hour later, the three of us are stumbling down the street, weaving around the Saturday night crowds. Barrett is trailing behind us, one arm slung over the blonde girl's shoulder, the other arm wrapped around her tall brunette friend's waist. At first, I think the tall girl was interested in Lachlan or me, but we've both steered clear.

Lachlan pulls out his phone.

"No way." I grab it out of his hands, his reflexes even slower than mine at the moment. "No texting her."

Lachlan groans and stops in front of Horsetooth Brewing.

"Remember when we were here, and Melissa was out of town?" Lachlan nods to the busy restaurant, tables filled with people, crowds standing around the bar. He's got a dreamy look in his eyes that turns miserable. "Was she even out of town for the reason she said? Or maybe she *was* at her sister's, but planning on how to break it off with me."

"I'm sure it didn't happen that way."

I'm sure of no such thing. I think that woman was just fucking around with Lachlan all summer for entertainment, but she was never going to accept him in her snobby academic life. Maybe he was her trophy, but when it came down to it, she couldn't swallow that he was an athlete without a college degree. Maybe her colleagues shunned her. Maybe a hundred reasons.

My eyes scan the tables to look for the one we all sat at together those weeks ago. That was before anything happened with Raleigh. Before I had a clue how hard I was falling for her.

Fuck! I'm not falling for her.

"Hey, is that Raleigh?" Lachlan says, pointing to the far corner.

"Huh?"

My eyes follow his finger.

Raleigh is sitting at the table. My heart does a little leap, until I see who's sitting across from her.

Her ex-husband.

"Who the fuck is that dude?" Lachlan rolls his neck. "Want me to fight him?"

Right. I chose not to tell Lachlan all the dirty details, so he has no idea that I know exactly who the man is.

I don't answer Lachlan, but I watch Raleigh and her ex. They are leaning close together, talking intently. She's got her fingers wrapped around a glass of wine, and he has a pint glass of amber liquid. I can't tell if they're arguing, but they are far too close together for my comfort.

"Atter? Wanna go fight?"

I shake my head.

Wasn't she supposed to be home? Video calling with her mom and my sister? Wait—she wouldn't be video calling with Lucy and January in the evening anyway, since they are seven hours ahead in England.

I'm such a sucker.

She lied to me. Her plan was to go out with her ex-husband instead of with me, and then cover it up with a lie about talking to my own sister. A lie that I could easily uncover.

Fuck this.

I want to go in and rage at them. I want to see what she has to say to me when I walk up to their table. I want to punch that asshole in the face for having the absolute fucking nerve to show up here in Fort Collins uninvited and try to get Raleigh to take him back.

She doesn't want him. She's told him that.

She's told *me* that.

But what if that's not the whole truth? Would he really show up at her RV across the country six months post-divorce if he didn't think there was a real chance of her taking him back?

As I watch, she shakes her head and he reaches over and touches her forearm. She glances down at the contact with a furrowed brow, but doesn't pull away. I can read his lips: *please, Raleigh*. She sighs and shuts her eyes.

"Look at Barrett." Lachlan elbows me and nods behind us, where Barrett is getting into a hired car with both women. He lifts a hand at us with a smirk before disappearing into the vehicle. "That should be us, dude. Fuck relationships. Fuck women who only want to mess with our tender hearts."

I snort and watch the car pull away with Barrett and the two women.

Back in the restaurant, Raleigh's ex stands and weaves his way to the back of the restaurant.

I could go pop in and talk to her now before he gets back. Find out what's going on. Be a mature adult.

But as I watch, she pulls out her phone and starts typing.

Maybe she's messaging me.

I look at my phone, but nothing pops up. Then I do something I know I shouldn't.

ME

hey, how are you?

Raleigh stares down at her device. She taps some more, then flips it over and looks in the direction Jacob disappeared.

Well, shit. I'm getting ignored. Plus, she's messaging someone else. Lucy? For her to read when she wakes up in the morning? Not me, that's for sure.

"Let's go," I growl.

"Where to? Wanna go try to find girls?" Lachlan's slurring his words. He's got bags beneath his eyes, and his blond curls are wild. Maybe now that Melissa's gone he'll grow his hair long again.

But there's no way this dude wants to go find girls. And I sure as hell don't either.

"No. You're going home. And so am I. Then we're going to wake up and go to the gym and sweat all this out. It's time to start getting ready for hockey season."

I give Lachlan's considerable forearm a push.

"Hey. Fine." He sighs.

I cast one final glance at the table. Her ex is approaching and Raleigh offers him a tight smile as he sits.

They look like a married couple working their shit out. And that's pretty close to what they are. So they're divorced—that doesn't have to be permanent. They have history.

Fuck this.

I'm done.

Done with pretending to be someone who I'm not.

Done with going down a path that will only lead to heartache.

I'm gonna go tuck the Aussie into his bed and then head home and do a hundred pushups. Remind myself of who I am.

And it's no one's boyfriend.

## CHAPTER 23

# Pucked Around and Found Out

## RALEIGH

Sunday, July 27

I should not be coming up with new cross-stitch ideas, but here we are.

After the Atticus video, which is at six hundred thousand views and still slowly climbing, I got messages from customers asking for hockey-themed designs.

What I also got was a ton of comments detailing what women would do to Atticus if *they* were sitting next to him on the couch. Also—and this is when I stopped looking—many comments questioning whether I was hot enough to be dating him.

The answer was unanimously no.

Some even wondered if I was his sister. Then the conversation in the comments switched to his actual sister, my best friend, who is dating the Blizzard team captain.

I lay my notebook down next to my open laptop and reach for my lukewarm coffee. *Pucked around and found out* is accurate for my current situation.

My eyes spot something brown tucked into the cushion of the table's seating bench next to me.

"Megghen!" I reach for the gift from my chicken. It almost blended right in—I'm lucky I didn't sit on it and get raw egg on my ass. I really need to stop letting her wander around the RV. I groan and shut my eyes, egg still in my palm.

It felt wrong to be out with Jacob last night.

His words keep spinning around my brain.

*I am still in love with you.*

*I can wait as long as you need me to.*

*I'm building a life for us back home.*

*We can start over.*

But the more time I spent with him, the more confident I became. Especially when Atticus texted me. My brain lit up in a way that it doesn't with Jacob.

At the end of the night, I was profoundly clear with him: No more money. No more showing up. No more texts, phone calls, emails.

It's over.

I'm emotionally rung out this morning.

My phone rings again with an incoming video call from Lucy. She's heading back here from England soon—in my chaos I can't remember the exact date. But I'm not ready to face her yet, so I press ignore on the call.

Because while I finally understand my feelings about Jacob and how I haven't been clear enough with him about my boundaries, all of this affects my relationship with Atticus.

I'm in no place to be getting so emotionally involved with Lucy's brother.

I've been so concerned with *myself*. So obsessed with living some kind of imaginary exciting life where I travel across the country in an RV and do things like kiss hot hockey players who I've had a secret crush on since college.

But I'm going to hurt him. I'm going to *get* hurt by him. Atticus is confused too. This isn't him. Pretending to be in a relationship? Being the doting boyfriend to a pharmacist from Connecticut?

Nah, that's not who he is.

My phone vibrates with another incoming call, like it's emphasizing that thought.

"Mom." If I didn't answer, she'd keep calling. So will Lucy and January, actually.

"How'd last night go with Jacob?" Mom is quick and to the point. I know she wants me to end this lingering relationship with Jacob once and for all, even though she feels bad for him as well.

"It was painful." I don't want to rehash the whole night, and I don't think she'll push me on it. "I told him it's over. For real."

"Good for you. I'm sorry he figured out where you were from me, but maybe it's for the best that you got to talk to him in person before you return to Connecticut."

"Sure, but I didn't need the jump scare at my door." I stand and deposit the egg in my small refrigerator.

Mom ignores the comment and clears her throat. "Well, I sent a new spreadsheet just now. It's been years since we started a fresh one."

"Mom, really? I'm thirty-four years old."

"I know. But I put a few different scenarios in there that will at least get you thinking about your future."

I sigh and pace the RV. I'm sure she put a path that would have me running the entire region's pharmacy departments. But at this point, I don't even want to think about the day I have to go back to work.

Two weeks from tomorrow.

"Did I tell you I've been hanging out with Atticus? Lucy's brother."

There's silence on the other end of the phone.

"Mom?"

"Don't do this, Raleigh. Don't get involved with someone so fast. Again."

My insides twist.

"I'm not."

"Then put that boy out of your mind."

I scoff, thinking of Atticus Knox being referred to as a boy.

"You loved Atticus." I don't know what else I expected her to say. Of course she's not supportive of me doing whatever it is I'm doing with Atticus.

"Yes, back when you were in college," she admits. "He was sweet."

He still is. I bet she'd love him now, too. What's not to love? He's handsome and charming and kind and funny and—

"Raleigh Hayes. Pack up your stuff and get your butt back to Connecticut to restart your life. Forget Atticus Knox. Forget your ex-husband. Start over *here*."

"I'm not leaving yet. The whole point in me coming to Colorado was to see Lucy, and I haven't done that yet."

"When does she get home?"

"Soon? Tomorrow? The next day, maybe?"

"I can't believe you don't know."

I'm my mother's worst nightmare right now. Disorganized, unmotivated, drifting through my days without a plan.

I sit and click through the updated spreadsheet she sent. Already open are a few other spreadsheets: one for my RV and the one I started for Megghen but didn't let myself continue.

"Here's my plan." I go over the timing in my head real quick. "I'll stay here another week, tops, so I can see Lucy for a few days. Then I'll drive the Pink Palace back to Connecticut."

"Cutting it a little close, aren't you?"

"Mom! Take what you can get from me, okay?"

"Fine, child."

I chuckle and we hang up a minute later. I stare at those open spreadsheets and a visceral reaction builds inside me. Why does my life have to be so perfect? So carefully planned? Why not accept a little mess? Isn't that what I've been doing this summer? I pushed myself out of my comfort zone in so many ways.

With a few clicks, I delete the spreadsheets.

Half-started chicken spreadsheet: gone.

RV spreadsheet: gone.

Updated life spreadsheet from Mom: gone.

I lean away from the table and laugh. Living a life without spreadsheets? The idea is freeing. And a little scary.

Maybe I shouldn't have deleted all the RV maintenance records, but that's a problem for another day. Also, it's in the trash for thirty days before it's permanently gone.

There's a knock and I jolt. It better not be my ex-husband.

I walk to the door of the Pink Palace like it's my funeral procession, reaching slowly for the handle, eyeing Fred, still leaning against the wall.

But it's not Jacob.

"Hello." The man in front of me is young, probably late twenties, and has long, curly brown hair and dark eyes.

The guy Atticus hired to repaint the Pink Palace. A week ago, he started showing up to work a few hours a day. I have no idea what's going on under the tarp he has covering my RV from the door all the way across, with a hole cute out for the window. It's definitely more than a simple re-paint of the peeling side of the vehicle.

"Hi. Still painting?"

"Yup. Almost done."

"Need anything?" I'm very curious to what Atticus meant by *permission to be a little creative.* It seems unnecessary to be creative when my summer with the RV is almost over, but it's hard to say no to that man.

But now I think I need to.

"No, thank you." The artist turns and heads back to the popped trunk of his car.

I gotta go talk to Atticus. It's a conversation I'm absolutely dreading. And ten minutes later, I'm in my SUV heading into town.

I park a few blocks from his apartment and wander around, past Rocky Gifts, the gift shop where I stopped when I first arrived in Fort Collins and asked if they had any cross-stitch in their local artist shelf, past the bookstore where Rose works and then Deep Roots, the coffee shop. I avoid the brewery where I met up with Jacob last night. Avoid Black Diamond, the bar I've been frequenting with the hockey boys.

Too soon, I'm in front of his apartment building with a dreadful truth swirling in my head.

I need to break up with him.

There's one thing Jacob said last night that broke me: *please don't go off and marry someone else as a rebound.*

I was angry, but then the words sunk in. And the fact that I'd used that exact word—rebound—with Atticus as a joke.

It feels a lot less funny now.

My phone buzzes—it's Lucy again.

I ignore her. Again.

ME

Can you come down here?

ATTICUS

hey. I'll buzz you up

ME

No, please come down

I can't go upstairs with Atticus. I can't be in that apartment with him again. My clothes will fly off and I might accidentally tell him I'm in love with him.

Because—dammit—I'm in love with him.

I know that now.

I knew it the moment Jacob said those dark words.

Because I know if I did tell Atticus I loved him, if we did actually get together, it wouldn't be a rebound. But no one else would know that. Everyone would think I'm doing what I always do.

Part of me hopes he insists I come upstairs. Maybe if he just buzzes me in, I'll head on up. Maybe if he doesn't listen to me, then it'll all work out.

But a few seconds later, the door opens and Atticus Knox is standing in front of me.

"Raleigh," he says, and it feels like goodbye already. I can see it on his face. Was he already going to break up with me? Maybe I should just wait him out and make him do it. Make him break my heart instead of forcing me to do it to myself.

"I can't do this anymore. Us." The words are hardly audible. I cross my arms on my chest, balling up my fists and tucking them under. I can't trust myself not to reach for him. My face heats and pin pricks tingle down my spine.

I'm doing the unthinkable.

"What do you mean, us?" Some of the color drains from his face.

For a second I wonder if me thinking there is an *us* was too presumptuous, but then his face gets even whiter.

No, he wasn't going to break up with me.

This horrific job belongs to me.

"Whatever has been happening between us this summer, it needs to be over now. I need to go back to Connecticut. Soon. And I need to make a clean break." I swallow and it's all I can do to not choke.

"Raleigh." He clenches his fists and shoves his hands in his pockets, like he's trying to hold himself back.

"I thought I was over my divorce. I thought I was past my ex-husband. Ex-husbands. I'm over *them*, but I'm not over what happened. And I don't think I can fully get over it while I'm with you."

I pause, but Atticus doesn't respond. Should I turn and walk away? But I can't bring myself to do that. Perhaps I should explain—

"I saw you last night."

His words are a hockey stick to my gut, even though I've never felt that particular pain. It's what I imagine it'd feel like. Awful.

"Last night?" I whisper.

He nods.

Last night when I was out with Jacob. During the time I told Atticus I was going to be home doing cross-stitch and talking to my mom and my friends.

That was the stupidest lie I've ever told.

"I sent him away," I say in a shaky voice. "He's gone now."

A laughing couple walks past us on the sidewalk, and I glance their way, hands linked together, striding away with their aura of happiness. The fact that we're in public is forcing me to try to hold it together.

Atticus doesn't respond.

"I've been sending him money every single month since our divorce was final." I look back at Atticus. His eyes are filled with sadness, the color a washed-out sage instead of the deep forest green I'm used to.

"For what?" His face pinches.

"To help him. Because I felt guilty for taking everything in the divorce." I rub the back of my neck. "We email and text all the time. I've been enabling him for the past six months."

Atticus presses his lips together and crosses his arms. He takes half a step back toward his building. I don't think he even realizes he did it.

Stepped away from me.

Yes, this is what I need to do. Show him what a fucking mess I am so he doesn't even want me anymore. Ruin it.

"Do you still love him?" Atticus asks through clenched teeth, his voice low and dangerous.

"No, I don't. But I'm done enabling. He's gotta figure out shit all on his own from now on."

I'm talking so much about Jacob. I don't want to be talking about my ex with Atticus. I hate it.

But I think this is what I need to do.

Show Atticus exactly who I am.

I can see in his face he's confused. He's not sure if he should be trying to convince me to stay or letting me go.

Well, the answer is to let me go.

"I have to leave." I step away from him and into the path of a man on his cell phone. The man dodges me and doesn't give me a second glance.

"Raleigh," Atticus says again, a bookend to when he first appeared in his doorway.

I memorize his face. His sharp jawline and the red curls falling over his forehead, popped out from the hole in his backwards baseball cap. Big eyes with dark lashes staring at me.

Maybe he's doing the same thing. Memorizing me.

We're done with each other. Neither of us are going to fight it.

"Goodbye, Atticus."

I spin around and stride away.

He doesn't try to stop me. Doesn't even say my name again.

Twenty minutes later, I pull up to the Pink Palace, my face sore and wet from crying, and it takes me a second to soak in what I'm seeing.

The tarp on the RV is gone, revealing what the artist has been working on for the past week. I laugh out loud through my tears and sit behind the wheel for a beat before slowly getting out of my car.

It's not a paint job. It's a mural.

A beautiful mountain with a still lake, a pink and orange and yellow sunset reflected in the water. And on the banks of the lake is a single white chicken that looks just like Megghen.

I slam the car door behind me and step toward the Pink Palace, which looks decidedly less old and crappy.

Atticus did this.

I bite my lip as fresh tears spring to my eyes.

"Raleigh!"

I spin in the direction of the voice, which came from the front of Elizabeth's RV.

Then I see the tall, red-haired woman standing next to my neighbor.

Lucy.

CHAPTER 24

# The Unthinkable

ATTICUS

"You are all fucking pathetic." Barrett shakes his head at us and makes a disgusted grunt. He leans back in his chair, hands linked over his abdomen.

"Who is this kid?" Harley—who just arrived back in town from Maine with bad relationship news of his own—glares at Barrett Steele like he's a random dude we picked up on the street corner. Harley knows very well who Barrett is. But I can always count on Harley to be a dick to someone like Barrett. He was the same to me when I met him years ago.

Besides, Barrett tends to bring the worst out in people when he first meets them. I chuckle.

"Barrett Steele. How do you not know who I am?" A puzzled look falls on the kid's face, like he truly doesn't understand how someone wouldn't know who he is.

Arrogant prick.

But, he's kind of grown on me. Like a foot fungus.

"Yeah, I know who you are." Harley scoffs. "I'm just not sure why you're here. In Fort Collins. In this bar. At this table with us. Right this very moment."

This is harsh, even for Harley. He's not himself at all. I feel the need to jump in.

"Come on, Harley. You know he's our new second line right wing." I glance at Barrett, who looks at me with raised brows and a bright smile. Whatever. He needed my help. I'll punch him in the arm later to set things right.

"He's one of us now." Lachlan reaches for the pitcher of beer and fills his to the very tippy top, then splits the last few drops between the rest of us.

"And I'm not sure of the second line bullshit," Barrett says, but everyone at the table gives him a hard glare. "Woah, fine, okay. Second line." He holds his hands up in mock defeat.

"What the fuck ever." Harley shakes his head and looks away from Barrett.

"I don't understand." I stare at Harley. "What the hell happened with Emily?"

Harley showed up a few hours ago, back early from his summer in Maine. He goes back home every offseason to spend time with his long-term girlfriend.

*Ex*-girlfriend.

"I told you not to bring it up." Lachlan lets out a frustrated sigh.

"I don't want to talk about it." Harley's words are clipped and and angry. "I don't ever want to talk about what happened with her."

"I'm sorry, mate." Lachlan lets out a deep breath. I swallow and nod. Barrett rolls his eyes.

"Sure, dude. Whatever you say." I hold my hands up. We'll find out eventually.

The whole world has gone absolutely insane if Harley is single. He's thirty-five years old and is one or two seasons max away from retirement. He's always talked about going home to marry his girl-friend and have a bunch of babies after hockey. There's never been any drama or questions about his relationship. Actually, we don't know much about it because he doesn't share many details. And Emily never came to Fort Collins. Not once in the entire time he's been here, as far as I know.

Which, now that I think about it, is quite the red flag.

"Great." Barrett scoffs. "Let's not talk about this again. I'm on board with that. Ever since I arrived, one of you has been crying over a woman." He shakes his head. I think Harley might actually go ahead and murder him now. Might as well get it over with, I suppose. "But the good news is that now everyone here is single. Think of the women you get to fu—"

"Shut up, Barrett," Lachlan growls with a sideways glance at Harley, who might have real steam pouring out of his ears. "Besides, Atticus isn't single." He waves a hand at me.

Everyone's head swivels to me.

"You're not single? Who the hell are you dating?" Harley's eyes widen.

Well, fuck me. I didn't want anyone to know I *wasn't* single, and now I really don't want anyone to know I *am*.

"I am single," I say firmly, a stabbing in my chest saying the words out loud.

Lachlan's brow creases. "What about Raleigh?"

"Raleigh? Lucy's friend?" Harley's eyebrows lift and he looks remarkably less destitute than he did just a minute ago. Turns out other people's problems are a good distraction from our own.

"Yeah. She's been in town."

"Doing what?" Harley asks.

Harley, Lachlan, and Barrett all stare at me.

"Go on, Atter." Lachlan waves his hand in the air to get me to continue. "Story time."

Fuuuck. Much like Harley, I really don't want to talk about this.

"We've kind of had a thing." I grumble and chug my beer, hoping they'll all magically disappear. "But it's over now."

"What? When did that happen?" Lachlan's face drops. He

looks as devastated as I feel. Shit. I guess he was more invested in me and Raleigh than I thought.

"Today. She's got drama with her ex-husband that she needs to work out in her head." I attempt to sound casual, but I'm immediately filled with the urge to go punch that guy. "And she's heading to the East Coast soon to start back at her job."

Fuck, I want her to stay here. But I can't think of a logical argument for her to do so. For my immature ass? I'll never fit in her spreadsheet.

"Man, I'm sorry." Harley shakes his head and looks genuinely sorrowful. "I know you've had a thing for her."

"Why would you say that?" I blink at him.

"I mean, the flirting, the video calls, New Year's Eve? We're not stupid." Harley shrugs. "You've not been your normal self since then."

"Agreed." Lachlan nods.

"Fuck yeah!" Barrett jumps in, completely bereft of all emotional intelligence. "We really are all single then. Let's get drunk and—"

"Fuck off, Barrett," I interrupt, not sounding as harsh as I mean to.

"You guys are depressing as shit," he sighs.

"Who's depressing as shit?" A familiar voice rings out from behind me.

Kellen appears behind my chair.

"Hey, you're back," I say. Kellen slaps me on the shoulder before reaching behind him to grab an empty chair from the next table, pulling it over and sitting in one swift move. Relief cascades through me. It's like the team dad just returned. Maybe he can get his brokenhearted children under control.

Kellen looks around the table and grins at Barrett.

"Welcome to Fort Collins, Steele. How're you settling in?"

"Good, but these assholes are all crying in their chocolate milk about women. Miserable about being single, when they should be basking in it." Barrett stands. "I'm getting another pitcher of beer, and before any of you whine about it being two o'clock in the afternoon, I don't give a fuck."

"That guy's a character." Kellen snorts as Barrett walks away. "Hey, sorry about Emily," Kellen says to Harley.

Harley nods and stares sightlessly into his pint glass, apparently not willing to snap back at our team captain like he snapped at the new guy.

"Uh, just so you know, we're not talking about that." Lachlan leans over to Kellen and fake-whispers. Harley glares at him. "And we're definitely not saying her name."

"Ah, okay. And sorry about Melissa," Kellen says, this time to Lachlan.

"Thank you." Lachlan pales.

"But you and Raleigh, huh?" Kellen turns to me with a wicked grin.

"Over." I shake my head.

"Oh, shit." Kellen sits up a little straighter. "What the hell happened?"

"She's going back home." I shrug. It's the simplest answer. And I don't have the strength to bring up her ex-husband again.

"Lucy's with Raleigh right now." Kellen runs a hand through his dark hair and watches me thoughtfully.

I don't know how to feel about my sister talking to Raleigh about this. Not that there's any way to stop it. But they're gonna talk about *everything*, and it's been such a private summer without friends and teammates around to witness and judge and jump in on my relationship with Raleigh.

I'm not sure I can go back to normal. I don't even know what normal is anymore. Bringing girls back to the hotel room when we travel? Sounds heartless and empty. Not after I know what it's like to sleep with someone I have real feelings for. Someone I lo—

Woah.

Wait.

No.

Black spots edge around the corner of my vision and heat washes over me.

Abso-fucking-lutely not.

I did not just think that.

Really, I didn't. I definitely cut off that dirty word halfway through.

"Fresh pitcher," Barrett announces and stays standing to refill glasses.

"Thanks," I manage. Kellen chuckles and I glance around the table at despondent faces. We really are pathetic.

"A toast." Barrett lifts his glass. "Love sucks. Avoid it at all costs." He chugs half his pint.

"I'll drink to that," Lachlan says and follows suit.

Love sucks.

Love?

Oh, for fuck's sake.

I didn't go and fall in love with Raleigh Hayes this summer, did I?

But even as I think it, my chest fills with warmth around those three little words, so much so that my heart might burst out of my body.

I fell in love with Raleigh.

I love her.

And I have a feeling it happened before this summer.

Have I loved her since New Year's Eve, when I finally got to fulfill my college dream of kissing her?

Or did it happen long before that?

Have I loved her since college?

And this summer was my chance to get her to fall in love with me.

My second chance. Or third, if you count freshman year of college as the first.

And I didn't understand the assignment.

I think I fucked it up.

"Atticus, drink!" Barrett demands. "Or it's bad luck."

I gulp my beer toss and let my revelation settle.

I love Raleigh.

But she still broke up with me.

She's still leaving.

"You okay, dude?" Kellen says quietly from next to me.

"I really fucked up." My voice is low, only for my best friend.

"What do you mean?"

"I let her walk away." I close my eyes and crinkle my face.

It's so obvious now. She was pushing me away. I don't give a fuck that she was sending her ex-husband money. She cared enough to help him because she's a good person. When I asked her if she loved him, she told me no without hesitation. But she doesn't trust herself to let herself go with me.

But I trust her.

I let her go because I'm scared of myself. Scared of who my father is and how I would treat someone like Raleigh.

If I could go back to when she said goodbye to me at the door to my building, I'd do it all over again. I'd refuse her goodbye and drag her inside—respectfully, of course—and make her understand that she can trust herself. That maybe she can help me trust myself.

But it's too late for any of that.

"Want to get out of here and talk about it?"

I shake my head. What's the point? I'm not going to have some stupid happily ever after like Kellen and my sister.

My phone pings in my pocket and I fish it out, too eager.

It's Raleigh, and my heart leaps.

RALEIGH

Thank you for the mural

I wait for more, but that's it.

What am I supposed to say to that?

You're welcome, I did it because I'm madly in love with you?

I love you, please don't leave me?

Just... I love you?

I glance up and Harley is studying my face astutely. He's the polar opposite of Barrett, with emotional intelligence too high for his own good.

And look where that got him.

Dumped, like the rest of us.

I love Raleigh Hayes.

Now that those words are in my head they feel so damn right. Painfully fucking right. But even if I had told her how I feel, even if I had realized it in time, I would've just come off as pathetic. She would still be leaving. Dealing with her ex-husband.

I'm the rebound after her second divorce. The third dude she's ever slept with. Now she can check off a summer fling with a pro hockey player.

Then she can go look for her next husband. Or one of her ex-husbands.

I'm an asshole. I know it.

And that's the point.

It's who I am. Maybe Raleigh hurt me more than I hurt her this time, but it was inevitable I'd do it eventually.

No one would talk marriage to me.

Not ever.

I'm my father's son.

A player. A hook up guy.

And this season, Lachlan and I will go back to being our old selves. Barrett will happily join us. Maybe we'll even rope Harley in, now that he's inexplicably single.

I'll forget about Raleigh Hayes.

And that will be that.

## CHAPTER 25

# Say It Again



"You're back! Why didn't you tell me??" I run the last few steps to Lucy and throw my arms around her body, squeezing tight.

"I mean, I tried calling, but you didn't answer," she says with a strangled voice.

"Oops. Sorry, I'll let you breathe." I step back and look at her. Lucy's red curls are mostly held back with a big scrunchie. Her green eyes—so much like Atticus's—sparkle in the bright afternoon sun. Man, I really missed her. "I've been a bit scatterbrained."

"And then I figured I'd just surprise you. We've changed our return flight a few times, so I figured you didn't remember my latest date and time." She scrunches her mouth to one side. "Or maybe I didn't tell you. Either way, six weeks was enough time away from Fort Collins. And Kellen missed his daughter, even though she spent time with us in London."

"Well, I missed you too." Even though we don't live in the same place, being on different continents was too much.

Lucy glances over at the mural. "Wow. That's gorgeous."

I nod, a lump still in my throat.

"Your neighbor was telling me how there's been some artist here all week working on this."

"Yeah. Atticus arranged it." I sigh and pull at my hair. "A surprise."

The best surprise.

Lucy intakes a breath sharply and turns to me. "Oh no, Raleigh."

"Oh no what?" I turn to her, my brow furrowed.

"The way you just said his name." Lucy crosses her arms and chuckles.

"What way? I said his name."

"Say it again, sis."

"Fine." What did I do the first time? "Atticus."

"See? You did it again." Lucy shakes her head, a smirk on her freckled face.

Shit. Yeah. Even I heard that. His name came out of my mouth more like a sigh than a three syllable word. Like something treasured and reverent.

Someone loved.

"Damn," I whisper.

"Did you seriously come here and fall in love with my brother?"

"What?" How did she already figure that out? What the hell? Am I that transparent?

No. But she's my best friend. It's probably written all over my face, and she knows me like no one else.

"You heard me."

"No, of course not..." my sentence trails off and I gaze back to the mural on the Pink Palace. Why bother lying to her? I'm desperate to talk about this with someone, and why not let it be my best friend and Atticus's sister?

She waits while my eyes trace over the colorful strokes on the side of the RV.

I only now realize that my name is woven into the painting in the most subtle way, *R* a part of the chicken—which looks adorably like Megghen with her spikey white feathers—and *aleigh* integrated into the tall trees and swooping mountain. It's like a Where's Waldo of the letters of my name.

"Raleigh Durham. You're crying." Lucy steps forward and drapes her arm over my shoulders. Whenever she uses my old nickname, it makes me revert back to our college years. "Are you ready to talk about it?"

I don't know what there is to talk about. What can Lucy say that I haven't already worked through in my head?

"Yeah."

"Let's grab coffee in town. The jet lag is killing me and I missed Deep Roots."

I wipe the tears from my cheeks and nod.

* * *

A half hour later, we are settled at a table at Deep Roots back in downtown Fort Collins.

I explain the last few weeks to Lucy and she listens carefully while sipping her vanilla oat milk latte. I leave out any mention of sex after the first face that Lucy made. She requested I give no further details on that aspect of me and Atticus.

"That's a lot, Raleigh."

"Yeah." It feels so good to be face-to-face with one of my best friends instead of seeing her on a video call.

"I can't believe Jacob came here. Think he really understands it's over?"

I nod. I do. The emails and text messages and phone calls have all stopped. He went back to the East Coast. It's only been a few days, but I believe it's truly over.

"And you really think it's done between you and my brother?"

"Yes." I shrug, but my shoulders are tight and it's more like a flinch. "What kind of future could we have? We're not like you and Kellen were, you know. It's not some big romantic love story."

"Hmm." Lucy makes an unconvinced face. "I mean, it's not *not* a big romantic love story."

"No." I shake my head, thinking of the way the two of them fell in love last fall. It was truly special. "You don't understand."

"Try me."

"Most of it's probably in my head anyway. Do I really love him? Or am I just jumping on the first guy who pays attention to me post-divorce? That's my pattern, you know."

Lucy take a deep breath and nods.

"You have to take that into consideration, sure."

"And I have a life to get back to." Don't I? Yes, I do. This sabbatical has been... something, but now it's time to get back to my reality. "I need to drag my ass back to the East Coast."

I think of the Pink Palace and the gorgeous mural on its side. What am I going to do with that big pile of scrap metal? Sell it? Live in it? Drive it off a cliff?

How do I not have a plan for that?

"There are other options, you know." Lucy's voice is soft and she watches me as she sips from her ceramic mug.

"Like what?" I narrow my eyes at my friend. I shouldn't even entertain this conversation. Lucy doesn't understand.

"A few questions first."

"Ohh-kay."

"One. Are you going to keep the house you and Jacob bought together as a married couple, filled with memories and ghosts of your failed relationship, or will you live somewhere else so you can move on with your life?" Lucy cocks her head.

"I feel like that's a leading question." I sigh. "Alright. I guess my plan is to sell it and live in an apartment or something."

But that sounds awful. I don't want to live in a sad one-bedroom apartment in Connecticut.

"Cool cool, so no great housing roots there." Lucy taps her lips with her pointer finger. "Second—your pharmacy job is waiting for you, yes?"

"Yup. Talked to my manager yesterday." After avoiding even listening to Stacey's voicemail, I forced myself to call her back. She was checking in on how my sabbatical has been and confirming my return date.

"Great." Lucy takes a deep breath through her nose.

What's her game here?

"I just need to show up two weeks from tomorrow." My voice hitches on the last word.

Lucy blinks at me. I clear my throat.

"Don't you work at a chain pharmacy?" Lucy tilts her head.

"You know I do."

"Don't they also have branches here in Fort Collins?" Lucy nods. "Like a bunch?"

Yup. There are at least three locations around Fort Collins.

And now I understand exactly what Lucy's getting at.

"Are you seriously suggesting I stay here?" She's gotta be out of her mind. I scrunch my face and squeeze my eyes shut. I won't even let myself picture that. It's not a reasonable option for me.

Definitely not on the spreadsheet.

But didn't I delete the spreadsheets?

"I mean, yeah, Raleigh, I kind of am."

"That's not what I came here for. That's not who I am." I open my eyes and focus on my coffee. "I left Connecticut thinking I could be someone else. Someone more interesting, exciting, whatever. But that's just not me." Talking to Jacob the other day made me realize it. I've been playing a part out here, trying out different versions of myself, and it just hasn't worked. Chicken Mama. Kayak Warrior. RV Adventurer. Cross-Stitch Lady.

Puck Bunny?

"I'm gonna return to Connecticut and go back to work. And I won't have time to do cross-stitch or take care of chickens."

Again with the voice hitching.

"Okay," Lucy says, nodding her head. "I can see that."

But I don't know if she *does* see that. Why should she? Her life has proven otherwise. She gave up so much live in Fort Collins. Sure, she stayed for an amazing job and a hunky, sweet dude, but that's not me.

She's clearly got some serious opinions about where my life is headed. Where it should be headed.

And I don't want to hear it.

Still, the idea of packing my shit up and driving away from Fort Collins in my pink RV turns my stomach.

I groan and drop my head into my hands.

"Raleigh? You okay?"

"I'm fine," I say, but it's muffled. I lift my head up and plaster on a smile. "Can we talk about your trip now, instead? How's January doing? I can't believe you hung out without me for weeks!"

"Yeah. I can't either." Lucy leans back in her chair and crosses her arms.

"What's that supposed to mean?" I truly don't understand.

"I'm just surprised you didn't hop on a plane and come see us. There was literally nothing stopping you."

I scoff. "I mean, well…" I search for a reason why that never occurred to me. Why didn't I get on a plane to go see my friends in England instead of sticking around here? Getting into something I can't seem to extract myself from?

Why didn't that even cross my mind?

Lucy studies me, waiting.

"I had to take care of Megghen."

"Your chicken."

"Yes."

"That is technically not even your chicken."

"I mean, I guess that's correct."

"Aren't you going to have to give her to a farm or something before you leave anyway?"

I let out a little squeak.

There's been a few more responses to my posting, including offers to take Megghen if I don't find her owner. But I'm afraid I'll hand her over and they'll immediately chop her head off and make her into dinner. How can I trust anyone else with that chicken, the one who trusts me with her very life?

Maybe I could drive her back to Connecticut. And then what? I guess I could keep the house, but the HOA might not approve of a chicken in the backyard. And an apartment certainly wouldn't. She can't live in my tub or free range in an apartment, leaving warm eggs hidden everywhere.

I groan and squeeze my eyes shut.

My decision making has been absolute shit. But there's no going back. No fixing what I've done. Only making better decisions going forward.

Like finding a no-kill farm or a family with a backyard coop for Megghen.

Packing up the Pink Palace.

Going back to my job and my hometown.

That's the plan.

"I'm leaving next weekend," I say firmly. "I'd go sooner, but you just got here and I want to hang out."

Lucy leans over and pats my hand, but doesn't say anything else on the subject.

Then she starts telling me about her trip. I mostly listen, but a slideshow of the past month flies through my mind on repeat.

Atticus stars in every image.

I've done so much damage here.

I need to get back to the East Coast and let myself heal.

## CHAPTER 26

# Back to Normal

## ATTICUS

Wednesday, July 30

"Get your asses moving, gentlemen! Summer is over. Almost." Coach Jackson projects so impressively from on the bench, it's like he's got a bullhorn. "Time to get yourself in gear for hockey. And it's obvious some of you have been eating too much, drinking too much, and sitting on your asses."

I growl. It's still freaking July. But I don't say it out loud in case it brings Coach's wrath down on me. As if he hasn't been lying around and drinking and eating too much? Just because his career doesn't hinge on how fit he is doesn't mean he can throw it in our faces.

Well, I guess it does, actually.

Real practices don't start until pre-season in September, but most of the team steps up their workouts and skates throughout August in preparation. This practice is mostly informal. Not all the players are back or even participating in the upcoming charity event.

We're on the ice doing two-on-one drills with rotating partners. I attack with Kellen and we attempt to get past Lachlan to shoot on goal. Augustus, our goaltender, stands guard at the net. He looks relaxed and tan after a summer at the beach with some of the other guys. I bet they went for leisurely jogs on the beach every morning and played golf in the afternoon.

That's what I should've done this summer. Gone to the ocean and got a tan and worked on my surfing skills.

Not let myself fall for Raleigh.

I shake my head to get the repeating *I love her* out of my head, and instead focus on my next pass to Kellen. After I get him the puck, I skate ahead, but Lachlan knows this play, so when Kellen goes to pass back to me, Lach's right there and hits the puck past us to clear it from the net.

There are no smiles from Lachlan today. He's focused and stony-faced, channelling his heartbreak into hockey. That's the healthy way to handle it. Take it out on the puck.

I, on the other hand, am far too distracted. I can't focus. I can't think straight.

My father texted me again yesterday. I'm not a fan of him keeping in touch since Lucy's not been responding. And this time, when I responded, there was no sarcasm or snark. I told him I needed a break from him.

Because I don't want a reminder of who I am by nature. I don't want to see him or talk to him or watch how he treats women. Even if I can't have Raleigh, he's not who I am going to let myself be.

And that feels like quite the revelation.

It feels good to understand myself a bit more, but it doesn't help my current heartache.

I kind of want to kick Lachlan's ass for even suggesting Raleigh be my dating coach that first day we all hung out at Black Diamond. He was enthralled with his girlfriend and determined to play matchmaker. Maybe if that hadn't happened, Raleigh would've moved on, just using Fort Collins as a brief stopping point since Lucy was out of town for another month. Maybe I wouldn't have kissed her that night while we were watching the zombie movies.

There's a twist in my chest. My heart? My belly? Maybe I just need to throw up. Or maybe it's heartburn.

We skate around to the back of the line and rotate partners so I'm with Harley. His face is a blank slate, and he nods at me while we wait our turn to shoot at Augustus.

"You okay, man?" I ask Harley. He definitely does not look okay. He's not been acting okay.

He nods. "Fine. Feels good to be back on the ice." It sounds like he's talking through gritted teeth.

I think his breakup might have cleared his entire body of any emotions. Permanently. He's never been the outgoing extrovert, but he at least chatted with us, laughed at jokes, engaged with the guys. Now he's a robot going through the motions.

"I know what you mean." It does feel good to be back on the ice and around the team. Hockey season means something huge and all-encompassing to focus on. It's not just our job, it's who we are.

This time, I get the puck back to Harley and he manages to sail it past Jasper. It almost goes in, but Augustus makes an impressive save with his glove.

After another ten minutes of this drill, Coach sets us up for a passing drill where we're all positioned around the ice with the goal of keeping the puck moving in a continuous motion, mimicking the intense pace of passing during a game.

There's not much time to think. And for that, I'm grateful.

The best part of today's practice is the fact that I'm pushing myself hard and my body feels one hundred percent ready. Those twinges in my groin that lingered over the summer are gone. Even the phantom ones.

We end the practice with a twenty-minute intense scrimmage.

We always take these seriously, but especially during preseason—or pre-pre-season, as this is—because Coach Jackson and sometimes other people from management are on the sidelines assessing us.

But this time, halfway through the scrimmage, Coach Jackson mixes up all the lines in a way that makes me feel sick.

They pull Barrett up to the first line as left wing—even though he normally plays right wing, my position—and move Harley down to second line. Then they move the second line left wing down to third line and swap that dude... it's a lot of movement.

But the intention is clear.

Coach is testing different lines.

It's not that unusual to switch sides during practice to make sure we're comfortable playing both positions. Sometimes it even happens in a game situation. But moving Harley down to second? That's not normal.

I'm hoping it's just for this scrimmage, and not for the season. Why would he mess with a good thing? Kellen, Harley and I are like a well-oiled machine up here.

But Barrett Steele is really good. And young. And powerful. And I'm sure the Blizzard paid a shit ton of money to get him on the team.

And today, he shows his worth. He does a pretty fucking good job sliding into Harley's spot. He's faster and more powerful. It's obvious.

Fuck.

Is Barrett fucking Steele legit ambidextrous? Why the fuck is that kid so good?

Grayson and Elias—the second line defensemen—do an amazing job keeping us at bay. Looks like some of the other guys have been working hard over the summer. Or are at least coming in with determination.

Things might be different this season. I don't like change. Especially as I'm on the first line with two of my best friends.

The scrimmage ends and Coach Jackson calls us all over.

"Nice work, everyone." He claps his hands three times. "As you saw, we're playing around with some of the lines. These charity games are the perfect time to test new lineups and strategies."

There's some grumbling from the group, but Coach holds up his hand to stop the noise. I sneak a glance at Harley, but his face holds zero expression. I wonder if he's going to talk to Coach. Harley's so close to retirement—still a top hockey player, but it's hard to compete with twenty-five-year-old bodies when you're in your mid-thirties. I let my eyes land on Barrett. He's got the common courtesy to not be smirking.

I guess I'm lucky Coach didn't push me down to second line today as I've crossed that old-as-shit-for-hockey thirty-year-old line in the sand. Because really, Barrett should be the biggest threat to me, not Harley, as we play the same position.

I'm overthinking all of this.

All I can do is play the best hockey I can.

"I want to go over a few things. This here is the group for Skate for Kids, our upcoming tourney." Coach gestures to us. "This is a fundraiser for several different prominent children's nonprofits, including one that focuses on childhood cancer, so we want to give our full effort. Consider it a preseason game."

We all nod and there are some murmurs from around the ice. A few guys glance at Kellen, whose young daughter is a childhood cancer survivor.

"We'll be playing two games. Thursday we're against Calgary, and Friday it'll be Vegas. The private plane will leave to come back to FoCo on Friday right after the game, although I know several of you are spending the weekend in New York City."

Barrett and Lachlan are staying the weekend, and they're trying to get Harley and me to as well. Why the fuck not? What else do I have to do? Might as well have some fun in the city. Maybe I'll meet someone to help me get Raleigh out of my head.

But even thinking that disgusts me.

I don't want to get her out of my head.

I don't want to kiss anyone else.

I just want Raleigh.

Ah, fuck.

I hate the tightening of my chest when I think about how I've lost her.

"That's all. Flight leaves in five hours. Don't be late."

Coach Jackson dismisses us and we all head to the locker rooms for showers.

No one mentions the line mixups.

"How are you feeling out there, Atter?" Kellen asks me as he slides on his sneakers post-shower.

"Good. Healed."

Kellen casts a side glance at Harley's cubby. He showered and sped out of here so fast. Barrett and Lachlan followed shortly after.

"I'm afraid everyone's heads aren't going to be in these games." Kellen sighs. "I might have to give a bunch of pep talks."

I nod. Kellen's good at that kind of stuff. Better him than me, especially in my condition. It's one of the reasons he's our team captain.

Kellen stands and grabs his phone and wallet from his shelf. "You're doing okay though? Mentally?"

"Course. I feel one hundred percent." I pretend not to know that he's really asking about Raleigh. I don't want to talk about her right now. But I won't be able to avoid spilling my guts to him for long. We always share a room when traveling, so for the next two nights it'll be just us for at least some amount of time.

"Right."

I don't add more or look at him, but I can feel Kellen's gaze on the side of my face as I slip on my shoes.

"I'm gonna go hang with Lucy and Ava before we leave. See you in a few hours."

Kellen leaves to go see my sister and his daughter.

I let out a deep breath.

I'm never going to have what he has. I've known my whole life that it's not in the cards for me.

I can't wait to hear how Kellen tries to convince me I'm wrong while we're in NYC.

# boc boc boc

### RALEIGH

Friday, August 1

I'm almost caught up with my cross-stitch orders. And the good news is I've started to sell some of my kits, which require much less effort on my part. I added a new one today that has a cute chicken design and simply *boc boc boc* as the quote. I have a big enough following now, thanks to that viral Atticus video and continuing to post on my socials. I did manage to put a max number of orders per day on my account so there's an actual wait list. I'm less freaked out about falling behind now that I have more of a control on the business.

I knock on the door to Kellen's house, and Lucy opens it seconds later.

"Hey!" She throws her arms around me like she didn't just see me yesterday. Waffles—her adorable Boston terrier—tries to run out the open door, but Lucy reacts fast and scoops up the adorable little escape artist before he succeeds. "Come in. I can't wait for you to meet my new friends."

Lucy spent most of the day traveling to and from the Denver

airport to pick up the couple she met overseas. While Lucy was in London, January introduced her to a bunch of friends, including Reese, who is American but lives in Scotland with her Scottish husband, Oliver.

Turns out Reese's daughter—who plays college soccer but has professional ambitions—has a big tournament outside of Denver, so the couple is visiting pre-tournament.

I follow Lucy down the stairs and take in the enormous television and big sectional couch. There's a row of leather reclining chairs that give movie theater vibes, and the walls are lined with framed signed hockey jerseys with famous last names.

A pretty brunette woman in her late thirties or early forties is sitting close to an attractive blond man. He's athletic looking, but not as bulky as the hockey guys.

"This is Reese," Lucy says. Reese stands and reaches over to shake my hand, her long, dark hair falling over her arm.

"So nice to finally meet you! Lucy and January would not stop talking about you in London."

Lucy laughs. "What can I say? It was weird not having her there while January and I were spending so much time together."

"I'm Oliver," the man says. "Nice to meet another one of January's American friends." He's got a thick Scottish accent. I know from Lucy's earlier description of the couple that Oliver is an ex-professional soccer player.

I'd love to hear the story of how an American single mom of a teenager and a Scottish ex-pro soccer player with a young son got together. Seems like something that would be impossible to make work.

I follow Lucy to the fully stocked bar in Kellen's basement.

"Remind me why you don't just live here with Kellen and his daughter?" I stop as she steps behind the counter and examines the tabletop wine rack. There's also a wine cellar room on the other side of the bar, because of course there is.

"Because." Lucy pulls out a bottle of red wine, examines the label, and then pulls out a corkscrew from a drawer. "I like having my own place. It's one hundred percent me and I love it."

"That's true. It is adorable." I watch Lucy twist the corkscrew into the bottle.

Lucy has a one-bedroom apartment in downtown Fort Collins. It's not over the top as she pays for it with her salary working in PR for the Blizzard, but it's bright and clean and decorated exactly for her personality.

"One day I'll move in here with Kellen. But for now, I appreciate my independence."

"And eventually you'll give in to his requests to marry him?" Apparently it's a regular topic of discussion, but Lucy wants more time to live on her own. I don't blame her. Not after what her ex put her through.

"I mean, yeah." She pops the cork out and grabs two stemless wine glasses. "And I can't believe you chose your RV over staying here for the past month."

"I love the Pink Palace." My voice hitches at the end. At some point, Lucy had offered her boyfriend's house after she realized I'd be in town for more than a few days, but I declined.

I also wanted to explore my independence and not rely on anyone but myself.

"Aw, you love the Pink Palace, huh." Lucy slides a glass over to me and picks up her own. "To the Pink Palace, the ridiculous contraption which has served you well."

Over the past few days I came to the conclusion that I need to sell the RV and just fly home. What's the point in spending a week driving across the country when there's another option? I don't even enjoy driving that thing. It's a lot of miles on the road to just put it up for sale back in Connecticut. In another universe, I might've liked being a passenger princess in the RV, but part of the reason I stayed so long in Fort Collins is because of how much I disliked driving that beast.

Part of the reason.

The other part of the reason causes me physical pain to think about.

"To the Pink Palace." I clink Lucy's glass and take a big sip of wine.

"This is from my mom's vineyard," she says after lowering her glass. "Kellen orders it by the case. I think he's the only one."

"Nope, so does Atticus. He told me about it when I first arrived." Lucy and Atticus's mom is so sweet and supportive and doesn't pressure them to be a certain way. She certainly doesn't give them life spreadsheets.

Maybe they don't need them.

"I didn't know that," Lucy says.

Always drinking good wine is a benefit of dating a Blizzard player, I guess.

Not that Lucy is doing it for that benefit.

She'd love Kellen if he was unemployed and living in a cardboard box.

Just like I... shit, don't even think it.

Too late. The thought's already formed.

Just like I love Atticus.

I cannot stop thinking those words. It's distracting, and unhelpful, and distressing.

I'm glad he's out of town. I don't know what I'd do if he were only a few miles away in his apartment. I don't think I'd be able to stay away.

Because I really want to tell him how I feel.

I shouldn't. I won't. But I want to. It would make it harder for both of us, because it wouldn't change anything.

After the game tonight, Kellen is flying back here on the Blizzard's private plane. But Atticus and the other single guys—which is most of them at this point—are staying to hang out in NYC.

I don't even want to think about what's going to happen when a group of gorgeous hockey players descend on the city. The idea of Atticus showing up with that slutty backwards hat and the touchable curls and forest green eyes... heat washes over me. He won't even have to try. The women will inhale him.

Not that it's any of my business.

We've not shared one single text message since breaking up.

And that's the way it should be, no matter how tempted I've been.

I've gotta be gone before he gets back in a few days so I can avoid any confrontation.

I put the RV up for sale three days ago and have had several potential buyers come see it.

One couple loved it, but I heard them talking about painting over the mural.

Painting over that mountain, beautiful sunset reflected in the lake, and Megghen, like it was never there to begin with.

Saying goodbye to my chicken will be another story. But luckily, there's a great plan for her and her giant coop that doesn't involve dropping her at a farm where they'll probably make her dinner.

I follow Lucy back to the couch.

"I canna go back to our wee television when we return to Scotland," Oliver says. "Lucas will never forgive us."

I mean—that accent—it takes a lot of concentration for me to follow along, but it's delicious. Instead, I let my mind wander while I stare blankly at the muted pre-game coverage.

The Blizzard won their first game of the charity tournament yesterday. I was at Lucy's apartment and we watched it from her couch with Waffles stretched out on our laps. I tried not to watch, actually, and spent a lot of time scrolling on my phone so I didn't accidentally meet Atticus's eyes through the television screen. At one point Lucy grabbed my phone and threw it across the couch. At least you can hardly tell who each player is under their uniforms and helmets, and especially on Lucy's tiny flat screen.

But Kellen's television makes the players practically life-sized.

"How did you guys get together?" Lucy asks her friends with a sideways glance at me. "Reese, I've only heard the story from your sister. I heard it's a good one."

I make a face at Lucy. Last night she was trying to convince me to talk to Atticus again. She even asked if there was any way he and I would consider trying to work it out. I told her no. For so many reasons, no.

I guess she's trying again, but at least it gives me an excuse not to look at the screen, where any second now the players will come out onto the ice.

"Well, I was in Scotland with my daughter for an elite soccer camp back when she was still in high school." Reese's cheeks turn rosy as she talks.

"And I'd just left Winchester FC due to an injury. I was a coach for the camp that Chelsea was attending. She was so good at football. *Is* so good." Oliver's voice lilts up and down in his soothing Scottish cadence.

"Soccer," Reese says to me. "We were, uh, kind of pushed together." Reese smiles, and Oliver reaches over and grabs her hand.

"Reese left Scotland, but then I chased after her. It was complicated, aye. We both had to compromise. But we've made it work."

"There was no other option, really." Reese squeezes Oliver's hand.

"The obstacles didna matter, as long as we ended up together." Oliver leans over to kiss Reese.

Oh, for the love. I roll my eyes while their lips are locked and glance at Lucy for solidarity, but she's got actual fucking tears in her eyes.

I have to get out of this town.

"It seemed impossible," Reese says when they break apart.

Was this rehearsed? Are they reading from a script? Because it's ridiculously sappy and dramatic.

"Yeah, it often does," Lucy sips her wine and leans her head back on the couch. "I mean, Raleigh, did you ever think I'd end up here? Staying in Colorado?"

"No. Your dream was England." I don't mean it to come out so cross.

Lucy looks at me, and her face betrays a flash of hurt.

"Sometimes dreams change," she says in a steady voice. "And sometimes we need to figure out why we feel like we must do something. Why the rules are there—if they're even really there, or if we've made them up and trapped ourselves voluntarily."

Ouch.

I scoff and break eye contact with Lucy, pretending like her words aren't twisting a knife in my gut. She's absolutely passive-aggressively continuing the conversation we had when she questioned why I couldn't stay. Why I couldn't actually date her brother.

Reese and Oliver are watching our exchange with wide eyes.

"I feel like we missed something," Reese says slowly.

"Aye. I'm sure of it."

But I cross my arms and Lucy keeps her lips zipped. She unmutes the television and we watch the Blizzard players skate onto the ice. I look away when they show Atticus.

My stomach rolls. Why am I fighting with my best friend? The person I've missed so much this summer and was exactly who I needed to see after breaking up with her brother?

Is it because I can't help but wonder if she's right?

She implied that I've made up the rules to my life, and that I don't really need to be following a perfect life plan anymore. Well, I get it, which is why I deleted my spreadsheets.

And now I have a blank next chapter in front of me, waiting to be written.

How will I pen it?

I'm a bit afraid that if the story is that I sold my RV and flew back to Connecticut to my old life—but worse—than maybe I don't deserve to be the main character at all.

So what *would* a main character do? Because I want to give off that energy. I don't want to be a side character.

I wasn't acting like a side character this summer.

But now I'm gonna go back to my old life?

Just like that?

And it's happening soon.

## CHAPTER 28

# Tourists

## ATTICUS

Friday, August 1

Fresh off a win in the charity tournament, everyone is in a good pre-game mood in the locker room.

I send Lucy a picture from earlier today before clicking off as Coach Jackson walks to the middle of the locker room for his pep talk. Like a bunch of middle school kids on a field trip, a group of us took the ferry over to the Statue of Liberty and Ellis Island this morning. It was actually really moving. I never went as a kid. There was a New York City field trip in high school, but I was so wrapped up in hockey there was no way I could take four days to do tourist shit.

And now I have group photos of me, Kellen, Harley, Lachlan, and freaking Barrett Steele in front of the Statue of Liberty, taken on the ferry by an attractive middle-aged woman who definitely didn't know who we were but stared at the group of us with wide eyes. Barrett kept staring at her like he wanted to gobble her up. Maybe the kid's got a thing for older women.

Coach Jackson launches into a speech about working together, staying motivated, skating hard, and the weaknesses of the other team. He wraps up with the lineups for the game, as he always does.

I half zone out, as there aren't usually surprises or major shifts.

"First line offense: Kellen in center, Atticus as right wing, Barrett as left wing. Starting defensive line is Lachlan and Jasper."

Oh, shit.

A heavy silence settles on the room and seems to stretch unnaturally long. Not that we weren't respectfully listening before, but starting the game with Barrett in Harley's place on the first line?

Everyone takes a pause at that.

Fucking intense.

During last night's game, things were as they usually are, with the exception of Barrett on the second line in place of Armas. I thought we were good to keep status quo.

I sneak a sideways glance at Harley. He's watching coach with a stony face and arms crossed on his broad chest. He's usually a bit more relaxed than this, but Harley takes everything very seriously. He never cracks a grin during pregame speeches or steals a look at his phone. He's dead focused on his career.

And his relationship.

All that seems to be falling apart. Dude must be freaking out inside.

Coach warned us he'd be trying out new lineups and strategies during these games. I guess I didn't really believe he'd swap Harley down.

"Second line offense: Finn is center, Rhys right wing, and Harley left wing."

I shake my head subtly as Coach goes through the rest of his speech. I can't focus on the Harley issue right now. Maybe I'll try to talk to him about it over the weekend while we're out in the city post-game, but he probably won't want to.

Like last night, the crowd goes absolutely wild when Barrett is introduced onto the ice. I guess I'm not surprised. He's top talent and quite the fan favorite, I guess because of his good looks, arrogance, and famously promiscuous behavior.

The game starts and it's absolute bliss being on the ice playing a game again. Summer offseason is needed and appreciated, but this is where I want to be. On the ice fighting for the puck and kicking other players' asses.

The crowd is mixed—some here to support their team, but some are just hockey fans taking advantage of a bunch of different NHL teams being in the city at the same time. It's a fun, high-energy environment.

We look good in the first period, and the other team is not prepared for us.

I speed past one of their defenders and give him the slightest little nudge into the boards. He hits them with a completely over-exaggerated slam, and the crowd gets excited, their reaction to a potential fight over-the-top.

I don't *not* know how to feed a hockey crowd.

Lachlan might be the one most likely to start something on the ice, but I'm right behind him. I tend to get in slightly less trouble than the Aussie, enough that the attention is usually on him, so I mostly slip under the ref's radar.

Two of their defenders come at me from either side, probably as revenge, and when they slam into me, my stick goes flying into the air.

Fuuuck.

I skate forward with momentum, my eyes up as my stick spins and I just know it'll hit the ground right behind me. But then Barrett fucking Steele swoops in like a knight in shining armor and gracefully catches it by the edge of the blade.

The crowd loses its collective mind as I slow so he can skate past me, handing me the stick with a smirk on his face. I cannot help grinning back as I nod to him.

That was a slick fucking move.

Kellen gets the puck to me a second later and I strike, easily scoring past their goaltender, who must've been lazing around all summer to be that slow. And he doesn't even have Augustus's tan.

I chuckle and skate away from the net.

Coach swaps us for the second line and I tap Harley's stick as we pass each other. He nods at me and skates out, looking strong and motivated on the ice.

The first period ends, and we have a fifteen-minute break in the locker room. Score is 1-0 and the feeling in the room is light and positive. I'm not the only one loving being back on the ice.

"Alright, listen up," Coach barks. "You're doing well out there, but keep it together. This is the time to figure out what's working, and for fuck's sake, fix what's not. We want to take both games and let everyone know we're the best team in the league."

There are grunts and shouts in the room.

Ten minutes into the second period, the Vegas Golden Nights are skating angry. They're hammering away at Grayson and Elias, our second line defense. Augustus makes a huge glove save on a short-handed breakaway.

But then Lach—bless his short-fused soul—gets pissed when someone checks Augustus. He tackles their center forward, football player style. Completely illegal. The crowd goes absolutely wild and I do a swan dive to join in. Barrett Steele is right behind me.

It's a beautiful thing.

Fuck anyone who dares lay a hand on our goaltender. Augustus is a goddamn team treasure.

I love hockey.

Lachlan gets sent to the penalty box for two minutes but we kill the penalty, and as soon as he's back, I watch Rhys from the second line bury our second goal of the game. Textbook backdoor tap-in that was only possible because of Harley's skilled moves getting their defenders to follow him, and then threaded a perfect cross to Rhys for the finish.

It's thirty seconds before the end of the second period that I take a hard fall after a check from the other team's right wing.

I feel something in my groin—a twinge that reminds me of when I got hurt last season. I panic as I stand and get back in the game, but our defense immediately lets in a second goal and the period ends.

I'm not sure anyone even notices, and I try to quell the terror building inside of me as I follow my teammates into the locker room. I grab a sports drink and chug it, my back to my team. If Kellen or Lachlan—or even freaking Barrett—spots me, they'll know I'm crashing out.

My breath is catching in my throat. Fuck me. I'm afraid to even stretch and check for damage. I down the entire drink, then reach into my bag for my phone. There's a meditation app that might help calm me down. Not that I've ever used it, but I at least downloaded it.

That's when I see the text messages.

RALEIGH

Hey, I saw you go down. Are you okay? You've worked so hard on your recovery this summer, I hope you're not freaking out. But remember, it's probably all in your head. Not that you're imagining it! But... didn't your skating coach tell you it's all a mental game at this point?

Go check in with one of the trainers

I'm sorry, I know I have no right to even message you, and you probably won't even see this until later

Good luck, Atticus

Oh.

Yeah. Okay. I should go talk to someone. Obviously. I turn around and catch the eye of one of the athletic trainers, and he comes over right away.

Fifteen minutes later, I'm skating back onto the ice, given an all clear by the trainer after some targeted stretching.

I feel completely fine. I almost laugh with relief.

All thanks to Raleigh's encouragement.

Harley almost scores in the third period, and I'm already cheering when the puck rings off the cross bar.

Fuck.

Kellen scores one more for the Blizzard, the other team scores, and we win the game 3-2. The crowd goes wild.

Now that I'm off the ice, my thoughts rush back to Raleigh.

Coach gives us a final pep talk, reminding us to work out and *get your asses in better shape before preseason practices start in September.* He reminds us that we'll continue informal practices and workouts in August for anyone who is around.

"Buses will take those of you who are heading home to the Blizzard plane right away. For those of you staying here for the weekend or longer—try to behave yourselves, alright?" There are chuckles around the room. A big group of players are staying in New York, not just me, Lachlan, Barrett, and Harley.

Guys shuffle in and out of the showers, and Kellen pulls me aside before heading to the team bus.

"You sure you want to stay?" He furrows his brow.

"Why would I not stay?" I don't mean the words to have an edge to them, but they do. "I don't have shit to do in Fort Collins."

Kellen assesses me calmly and raises his eyebrows. I can only imagine what he'd say if he knew about Raleigh's texts.

I don't even know what to think about that.

"Lucy tells me Raleigh isn't leaving until Monday," he says, his voice slow and steady and heavy with implication.

"Cool." I knew that, kind of. I've heard that she's selling the Pink Palace and giving Megghen to Bri and isn't everything working out just perfectly for her?

Meanwhile, I'm a hot fucking mess.

Maybe not on the outside. But inside.

I'm in love with that woman, and she's currently getting ready to leave Colorado to go back to her old life. Fuck. I wish I could get her to stay. I wish I could change her mind. I wish I had the nerve to try.

"If you wanted to see her once more, maybe see if you two could talk things out..."

"There's nothing to talk about." This time I mean to sound curt. I need to remind Kellen—and myself—that it's truly over.

Isn't it?

"Yeah, well, that's what I thought—" I know he's about to launch into a speech about my sister and him and how things magically worked out for them.

"This is nothing like you and Lucy, Kellie," I interrupt. I sigh and run my hand over my face.

"Right. It's not like me and Lucy." He pauses for dramatic effect. "It's you and Raleigh."

"There is no me and Raleigh." But my objection sounds weak.

"Ready to go, mate?" Lachlan slaps his hand on my shoulder. "There's a bar across the way we might swing by before heading to the club."

"Bad choice." Kellen shakes his head. "There are going to be so many people there who were at the game. You sure you want to deal with that?"

"Yup." Barrett pops between us like an annoying little brother, draping his arms over our shoulders. Him being taller than me is infuriating. "Hopefully, all the hot women who were in that one section make an appearance."

"The ones you kept winking at?" Lachlan rolls his eyes and laughs.

"Yep. Those women."

"Let's go then." Lachlan heads toward the door and looks back over his shoulder at me. "Coming?"

That dude is totally burying his feelings about Melissa. There is no way he is over the breakup. This is a complete cover-up. And it'll be painful to witness how he takes it out on poor girls at the bar."

He's gonna have so much sex getting over his ex.

And I will too. Yeah, that's what I'll do.

But the idea of sleeping with someone else is revolting. Like honestly makes me want to gag.

"See you next week," I say to Kellen without another glance, following Harley out the locker room door.

I force myself to leave the arena, heading down the crowded New York street where we all but blend into the throngs of people, and into the bar they've chosen. It's an Irish pub packed with Friday night drinkers, some dressed in business casual, maybe leftovers from office happy hours, and some in far less clothing out for the start of their night.

A trio of women immediately notice us, and Lachlan and Barrett waste no time going over to talk to them. Harley gets the first round and we stand in silence behind the boys and the two women they've descended on. The third woman gives us both interested eyes, but neither of us looks her way.

"Why aren't you going after Raleigh?" Harley asks me, anger in his voice.

"What?" I turn to him, confused by the hostility.

"If I had a chance to convince the woman I love—because from what I've heard, you're in seriously deep—to stay with me, I would do it in a second."

"I'm not in love—"

"Oh, fuck off." Harley runs his hand over his newly grown beard. I have a feeling this is going to be an intense year for my friend. "You obviously are. And by the look on your face right now, you know it. Whatever's happened with Raleigh this summer has changed you. You're different because of her. Yet you're here at this shitty bar, to get drunk, and I'm gonna guess *not* hit on women?"

I swallow and dip my chin. I know I love Raleigh. I'm ashamed I even tried to deny it.

"Yeah. You're right." I stare into the amber liquid and drain half the pint.

"I lost Emily. She's gone. I can't go fight for her anymore, because I already tried and failed. I did the whole romantic gesture thing to win her back... but I crashed and burned. It's over with her. It's over." I look up and Harley's clenching his teeth, like he's trying not to scream or cry or bite something. "Tell me: is Raleigh in love with someone else?"

I think about her ex-husband. About the flowers he sent her, the way he just showed up at the Pink Palace, all the money she's been sending him since their divorce.

That shit is complicated. Messy. So much baggage.

But is Raleigh in love with Jacob?

She told me she isn't. And I believe her.

I think about the way she looked at me the last time we slept together. She was the most beautiful thing I'd ever seen, lying out in front of me, all mine. All fucking mine. For that night, anyway.

She's smart and interesting and knows me. Likes the real me, not because I'm a pro hockey player. Probably despite being a pro hockey player.

Could she love me?

I don't know. I don't think so.

But maybe. She texted me earlier because she was worried. She knew how to calm me down.

And I think maybe Harley is right. I'm an asshole if I don't try one more time. Because what if? What if I could convince her to stay with me in Fort Collins? What if I was enough for her?

"Oh, shit."

I've messed this all up.

"Go get on that plane." Harley turns me to the door and physically escorts me outside, taking my half empty pint right out of my hand. "Order a car immediately."

I do as he says, putting in the destination as the small airport the team plane's flying out of, with a stop at the hotel to grab my bag.

"Done."

"Now text Kellen and tell him to hold the fucking plane."

I huff a laugh and do as he says.

"What about you? You coming?" I look up and meet Harley's dark, sad eyes.

"No. I might as well stay and babysit these assholes."

I want to ask him how he's handing the fact that Barrett might be pushing him to the second line, and how can he even want to babysit his possible replacement? But I don't, because I don't think it's the right time to push him on that.

"You sure?"

"Yup." Harley nods as my car pulls up. "Good luck."

I open the car door and confirm that it's the right one, then turn to Harley.

"Thanks, dude."

He raises his hand as we pull away.

Thirty minutes and a very expensive ride later, I'm jogging onto the runway and up the steps to the plane with my duffel.

"Finally." Kellen grins at me from his seat, already half-reclined.

"We were about ten minutes from leaving your ass in New York," Coach grumbles loudly from three rows back. He pulls an eye mask over his face and sighs. "And Kellen here was starting to doubt you'd show up."

"Any day now, Atter, whenever you're ready," Grayson, one of our defensemen, calls from a seat toward the middle of the plane. He's got a serious girlfriend back in Fort Collins, one he met while she was secretly driving a Zamboni to cover her father's shift. Now *that's* a good story.

About half the team is spread out on the plane, some with headphones, some already snoozing, a few chatting with each other and snacking on the food distributed by the flight attendants. These guys are all the ones with girlfriends or families or other plans for the month of August that don't include getting trashed in New York City.

"Any second now, I was just thinking," Kellen says as I settle in a comfortable seat facing him, a table between us. "What are you gonna do?"

What am I going to do? I've got a couple hours on the plane to come up with a plan. We'll arrive too late to see Raleigh tonight, but in the morning, I intend on showing up at the Pink Palace.

"I guess I'm going to go and tell her I love her." Why does that thought simultaneously make me so happy but also make me want to vomit and then hide under a rock somewhere?

"Good for you." Kellen nods and assesses me for a moment. "But you need a bit more than that."

He's right. I can't just show up at her door. I need to come up with some way to win her over. Because I don't just want to tell her I love her.

I want to convince her to stay with me in Fort Collins, when she's already made it crystal clear she intends to go back to Connecticut.

## CHAPTER 29

# My Boyfriend Works Out

## RALEIGH

Saturday, August 2

"I'm sorry to hear your grandmother's so sick." I'm lying in bed, my eyes tracing the scuffed ceiling of my bedroom in the Pink Palace. The cross-stitch project I was working on late last night and as soon as I woke up an hour ago lays next to me.

"Thanks. Apparently, they think it'll happen soon." January's voice is steady, but I know she was close to her grandmother when she was growing up. Not so much as an adult.

"Are you going to come home?"

"Probably." January's family lives in Rhode Island. As far as I know, she hasn't been back there in years. When she occasionally sees her parents, they meet her in Boston. She's never said much about them. Only that when she left for college in Virginia and then moved to Europe, they drifted apart. She definitely talked about her grandmother.

"Well, let me know. Maybe we can see each other." I sniff. "It's not fair you and Lucy had all that time together in England."

"We missed you for sure," January says, not commenting any

further about her family. "But can we talk more about what you've been doing this summer? Or *who* you've been doing?"

"Nope, we sure can't." Because it's all I've been thinking about, and I'm not sure I can handle vocalizing all of that.

"Raleigh." January chuckles, and while she still sounds strained, it's nice to hear her laugh. "You're not even going to say goodbye to him? Get one last kiss?"

"Hush. No, I'm not going to see him before I leave, which should be on Monday, as long as I can close the deal on the RV later." I stand and straighten up my bed.

Obviously I'm not going to see him. I'm not waiting around to have another painful conversation about how we can't be together. Why would I do that?

But something shifted in me last night when I was talking to Lucy and her friends. The stupid Scottish love story actually made me wonder if there was a way. Maybe I am the one who created the rules that are making me unhappy.

But I texted Atticus. I probably shouldn't have. He read it but didn't respond.

'Raleigh." January groans and I sink back down on the bed.

"What?"

"This is such a huge deal that you finally hooked up with Atticus."

"Finally?" I mean, okay, she's right that it's a big deal. And in my head, yeah, I guess it's been a long time coming.

"Lucy and I have been predicting it since he showed up at JMU."

"Seriously?" I can't seem to manage more than one-word answers.

"Um, yes? The way you two flirted back then was ridiculous. I can't believe it never happened, boyfriend or not."

"Well, it didn't."

"I'd at least go find him for one last fu—"

"January!"

"What?" she says with fake surprise.

"Can we talk about something else?" My mind is swirling. Damn, I'm so confused. I should be sure of my decision and getting ready for the next chapter of my life, not questioning everything.

She scoffs. "Fine. I can't believe you're selling the Pink Palace. I thought maybe you'd decide RV life was permanent."

"Definitely not." I shake my head. RV life is definitely not my permanent state. But I feel like this topic is in the same category as leaving Atticus behind.

I also can't believe I'm selling the Pink Palace.

Especially with that gorgeous mural.

The one the buyers were talking about painting over.

I rub my face. I need coffee. I've been lying in my bed awake for hours, googling things I shouldn't be googling. And last night I couldn't sleep after getting back from watching the hockey game at Kellen's house.

"I met your friends last night," I say, trying to change the subject. Trying to distract myself.

January squeals. "Aren't Reese and Oliver amazing? I went with Reese and her sister on a trip to Ireland this summer to visit their other sister, who lives in a seaside town with her gorgeous Irish bartender husband."

"They were nice."

January launches into a story from their trip to Ireland and I realize that hearing about Reese and Oliver's love story is not a distraction. It's the whole point.

I eventually say goodbye to January and head to my tiny bathroom, chuckling when I go to slide on my slippers. I honestly have no idea how she did it, but Megghen's left a final present for me in one of them. A warm, brown egg. Tears sting my eyes.

Am I crying over a chicken?

"Thanks, Megghen." I look across the RV at my chicken,

waiting patiently at the door of the tent for me to put her into her coop outside. "You've been a good friend this summer."

I swipe at my eyes and grab the egg so I can stick it in the fridge and start my coffee before going back to clean myself up and pull on leggings, a tank top, and a Blizzard hoodie.

Somehow, my relationship with Megghen went from *why is there a chicken in my RV* at the beginning of the summer to *she's my sounding board and friend*. I really need to hang out with Lucy and January more.

To be honest? I've been fantasizing about a life in Fort Collins.

"But it's not going to happen," I remind myself as I pour creamer into my coffee.

I've looked up so many things.

Local cross-stitch groups that meet in person.

The best places to kayak.

What it's like to live in Fort Collins year round.

Apartments to rent.

I'm just torturing myself, and I know it.

A knock at the tinny RV door startles me as I'm about to sip from my steaming coffee.

Who the heck could that be? The potential buyers are due to come later today—maybe they came early? Hours and hours early. Or maybe it's Bri's friend with the pick up truck here to get Megghen. Ugh, I thought I had until tomorrow with her.

But when I pull open the door—first making sure Fred is within easy grabbing distance—all the breath disappears from my lungs.

It's Atticus.

A dull buzzing sound fills my ears and I struggle to make my body function. I'm tempted to rub my eyes to make sure he's really there, but I blink a few times instead.

He's still standing in front of me.

"Hey, Raleigh," he says as if he's supposed to be here to pick me up for one of our early summer dating coach dates or go out on the lake.

"Hey." I grip the side of the doorframe.

"I'm sorry I didn't respond to your texts last night."

"It's okay." He looks so gorgeous. My heart can't handle it.

"It helped me get through. Thank you."

It's a warm morning, so he's wearing a short-sleeved Blizzard t-shirt with athletic shorts that show off his thick thighs and sculpted calf muscles. Honestly, professional athletes should come with a disclaimer on them as they walk around the world. One that says *don't mind me, I work out for a living.*

There might be an interesting cross-stitch quote in there somewhere.

"I thought you were staying in New York City after the game?" I manage to say, though my voice sounds strangled. The opposite of chill.

"I was going to. That was the plan." His serious green eyes hold me captive as a beat of silence rests between us.

"Good game," I say to fill the quiet. "I watched it with Lucy."

He nods and his neck ripples as he swallows.

"Raleigh—"

"Atticus—" We talk over each other and I press my lips together.

He's here in front of me. The man I realized maybe I could've fought harder for. The one I've been questioning whether it's possible to be with.

The one I fully regret breaking up with.

"You first," I say.

"I changed the plan." He nods. "I realized I had to come back here and talk to you. Before you left."

Atticus's eyes remain locked on mine, his baseball cap holding his red curls back from his forehead. There's a fluttering in my belly, like I felt when he kissed me on New Year's Eve. Sweet anticipation and excitement.

"I'm so glad you did."

It feels like a hundred years ago that I showed up at his apartment door and broke up with him, but it was only last Sunday. Six days ago.

I've lived and died so many times since then.

I've regretted my decision.

I've double downed on it.

I've rewritten that day too many times to count.

And in the past twelve hours, I've tried to come up with ways to fix it.

"You are?" He puts his weight on one foot, and then the other.

"I am." I nod. "What did you need to talk to me about?"

"I was hoping we could make another cross-stitch video." One side of his mouth quirks up.

I huff a surprised laugh. "Why?"

"To help you make more sales, of course."

"That might not be a great idea." I cast a glance at the pile of hoops on my table. "I'm still not caught up from the ones I got from that last video."

"How about to help you get more followers?"

"Last time I went from three followers to a thousand."

"See?" He grins at me.

My smile fades from my face.

"Atticus, I'm supposed to leave on Monday to go back—" My voice hitches. I almost said home, but it didn't feel right. "—back to Connecticut. And I start back at work in a week. I won't have time for doing cross-stitch anymore. At least not as a business."

I don't know. Is any of that true? Just a few days ago, I had resigned myself to being the boring, dependable pharmacist who will always have a stable job and make reasonable life choices. I'm my mother's daughter. The one with the spreadsheet life plan.

But right now, that all feels so wrong. It doesn't feel like who I am anymore. I've actually changed this summer. And I don't think I can go back to who I was.

And the way Atticus is looking at me right now... I want to grab his hand and drag him inside and kiss him until we can't breathe.

Instead, I step out of the RV so I'm standing right in front of him. I keep the door cracked open. If I invite him inside, I don't think we'll be able to work this all out logically. My clothes might remove themselves from my body of their own accord if we're near a bed.

But he's so tall. And gorgeous. And he's looking at me like I'm the entire world. So I'm not sure being outside actually helps.

Why is he here?

It can't be because he has the same feelings for me that I have for him.

Can it?

My heart surges at the thought.

To what end, though? Am I really considering changing my life for real?

Atticus doesn't step back, and we're standing close.

"I had some ideas, in case you ever decided to revive your cross-stitch side hustle."

From inside the Pink Palace, Megghen *boc boc bocs*. The gentle waves of the lake lap peacefully onto the shoreline. The warm summer breeze brushes past my bare arms.

And Atticus Knox is here.

He looks nervous, gnawing on his lower lip, adjusting the hat on his head, gripping his phone in one hand.

"I don't think I have enough ideas, so that would be great." I suppress a smile as we both know I've had so many good cross-stitch quote ideas this summer.

"I know! I wanted to make sure you accomplished that goal before you leave."

I press my lips together. "I'm ready."

"I'm going to read from my phone." He taps the screen a few times. "First one: *I like four things in life in the following order:*

*chickens, zombies, hockey, and RV life.*" Atticus looks up at me with wide eyes.

I crack up. "That is kind of perfect? But it might be a bit long for a hoop."

"Alright, alright, I hear ya." He grins and looks down at his screen again. "This one is simpler: *Chickens, cross-stitch, & hockey.*"

"I love that one. Simple, short, and to the point."

"And I bet there are a ton of people who have the same three priorities." He's got a super serious look plastered on his face.

"There must be so many." I cross my arms and let myself grin.

"Hundreds, at least."

"Yup." I nod. "Go on."

What is happening here? He's not here to actually give me cross-stitch ideas, is he? Or to make a video? But the other reason he'd be here is too much to dream for. Am I still tucked into my uncomfortable RV bed dreaming?

Atticus clears his throat and looks back down at his phone.

"How about: *Are you a chicken? No? Go away.* Or: *my house is an RV.* Or just: *hockey.*"

"You're really good at this, did you know that? Such a good cross-stitch student."

"Yes, I am a wonderful student in general."

"I guess I'm not a great coach though, since you fired me."

"It wasn't your coaching ability that lost you the job, I can assure of that."

"No?"

He shakes his head and raises a suggestive eyebrow. "I have one more idea."

"Go on." My stomach tightens and I draw in a breath, holding it while I wait for him to speak.

"*FAFO, my boyfriend is a hockey player.*" Atticus slides his phone back in his pocket and looks at me.

I swallow and can't squeak out a reply.

"That might work. But maybe too niche..." My voice trails off.

I want that hoop in my house. I want to be able to say that, in stitches or in texts or out loud. More than anything.

"Raleigh." Atticus shoves his hands in his pockets. His gaze pierces me. My heart. My soul. "I'm not just here to talk about cross-stitch. Although I have even more ideas than those, by the way."

I swallow and nod, my chest pounding. What do I do with my hands? They feel clammy. I clench my fists at my sides and release them again. It doesn't help.

"Then why are you here?" I whisper.

"I'm here because—" Atticus looks over his shoulder at his Wrangler, then adjusts his hat and meets my eyes again. "Since you showed up this summer. No—since New Year's Eve. Since *college.*"

He pauses and I flash back to New Year's Eve. The kiss in a dark corner. The one that was supposed to get it out of our systems. I swallow and it's like I'm choking on a bunch of chicken feathers.

"—all I could do after that kiss was think about you. It changed me." He takes a deep breath and I remember to let out the one I was holding. "You were always the college crush I had. A thing for my older sister's best friend. How original, right?" He cracks a tentative smile.

"Kind of the same as having a crush on your best friend's brother," I say and cross my arms.

A serious look falls on his face again. His hands flex at his sides.

"All winter I thought about you. All spring. And then, like freaking magic, you showed up here, in Fort Collins, in your giant pink RV."

"What was I thinking?" I let out a breathy laugh.

"I don't know," Atticus says with a wondrous look. "What were you thinking?"

"I've had no idea what I'm doing since the divorce." I shrug. "Actually, since a year ago, when I found out about Jacob's issues."

Atticus reaches out his hands and I immediately uncross my arms and put my hands in his. I sigh at the contact.

"You showed up and took my breath away." He licks his lips and glances at my mouth. "And I have a confession. The dating coach thing was a sham. I never wanted to ask out the bookstore woman. I never even noticed her... it was just a convenient excuse to get you to hang out with me."

I turn my hand until my fingers loop into his. It's like a live wire is connecting us, and I close my eyes to bask in its energy.

"I only fell more in love with you when we watched the zombie movies together."

My eyes fly open.

"What did you say?" I whisper.

He blinks a hundred times and looks confused, then appears to replay the last thing he said in his head. Atticus's eyes widen as he hears it.

Atticus is in love with me? Fireworks brighter than the ones on the fourth of July explode in my heart. Am I going to get what I want more than anything in the world?

Because it's Atticus. I'm sure of that now.

"Okay, I got there quicker than I meant to." Atticus squeezes my hands. "I'm in love with you, Raleigh Hayes. I've probably been in love with you since college. Since that first time I saw you and puked in the bushes outside of your apartment building. But if that didn't do it, it was the zombie movies. Or at the very least, our doomed kayak adventures. Learning to do cross-stitch from you. Hanging out with Megghen. Just... being with you."

All the breath has disappeared from my body.

Atticus loves me. He loves *me*.

His brow furrows and I need to say something back immediately.

I bite my lip and get lost in his green eyes.

## CHAPTER 30

# Best Places to Kayak

## ATTICUS

Raleigh doesn't know what to say.

If the response wasn't immediately obvious to her, I'd say this is not going to go in the direction I was hoping for.

I feel like I'm going to pass out.

Raleigh broke up with me and sent me away. She told me what she wanted—and it isn't me. So what am I doing here?

I'm clearing my heart.

Yeah, that's right. Telling her how I feel and doing everything I can to get her to stay with me. To *be* with me. And if it doesn't work, I'll know I tried.

She doesn't even look conflicted. I can't read her right now. Is she so sure of her decision to break up with me and leave?

"You don't have to say anything," I whisper and squeeze her hands. At least she's still touching me. At least we're connecting in this circle of electricity and sparks and... whatever this beautiful thing is between us. Even if she's not conflicted about her decision, she's gotta still feel this.

"I want to." She drops both my hands and covers her face for a beat, then runs her fingers through her wispy hair. "I need to explain to you."

Shit. Explain what?

This woman is so beautiful. So real. Standing there in her leggings and hooded sweatshirt. This is the woman I want to be with. She's perfect for me.

Raleigh is my person.

She crosses her arms and I brace myself for whatever she has to say. Because I can handle it. Raleigh's broken through the protective layers on my heart, ones that've been there for decades. Probably since I was a kid and realized I didn't *want* to be like my father, but that I was destined to be.

To that kid I say: *no you're not. You're not going to be like your father. You're going to be better than him.*

"All my life I've followed a plan. I needed to be perfect. After my dad left, my mother fell apart. I was babysitting and mowing lawns in middle school to help pay the bills while she put herself back together." Raleigh has a far-away expression on her face.

I hadn't heard that part of her story and my heart swells at the vision of thirteen-year-old Raleigh mowing a lawn for grocery money. I knew there was a tough time in her childhood with her single mom, but that things eventually settled down in their household.

"She didn't have her shit together at all when I was little. And the way she struggled after my father left? It was awful to witness. For years. Eventually, she went back to school and got a great job, and is kicking absolute ass. You'd never know what her past was like, seeing her now." Raleigh looks sideways toward the lake. "I swore I'd never struggle like that. And she agreed."

"That's a lot of pressure on a kid," I say softly, and Raleigh turns back to me and nods, her dark eyes on mine.

"So I spent all my time studying. Planning my future. When I was fourteen years old, Mom and I made a spreadsheet of all the possible careers I could pursue, including average starting salaries, education needed, and colleges that were the best value for money. We chose pharmacy as my career, and then did the same assessment for PharmD schools. We picked one, and I followed that plan perfectly from high school through to securing my pharmacist job."

It makes so much more sense now why she studied so much harder than the rest of us in college. How driven she was. It came from what she went through as a kid.

Which, same.

"But then it went to shit." Raleigh looks back at me. "I married the wrong guy, and I couldn't understand what I'd done wrong. Then I married another wrong guy." Her voice cracks a little at the end.

"That must've all been so hard, Raleigh." I don't know what she's gone through, but I want to wrap her in my arms to show I care about every bit of it.

Raleigh nods.

"I've gone on such a journey since my second divorce." She reaches her hands for mine again, and my body sighs at the contact, gently stroking her soft fingers with my thumb. "And that journey started with you in December."

I swallow and the world fades around us. It's just me and her, standing in front of the Pink Palace at the campsite in Fort Collins, Colorado. We're the only ones in the state. The country. In the world.

Me and Raleigh.

"New Year's Eve." She nods. "There was so much unspoken between us. At least on my side." Raleigh lets out a low chuckle. "I've thought about that kiss every single day. And maybe it gave me the courage to realize I wanted to go do things for myself. I never had time to travel or for hobbies. I was always working or studying or investing myself in those who weren't right for me. I want to be more than a blank canvas for other people to tell their story on. That's what's been happening my whole life." She bites her bottom lip. "Even my mother painted her story on me. The story she'd wished she'd lived from the start, not waited until she was forced to."

"Raleigh." I want to pull her into my arms and show her how special she is. I want to tell her I'd never try to brush my colors on her canvas. "You are not a blank canvas. You are already the most beautiful painting in the world."

Her eyes widen and lift.

"Thank you. I want to figure out who I really am."

I nod in support, but this sounds like she's going to go travel the world. Did those stupid memoirs work too well?

"But I know one thing." Raleigh steps closer and slips her hands out of mine, placing them on my chest. I reach forward and grab her waist.

"What do you know, coach?" I say in a husky voice.

One side of her mouth quirks up.

"I know that I love you." She pauses and the world spins around us. "I'm in love with you too, Atticus."

Could she really? Did I hear her right? I need her to say more. I want to hear everything. I move my hands to the small of her back and tug her closer until our bodies are touching. I'm not letting her get away. Not this time.

"I don't know when I realized it. Wait—yes I do." She laughs. "It was not long after I broke up with you. I'm so sorry about that." Her face breaks.

"It's okay." I pull her closer to me until our hips press together. "But I'd really like you to tell me you love me again."

"I love you, Atticus. I love everything about you. I love you because you're smart and loyal and funny and damn, you make me laugh. You love zombies and got me to go out on the water. You learned to do cross-stitch for me. You've never judged me and my weird choices. And you are so thoughtful." She looks pointedly at the coop holding Megghen, then over at the hammock. "Do you know what I've been doing all morning?"

I shake my head, unable to form words.

"I've been looking things up online. Kayaking. Cross-stitch groups. Apartments to rent."

"Here?"

"Here." She wraps her arms around my neck, pressing herself flush against my body.

A tiny, desperate sound escapes my throat. "I would do basically anything to have you stay here in Fort Collins. Fuck your old life back in Connecticut. You belong here with me—"

Raleigh pulls my head down and presses our lips together. I'm ready for her. She buries her hands in my hair, knocking my baseball cap off in the process.

The kiss is like coming home. Her lips are warm, her mouth inviting, and I could stand here forever with my arms wrapped around her. She makes a humming sound and it vibrates through my mouth and into my body.

She leans back an inch and smiles against my lips.

"I'm not leaving, rebound guy." She pulls me back and kisses me again.

Raleigh's. Not. Leaving.

The words swirl in my head like a tornado of autumn leaves, rearranging themselves and always falling back into the right order: *she's not leaving.*

"I could kiss you all day and all night—and I plan to—but can you please explain exactly what you mean by you're *not leaving*? I understand all the words, but I'm having a hard time processing."

"All I know is I can't imagine being apart from you. Maybe this won't last—"

"Are you kidding me?" I cut her off and move my hands up to cup her face. "This is forever." I kiss her long and hard. "Forever."

She lets out a noisy breath. "Forever?"

"Yeah. Do you disagree?"

"No, but, Atticus—"

"Let me guess. You don't want to get married."

I cannot believe I am bringing up marriage to Raleigh Hayes. It should be terrifying. The thing I've been avoiding my entire life. But I'd marry her. I would. I'd do it tomorrow. Today, even. And I'd spend the rest of my life making it work.

"Right. But not because of you. Because of me. And I'm not saying never. But I need to make sure I understand myself before I do that, and that might take a long time."

"I get it." I slide my hands into her hair and kiss her deeply before coming back up for a breath. "As long as I can fall asleep with you in my arms at night. As long as I can text or call you when I'm having a bad day, or I want to know how yours is going. As long as you'll come to my games when we're in town and wear my jersey. As long as you'll agree to be mine, Raleigh Hayes."

Raleigh's cheeks turn a deep shade of pink and she smiles at me, a promise in her eyes that I know mirrors my own.

"Your jersey! Wait here—I have something for you." Raleigh flies out of my arms and darts back into the Pink Palace.

"Okay?" I laugh and memorize this moment. The joy and anticipation.

She comes out a moment later, cheeks flushed, holding... my jersey? I knew I'd left it with her, but I wanted her to keep it. I wanted to know she'd see it when she opened her drawers, maybe wear it if she missed me.

"Last night... I realized I'd made a mistake breaking up with you." She shakes her head and clutches the jersey to her chest. "But I thought it was too late. So I, uh, stitched something onto your jersey."

"Um, what?" I cannot suppress a chuckle. I have literally no idea where this is going.

"I just kept thinking about how you've been fighting so hard to prove you're not like your father. You're not a player. You're a good person and, contrary to your request for me to be your dating coach, you are fully capable of being someone's boyfriend."

I feel a sweet, painful stab in my belly.

"Don't be mad I desecrated your jersey." She watches me with her brow furrowed. "I spent hours on it last night."

"Now I'm incredibly curious."

Raleigh holds out the front of my jersey, which looks just like it always does.

"Oops." She flips it around.

My last name is in yellow above the number 8, as always. But in between, there is a small set of words cross-stitched on. I squint my eyes and lean forward, reaching out to hold the sides.

"More than just a player?" I say.

"Yeah. Get it? Like works for you as a hockey player and also, you know..."

I look up and Raleigh's cheeks are bright pink.

"I get it." My heart squeezes.

"I realize I probably destroyed a $100 jersey. Are you mad?"

"Um, it's closer to $400, I believe."

She gasps. "Oh no."

"Raleigh. I love it. I love you."

"Really? Thank god. I honestly didn't think you'd ever see it."

"Hey." I grab the jersey and throw it over my shoulder, then pull her close to me again. I always want her close to me. "Ask me that dating question again."

I feel so damn full right now. Full of her. Full of love. Happiness. Everything.

"Dating question?" Her brow furrows.

"Yeah. Remember? You said you always want to know what people's plans are for five years from now."

"Oh." She moans. "It's the worst question, I know—"

"I know where I see myself in five years." All at once my future plan is perfectly clear in my head.

Raleigh presses her lips together. "Okay. Go ahead."

"I see myself with you. Maybe we'll have a house somewhere with a whole backyard of chickens." I love the smile on her face.

"Or maybe we'll be traveling the country in a very much upgraded Pink Palace."

"I'm never driving it."

"Done." I squeeze her sides. "Maybe we'll be married with a couple of kids."

Her eyes widen.

"We can talk about that," I say quickly, not wanting to freak her out. I'd have kids with her or not, whatever she wants. "As long as I'm with you. That's what I see most clearly five years from now."

"That's the perfect answer," she says with a sigh and kisses me again. And again. Her mouth opens for me and I swipe my tongue in until her breathing speeds up. Raleigh pulls back and nods to the Pink Palace with heat in her eyes. "Do you want to—"

"God, I've missed you." I bend down and sweep her up and into my arms, like a groom carrying his bride. She giggles and clings to my neck.

"You are ridiculous."

"Shut up, coach," I growl. We crash into the Pink Palace and I kick the door shut behind us.

CHAPTER 31

*Home Is*

RALEIGH

Sunday, August 24

"Kellen and Lucy want us to come over for dinner tonight," Atticus says. "If you're up for a trip to the suburbs after we all help you unpack for a few hours." Atticus leans against the doorframe of the kitchen in my new one-bedroom apartment, watching me unpack one of the boxes that just arrived.

After I decided I was staying in Fort Collins, I got on a plane back to Connecticut—with Atticus. We spent a week in my house, packing and donating and cleaning so it could be put up for sale. Atticus paid to have a bunch of my boxes driven out to Colorado, and some went to a storage unit. It was therapeutic having him there with me as I sorted through all of the things in that house. So much was left over from my marriage to Jacob, and some stuff even from my first marriage.

I donated almost all of that, especially what I couldn't use right away here.

And when the moving van arrived in FoCo yesterday, Atticus

297

ran up and down the stairs—why doesn't this building have an elevator?—along with Lachlan and Barrett.

Mom was really down when I told her I was staying in Colorado, but she said she'd come visit whenever she can. Her first trip is already planned for Thanksgiving when she knows she has time off.

She's nervous I'm going off-spreadsheet and will ruin my life plan.

She's nervous I'm going to marry Atticus and repeat my mistakes.

Somehow, I've managed to convince her to trust me to handle my own life. Probably because I'm a grown-ass woman who can make her own decisions.

And by the time she comes to visit, I should have a lineup of completed cross-stitch hoops for sale at Rocky Gifts, the gift shop in Fort Collins that I visited last week with an example hoop. They said they'd love to carry some hockey-themed hoops. Maybe that'll make her smile. Or roll her eyes. Hard to predict.

"Sure. Can we stop at Bri's to go visit Megghen and Peggy?"

"Obviously." He cracks a smile and crosses his arms.

"I can't wait to meet the new chicken." Bri got Megghen a friend, and her daughter named her Peggy. She was so excited to explain to us that she chose that name because it had *egg* in it, just like the way I chose Megghen's name.

"Kellen is bringing a bunch of eggs for us."

"Ha. I bet Bri doesn't have the problem of them laying eggs all around her house like I did." I grab the scissors and slice open the next box. "I miss Megghen."

I'm lucky Megghen got a good home with Bri. But one of the biggest conundrums I had with the whole staying-in-Colorado thing was what to do with the Pink Palace. I still had—have—buyers interested in her, but once that one couple talked about painting over the mural? I couldn't handle it.

Luckily, I have a rich hockey player boyfriend who is more

than happy to pay the fees at an RV storage park right outside of Fort Collins.

We have tentative plans to travel next summer in her, but Atticus declared that with my permission, he was going to completely gut the Pink Palace and make it as luxury as possible inside, including adding the most comfortable bed we can find that'll fit in the tiny bedroom.

"Have I told you how incredibly hot you look wearing my jersey?"

"You have, actually." I look down at the purple and yellow Blizzard jersey, at least two sizes too big, hanging below my shorts and making it look like I'm wearing nothing else. And yup, it's got *more than just a player* stitched on the back under his name. "I need one a little smaller for games."

"I'm on it." I glance over at him and his eyes are dragging down my body. I know that look. I freaking *love* that look. It means he has something in mind for the near future that involves me wearing nothing at all. Waves of heat wash over my body. I try to shake it off—we have company arriving soon.

"And you're really going to live here instead of with me, huh?" His eyes finally meet mine, but he remains where he is in the doorway.

"Yes." I pull out a stack of plain white dishes and sigh. Why did I pick out the most boring dishes ever when I married my first husband? But for now, they'll do. "We are only like five blocks from each other."

"I'd rather have you with me. In my bed. At all times." Atticus stalks toward me and takes the dish out of my hand and sets it on the counter before pulling my arms up and around his neck. "I can't believe you lived with me for weeks and after all that sex and love you're still leaving."

After we got back from Connecticut, I stayed with Atticus until my apartment was ready. I finally relented that his bed is really much more comfortable, so we chose to stay at his place over the Pink Palace. I felt all sorts of things when we moved her out of the campsite to the storage facility. That RV and the campsite meant a lot to me. It was even hard to say goodbye to Elizabeth, who had been keeping an eye on the Pink Palace while we were away. She and her husband and their dog, Tuna, were heading back to Cincinnati, and she invited us to come visit sometime and watch an FC Cincinnati soccer game or a Cyclones minor league hockey game.

"The sex and love has been amazing, and you can have me in your arms whenever you want." I lean up to kiss Atticus and can feel him smile against my lips. "But it's been my fantasy for a decade to live next door to Lucy again."

It really felt like fate when Lucy called me two weeks ago to tell me her neighbor was moving out soon and the building manager hadn't filled the apartment yet. We get to live next door each other, almost as close as we were as college roommates.

The only person missing is January, but she promised to come see us. Unfortunately, that might be soon as her grandmother's condition continues to deteriorate.

"I'm glad you'll have Lucy next door. Hockey starts soon. I'll be away a lot." Atticus presses his forehead against mine.

"And I'll be here when you're not away." I weave my fingers into the back of his red curls, tucked beneath his backwards baseball cap.

"Just don't be too depressed without me." Atticus gives me a crooked smile.

I huff. "I'll keep busy enough."

After Atticus and I officially reconciled, I called my boss at the pharmacy the next day. It was only a week before I was supposed to come back from my sabbatical.

I was really going off-spreadsheet, but I had a plan.

While I've got enough money saved to sustain me while I take some time to figure out what I want to be doing with my life, I need health insurance and some other kind of stability. Stacey made a call—okay, a lot of calls—and connected me with the regional office of our pharmacy.

One of the Fort Collins's locations happens to need a part time pharmacist.

I'm going back to work twenty hours a week at the pharmacy.

That'll give me time to fulfill the influx of orders I've received after the latest video Atticus and I made went viral. In this one, he first showed up shirtless. I made him go grab a shirt, but left the footage in the video.

I'm not surprised a million people—and counting—watched it.

"Do you remember what you said to me on New Year's Eve? When you were still resisting me?" Atticus slips his fingers under my shirt and onto the skin of my waist. A shudder vibrates through me.

"Hmm, not exactly, but we can reenact the situation."

I squeal as he lifts me up and carries me over to the wall in my small kitchen, gently leaning my back against it as I slide my feet to the ground.

"I definitely had you pressed up against the wall," he says, looking down at me.

"I think one of your hands was here." I push his hand up until it's above my head and my body immediately heats at being in this position with him.

"Is this right?" Atticus practically whispers, tucking a strand of my hair behind my ear. He's so close I can feel the warmth of his body. I let out a little sigh.

"Once and never again. That's what I said." I run my hands up his hard chest, so glad that I was wrong. *First and forever* would've been a better phrase for what that kiss started.

"You did say that, huh." Atticus leans down and presses a kiss on my neck.

"And you agreed." I can't stop the ragged breath that escapes my mouth.

"Then you called me a chicken, which, in hindsight, is hilarious."

I huff out a laugh that gets cut short when he kisses my neck again, this time with his mouth open. Atticus can't keep his hands off me, and I can't keep my hands off him. I know we're in the honeymoon period of our relationship, but I'm loving every single second of being his girlfriend.

There's a knock on my door and it opens immediately.

"Hello!" Lucy calls out. "We're all here to help!"

"Hey Lucy," I call, trying to regulate my voice. "Guess this is to be continued," I whisper to the gorgeous man who has me trapped, pushing against his chest.

"Fuck that, let's tell them to leave." Atticus hasn't move his mouth from my neck.

"Gross," Lucy says as she rounds the corner. "I love that you two are together, but I don't need to see my little brother making out with my best friend."

I push Atticus away and laugh. Kellen appears behind Lucy and lays his arm around her shoulders.

"I've got a dozen eggs. They're warm, which is kind of gross." Kellen glances behind him. "Couldn't get Barrett or Lach to come help, but we did bring the grumpiest man on earth. He's parking the car."

"Harley," Atticus states. I grab the eggs from Kellen and slide them into the refrigerator.

"Yep." Kellen looks over his shoulder again, as if Harley will secretly appear behind him. "Between the breakup and moving down to second line, he's a disaster. Not that he'll talk about any of it."

Harley is such a nice guy, I feel awful he's going through so much right now.

"He better pull it together in the next few weeks though..." Atticus trails off when we hear footsteps through the open door.

"Hey." Harley appears, nodding at me politely. "How can we help?"

I point to a few boxes stacked on the kitchen floor and the three of them get to work. I definitely could've done all this on my own, but it's nice to have the help. This group of guys acts like a family, and between them, Atticus, and living next door to Lucy? Nothing could be better.

Well, that's not exactly right. If January were here with us, it would be perfect.

When I left Connecticut in June to drive across country, I had no idea what I was doing. I just knew I wanted to be someone other than myself for a change. I wanted to do some things that the old Raleigh would never do.

Okay, so maybe driving an RV and learning to do cross-stitch isn't exactly the most adventurous thing anyone has ever done. But it helped me break the routine of my life so I could truly find myself.

I open a smaller box on the counter next to the one with dishes —this one came from Pink Palace via Atticus's apartment—and pull out the large completed cross-stitch that's right on top. Atticus steps behind me and slides an arm around my waist before peeking down at what I'm holding.

"I wish I hadn't screwed up the parts I stitched." There's a smile in his voice.

We've been working on this one together over the past few weeks. I won't sell it or post it online.

It's our cross-stitch.

It's us.

"It's perfect." I look around. There's an existing nail on the wall above the kitchen entrance. There's a lot of leftover hooks in this place—the last tenants didn't leave it in the best condition. "Can you hang it?" I nod to the empty space, way higher than I can reach.

Atticus takes the hoop from my hand and easily hooks it onto the nail. He steps back, and it's a little crooked, so he gently nudges it until it's exactly right.

The quote is way too long, which is why I picked a jumbo hoop for the project.

Atticus reaches for my hand and I meet his eyes with a smile before looking at the hoop.

It says: *Home is: chickens, hockey, the Pink Palace, zombie movies. And us.*

# Epilogue

## ATTICUS

1 year later

So much has happened over the past year, but all I'm focusing on is Raleigh Hayes.

"I can't believe how dark it is out here," Raleigh whispers, as if she will disturb the carpet of stars above us with a voice too loud.

I reach my hand over and grab hers.

We're lying on our backs in Arches National Park in Utah on a soft fleece blanket, staring up at the gorgeous carpet of stars above us. There's a remarkable quiet stillness in the national park at night. Sure, there are other people around stargazing, but we can't see or hear them.

I managed to snag a campground reservation at the Devil's Garden. It's the only campsite in the entire park and a tough slot to get. Six months ago, I had to wait at my freaking computer for the clock to turn midnight Utah time for reservations to open for this night.

The look on Raleigh's face when she woke up that morning was worth it.

We've been sleeping in the Pink Palace for the past three weeks as we've traveled around some of the western states. Well, it's more like the Pink and Purple Palace these days as we had that same artist who painted the chicken and mountain mural come back and paint a hockey inspired mural on the other side, including lots of Blizzard purple and yellow coloring.

Also, I had the Pink Palace basically gutted. If we were really going to drive around for a month—and we've spent time in Yosemite, Yellowstone, some gorgeous drives in California, and now we're working our way up through Utah—we needed some upgrades. Like, a lot of upgrades.

I'd have preferred to buy a bigger RV, but Raleigh insisted on keeping it.

Now there's real wood floors, a mini sectional sofa, a table that secures against the wall when we're not using it, incredible lighting, and the tiniest luxury kitchen we could fit in. Also, the bedroom is basically all bed, but it's raised a few steps so we could have custom storage built underneath. The bathroom is still my least favorite part as I can barely fit my body inside of it, but I'm surviving.

The RV is now basically a luxury studio apartment.

The view of the sky through the high stone arch—reddish orange in the day but a black outline at night—is incredibly striking. There's a poetic clarity to the pitch-dark skies and the bright stars and planets shining on the black surface of the solar system.

"This is what happens when there's zero light pollution." I squeeze Raleigh's hand. This is an astounding place to be, on so many levels.

"I remember reading that this spot is certified as one of the darkest skies in the world," she whispers.

"Pretty amazing." There are so few people around us right now. The parks are busiest in spring and fall. It's so damn hot in Utah in July and August that tourists tend to stay away. Today was no exception.

"I think this is my favorite place to see stars. And we've seen some incredible ones." Raleigh lets out a happy sigh.

"We really have." While in the national parks, we've been making it a point to find the best spots for stargazing.

It's been beautiful, that's for sure, but doing this with Raleigh is everything. She's everything I never knew I needed in my life.

All those years I insisted I'd never get serious with someone. But it turns out, I had already met the one for me. No one else had a chance.

And Raleigh? She had to go through a few husbands to get to me. But she's here now. And I try to convince her all the time to make me husband number three, but so far she's resisted the idea.

Maybe one day. I can be patient. I can wait forever.

"And we can see more planets here." I pull out my phone and click open the stargazing app we've been using. I point it through the majestic stone arches and let the app match the constellations with what we're currently witnessing in the vast night sky.

"Let me see." Still holding my hand, Raleigh scoots closer and peers up at my phone. "Wow."

"Milk Way." I point. "And that's Mars, Jupiter, Saturn... and there's Venus."

The night has offered us a relief from the high daytime temperatures. We've been doing hikes early in the morning before it hits mid-nineties in the afternoon.

I've also managed to continue to ease Raleigh out of her fear of water by bringing along the kayaks and taking easy paddles on calm, beautiful lakes.

She hardly ever flips the kayak these days.

And I hardly ever flip her on purpose.

Just occasionally.

"I don't want this trip to end," Raleigh whispers.

I lower my phone and turn my head to her, bringing our lips together. She rolls to her side and slides a hand onto my chest. I sigh with happiness.

This truly has been the best year of my life.

When I wasn't traveling with the Blizzard, Raleigh was my priority. My teammates endlessly make fun of me for making such an about face on love, but nothing they say could change how I feel and act about this woman.

Having her with me has made everything in my life better, even hockey. I have more to play for. More to motivate me. Much more to come home to.

I deepen the kiss, and Raleigh moans softly into my mouth, pressing her body against the side of mine.

"I love you," I say when she pulls away to take a breath.

"You're okay, I guess." She's aiming for nonchalance, but she gives herself away with her heated gaze and the way her breathing is heavier after kissing me.

In a swift motion, I flip her onto her back and lower myself between her legs. She's got a soft smile for me.

"Fine. I love you too." Raleigh wiggles beneath me, sending heat rushing through my body.

"That's better. Now let's go home and you can show me just how much."

And with that, I swoop up Raleigh and the blanket and carry her back to the Pink Palace.

The End

If you enjoyed *Any Second Now,* leave a review, it helps so much!

Check out the bonus chapter with Raleigh & Atticus (featuring chickens and spicy board games) by signing up for Chrissy's newsletter at www.ChrissyHopewell.com! Also, get hockey novella *Zamboni Kiss* and bonus chapters for every novel.

*Just One Season* is Lucy & Kellen's love story. It's a fake dating, brother's best friend, single dad, found family hockey romance.

Check out the completed Hart Sisters Trilogy:

*If We Pretend* is Reese & Oliver's love story. It's a fake dating, divorced mom, ex pro soccer player light sports romance set in Scotland.

*Unless It's You* is Stella & Ethan's love story. Set in London, this romance is a second chance, enemies-to-lovers, bucket list novel.

*Since We're Here* is Maddie & Patrick's love story. It's a grumpy sunshine Irish romance.

*One Hundred Lights* is a prequel novella to the Hart Sisters Trilogy and is a holiday romance featuring Britt & Adrian, both morally grey characters who can't stay away from each other.

Stay in touch:
Instagram: @ChrissyHopewell
Facebook: ChrissyHopewellAuthor
TikTok: @ChrissyHopewellBooks
Email: Chrissy@ChrissyHopewell.com
BookBub: ChrissyHopewell

# Acknowledgments

I'm incredibly grateful that I get to continue to write and publish novels.

Thanks so much to editor Brenda Chin, my incredible beta readers Sarah Brenton, Ericka, Talia Greer, and to my amazing hockey beta readers Shania, Melissa, Lou, and Emily.

I couldn't imagine doing this without a community of writers, especially Sarah Brenton, Jessica Booth, Dani Galliaro, Delaine Walsh, the rest of the Cincinnati Author Coven, and the Pitch Wars community.

And as always, thanks to my husband and four kiddos who (mostly) accept me for who I am, which is apparently a romance author.

Off to write the next one!

love, Chrissy

# About the Author

Chrissy Hopewell started her love for romance novels by sneaking her mom's steamy books in middle school. She has spent varying amounts of time overseas, including working at a pub in Dublin, waitressing at a hotel in the Scottish Borders, and studying and living in London. Because of these experiences, international flair and accents often show up in her writing. Chrissy now lives in the suburbs of Cincinnati, Ohio with her family, and she no longer has to sneak what she reads.

instagram.com/chrissyhopewell
tiktok.com/@chrissyhopewellbooks
facebook.com/chrissyhopewellauthor